Kindred Spirits

The Essential Elements Series, Book 1

Lauren Cutrera

Published by On My Way Up, LLC

ISBN: 978-1-944113-25-4

For Abbie, who read the ARC for this novel well before its release and asked me how soon she could read the next book in the series.

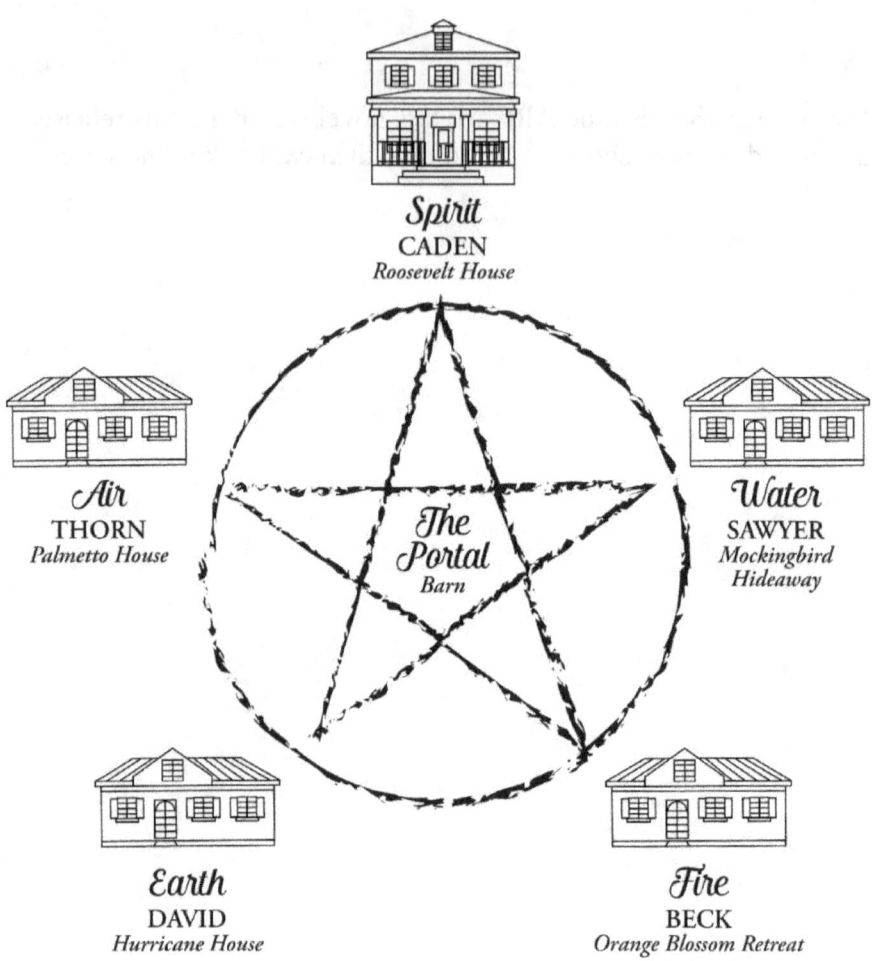

Spirit
CADEN
Roosevelt House

Air
THORN
Palmetto House

The Portal
Barn

Water
SAWYER
Mockingbird Hideaway

Earth
DAVID
Hurricane House

Fire
BECK
Orange Blossom Retreat

1 Rory

"Rory Roosevelt? It *is* you! I never thought I'd live to see the day *you'd* be on your hands and knees, scrubbing floors!"

Rory lifted her head as she pushed at some of the strands of dark red hair that had worked their way out of her braid. She was tired, annoyed, and didn't want to spend any time with Astrid Hass. The two women had known one another since childhood, but they'd never been friends.

"You *didn't* live to see the day," Rory informed her. "You're dead, Astrid." As her blue eyes widened, she whistled and then continued, "Too bad you didn't die wearing something more appropriate. You're stuck wearing that tight little piece of red sequined cloth I suppose is meant to be a cocktail dress." Returning her attention to the floor, she dipped the sponge into the bucket of water and then added, "Well, until you cross over to whatever's on the other side."

Astrid narrowed her eyes, squared her shoulders, and pushed some of her beautifully styled blonde hair away from her face before asking with feigned sweetness, "Whatever do you mean? I'm not dead! I'm just...." Suddenly looking confused, she stammered, "I – I'm only...um...."

"Only what?" Rory asked with irritation, throwing the sponge into the bucket and getting stiffly to her feet. "What are you doing here wearing an expensive but skanky cocktail dress and spiked heels? You moved away from Florida right after graduation in order to attend college in New York and afterward married some wealthy old man and inherited his fortune when he died. Last I heard, you were living the high life in Beverly Hills. All of a sudden, you're back in your hometown of Sage in the kitchen of one of the cottages of my B & B. Don't you find that a bit odd? Central Florida's a long way from southern California."

"But I can't be dead! I'm a beautiful, twenty-five-year-old millionaire!"

1

Rory shook her head, bent to grasp the handle of the bucket, and hauled it up before saying, "Trust me. You're dead. I just don't know why you ended up here."

"You were always weird, but now I know you're crazy!" Astrid snapped. "I'm *not* dead!" Then, sounding less self-assured, she asked, "Am I?"

Rory sighed. Lowering the bucket back to the floor, she decided it would be uncharitable not to try to help anyone in distress, even if that person was a bitchy, self-centered bully. Besides, if she didn't try to help Astrid move on to the next plane of existence, then she could be stuck with her for quite some time. Rory needed that like she needed a hole in her head. And speaking of holes in heads....

"I'm sorry to have to tell you this, but you *are* dead. You got shot."

"Shot? But who would want to shoot me?"

"Would you like a list? I could start from the time we were in kindergarten and go from there."

"That's not funny!" Astrid protested, but there was a hint of panic in her voice.

Forcing herself to sound as comforting as possible, Rory admitted, "I don't know who shot you, but at least you're not suffering now. The reason I know you've been shot is because you have a bullet hole in your left temple."

"What?!?" Astrid screeched. "You're lying! You're saying that because you're jealous!"

"I'm jealous, so I'm going to somehow transport you across the country and tell you that you were shot to death? Really, Astrid? Think about it for a minute. Why would I do that?"

"Where's a mirror? I have to see myself!"

"You can't."

"You can't stop me," the woman said imperiously.

"I don't need to. You're a ghost, and ghosts don't have reflections. Try to look if you like. There's a full-length mirror in each of the two bedrooms in this cottage."

Rory waited where she stood, as Astrid hurried from the room. A frustrated cry came from the closest bedroom moments later. Rory leaned her backside against one of the kitchen counters. The ability to see ghosts, interact with them, and help them move on had been passed down for generations through the Roosevelt line. Most of those blessed with the unusual family talent were male, but some were female. Rory's older brother, Nolan, and she both had the gift. Normally, she considered it a privilege to be granted the opportunity to assist the deceased who were in need.

It's more like a pain in the butt when it comes to times like these, she thought. *What a hassle. Nolan only attracts sexy female ghosts, but I get all kinds of people. Lucky me. I wonder why Astrid ended up here. Maybe she needed to tell me she's sorry for being such a bitch her whole life.* Shaking her head, Rory thought, *That can't be it. Astrid is clueless about that even in death.*

"Oh, my God!" Astrid exclaimed, as she rushed back into the room. "You're not lying. I can't see myself in any of the mirrors. I even looked at the little one over the sink in the bathroom."

"Believe me when I tell you that it's probably for the best. Having a hole in your head doesn't really enhance your looks."

"But I have things to *do*! I have my whole life ahead of me."

"Not anymore. I'm sorry."

"You have to help me! You have to find out who did this and make certain he's brought to justice!"

Rory hoisted the bucket again and asked, "If I find out who did it, will you accept it and go quietly into wherever it is you're supposed to be?"

Astrid looked coolly at her and said, "Maybe. It depends on who shot me and why."

"Let's go back to the main house, and I'll see what I can find out on the Internet. You'd be amazed at what one can turn up online."

Rory poured the water onto some plants before bringing the bucket back inside and placing it under the kitchen sink. She then locked the door to the cottage and came down the porch steps.

As she and Astrid walked along the path that led to the main house, the ghost asked, "Won't that soapy water kill the plants? You shouldn't pour cleaning fluids onto them."

"Are you seriously telling me you care about not polluting the planet? I thought all you cared about was yourself."

"I do," Astrid said nonchalantly. "But my husband made his fortune developing technology that could help save the environment. I learned about it before I began to seduce him so that he wouldn't think all I was interested in was his money. I'm not stupid. If I were, then I wouldn't have snared a millionaire for a husband. I'm a bright woman."

"I can't argue with that. As for my plants, they'll be fine. The cleaning products I use are all ecofriendly. Everything is natural. The mixture actually helps the plants grow. It's pretty cool. Although what I use is a little more expensive than the standard commercial products my parents used to buy, it's worth it to me." Pausing, she asked, "Why did you say earlier that you'd never imagined seeing me scrubbing floors? Were you being sarcastic?"

"I just never pictured you as the kind of person who'd do something like that. You were always a nerd while we were growing up, but I admired the fact that you were still such a girly girl."

"I wasn't a nerd; I was a geek. There's a difference."

Astrid shrugged and said, "If you say so. Why *were* you scrubbing the floor in that house? And look at your outfit! Little jean shorts and a Mickey Mouse tee is just so…common. You must wear at least a C cup, and your ass is nice and round. You could get so many more men if –"

"Enough talk about my chest and butt, okay? Wearing a cutesy dress to clean isn't very practical, is it? As for the cleaning, I do it because it needs to be done. Hiring someone else to do it would add to my overhead expenses. I might be a girly girl at heart, but I always had chores at home when I was growing up and was expected to do them well. It taught me the value of working in order to achieve success and the rewards of practicality."

"But that house we were in obviously isn't your home."

"No. I run a Bed and Breakfast. When my parents died in that small plane crash, everything was left to my brother and me. He wanted to sell this place and split the money. But our family has lived on this property for over two hundred and fifty years. So, I gave my brother his half of our inheritance by signing away my rights to most of our parents' investments while I kept the family estate. The main house is just for me. However, I do have four lovely guest cottages that I rent out to bring in an income that helps me maintain things. I was scrubbing the floor of Palmetto House because some of the guests spilled something and the floor was all sticky."

"Palmetto House? You named the cottage after a bug that's like a cockroach?"

"No. I named it after the palmetto palm tree."

"What are the other three cottages called?"

"Orange Blossom Retreat, Hurricane House, and Mockingbird Hideaway."

"Quaint," Astrid said derisively.

"They're white wood frame cracker homes built in the 1800s that have metal roofs, raised floors, and porches. In other places, they might be called 'shotgun' or 'dog trot' homes, because they have straight central hallways that run from the front to the back."

"Thank you *ever* so much for the history lesson, but I know what a cracker home is, even if I wouldn't dream of living in one."

Rory showed great restraint by refraining from reminding the woman that she would no longer be living anywhere. It wasn't Astrid's fault that she'd died and ended up back in her hometown. The haughty dead woman wasn't responsible for Rory's exhaustion after being up almost all night dealing with the unruly guests who'd been staying in Palmetto House. The ghost also couldn't be blamed for the hot, humid July weather that seemed to drain Rory's remaining energy.

"What's the name of your B & B?" Astrid suddenly asked. "Please tell me it's not something like Gator Cove or Mosquito Harbor."

Rory laughed in spite of her foul mood and answered, "Nostalgia Road Bed and Breakfast."

"I actually like that. It sounds…welcoming."

"That was the intent." Inclining her head, she said, "There's the Roosevelt homestead."

The ghost stopped moving and murmured appreciatively, "It's…well, it's just beautiful!"

"I certainly think so."

"A three-story Queen Anne Victorian," Astrid murmured appreciatively. "Lovely."

Surprised that the woman recognized the architectural style, Rory merely said, "I have five bedrooms, three bathrooms, and a wraparound porch along the first floor."

"How many acres of land do you own?"

"Thirty-five. Most of it is woods and wild pastures, but I do use the riding mower on the area surrounding the house. The paths to the lake and cottages are covered in gravel, so I don't have to worry about them. The back porch looks out across the lake."

"I love the way that you kept the house white like the cottages," Astrid remarked, as they began to move forward again. "Oh, my God! Is that a real barn I see off in the distance?"

Rory fought the urge to say, "No, it's a fake one." Instead, she said, "Yes, it's centrally located in relation to the houses on the property, which makes it convenient for me."

"Why'd you paint it red?"

"It's a fun color for a boring building."

"Boring?"

"The barn's where I keep the riding mower, tools, generators, and other things like that."

"Generators?"

"In case of hurricanes. If we lose power, then at least I have access to generators. I keep gasoline locked in a small outbuilding behind the barn."

"Isn't all of this a ton of work?"

"It's not so bad. It's only me in the main house, and cleaning the cottages after the guests leave doesn't usually require much work. Most stay for several days at a stretch. I'm an early riser, so cooking breakfast for guests each morning is no big deal."

"What do you do with the rest of your time?"

"Design websites for businesses."

"And what about men?"

"What about them?"

"Don't you like men, or are you gay?"

Rory chuckled then said, "I forgot how pushy you are…were. For your information, I'm straight."

"Have you ever had sex?"

"That's none of your business!"

"Who cares? I'm dead, remember?" Glancing at the house, she said, "I simply can't conceive of life without sex."

"Did you have sex with your millionaire husband?" Rory asked, thinking that two could play at Astrid's game of making indiscreet inquiries.

"Yes, I did. Glen wasn't bad for being in his seventies. He kept in shape. Granted, it wasn't like sleeping with someone around my age, but he was good in bed. Even if he'd been terrible, making love to him would have been the least I could have done. After all, he married me and left me half of his fortune. The other half went to charity."

"No one contested the will?"

"No. Glen had never been married before and had no heirs. He said he'd never wanted to get married until he met me. He loved me, but he was old and didn't want to start a family at his age." She paused then continued, "I didn't love Glen, but he was a nice man." Smiling, she said wistfully, "I did care for him. I hadn't anticipated that when I set out to seduce him. I was sorry when he died."

"Maybe you'll see him again when you cross over."

Which will hopefully be soon, Rory added silently.

"Do all people become ghosts when they die?" Astrid asked.

"Not that I know of. It's usually the ones who have some sort of unfinished business to take care of or those who had violent deaths. Some people just don't understand that it's their time to go and need to be told."

"What's the longest time you've had a ghost linger with you?"

"Two years. I was sad when she finally crossed over. We'd become friends."

"Two *years*! Who was she?"

"She wasn't from around here."

"Then why'd she come to you?"

"Because, unlike my brother, I help ghosts find peace so that they can move on. As for how it actually works, I have no idea why particular ghosts come to me."

"What did that woman want?"

"Her husband had stabbed her to death. She told me where the murder had happened, and I wrote an anonymous note to the police in the city where she'd lived. They investigated, found the weapon, and eventually recovered her remains. Once her husband had been convicted and sentenced to life without the possibility of parole, she was able to move on."

"But how did she know what happened to her? I still don't remember what happened to me."

7

"Some ghosts recall the circumstances of their deaths, while others never remember. I don't know why. I'm not aware of any handbook about these sorts of things." Opening her front door, Rory suggested, "Let's go in so I can get something cool to drink then take a shower. I have a guest checking in this evening and want to look presentable."

"Maybe I could help with that," Astrid muttered.

"I don't need your help. Once I've had a root beer and gotten clean, then I'll see if I can find out anything regarding your death. Perhaps by tonight you'll be at peace."

"I certainly hope so. I'd hate to be stuck here for two years. It is a beautiful place, but it's not really my style."

Rory thought of the Hass family mansion located on the other side of Sage. The town's residents knew that the palatial home had stables, an Olympic-size pool, tennis courts, and a large home theater. Astrid's parents were millionaires themselves, and all three of their daughters had married wealthy older men who'd died and left them their fortunes. Rory wondered whether the Hass sisters had killed their husbands or if the men's deaths had been coincidental. Their mother, who'd married her then sixty-year-old fiancé when she'd been in her early twenties, had obviously schooled her girls well in how to follow in her footsteps. Since Astrid's father was still alive, his wife was no Black Widow. But were her girls?

"Did you kill your husband to get his money?" Rory blurted out, as they walked into the living room.

"No. I know what people think, but it's simply not true. The main difference between me and my sisters is that I actually did like my husband, while they couldn't have cared less about theirs." Glancing around, she noted, "This is perfect. Who did your decorating?"

"Everyone who's lived here since the place was built over a hundred years ago. I do have modern kitchen appliances, but almost everything else in the house has been maintained or redone in the original style in order to keep that wonderful historic feel. Well, all of my electronics are fairly new. I did try to make everything blend well so that nothing I added or changed detracted from the decor of the home. I converted one of the bedrooms on the second floor into my home office, but it's still homey."

"Shabby chic. I'm impressed."

"Astrid, you don't have to pretend to be nice to me because you need my help."

"I'm not. It's charming. If I were still alive, then I wouldn't mind buying a little place like this for weekend getaways. Of course, I'd have a staff to cook and clean and wouldn't dare rent out those cottages!" Wrinkling her nose in what Rory surmised was disgust, she added, "The help could live in the cracker houses. Too bad I didn't think about something like that while I was alive."

"Yes, too bad." Going into the kitchen, Rory got a bottle of root beer from the white refrigerator, opened it, and then took a swallow before saying, "You have to know the rules."

"The rules?"

"I'll assign you a room to use as yours for as long as you're here. You can go anywhere you want, but you don't invade my privacy unless it's for a really good reason. No waking me up at night, watching me shower or change clothes, staring at me while I work –"

"Why would I want to do any of those things? How boring would *that* be?" Looking contemplative, she asked, "Can anyone else see me?"

"My brother, Nolan. I don't know anyone else like us, but we can't be the only people on the planet who can see ghosts. I just don't know of any others."

Licking her lips, Astrid said, "If I remember correctly, Nolan has sex appeal even if he isn't in *my* league. Do you think he'd be interested in me? Do I look like a regular woman or am I all hazy and white like ghosts you see on TV?"

"After everything you've just learned, you want to know if Nolan will think you're sexy?"

"You didn't answer my questions!" she pouted.

Sighing, Rory said, "You look exactly as you did when you died. This means you appear the same to us, but we can't touch you. It also means you're wearing a dress that's way too short, way too tight, and cut way too low. Nolan might like all of that." When Astrid brightened, she added, "I don't think he'll like the hole in the side of your head, even though I don't see any other evidence of your death like blood."

The woman's face fell, and she asked, "Do you think I could redo my hair to cover up the hole?"

"You're impossible! I'm going upstairs, stripping off these clothes, and taking a shower. I'll be down in a while. Make yourself comfortable."

"How do I do that? Every time I try to touch something, my hand goes through it."

"You evidently haven't been dead long. If you concentrate, you'll eventually get the hang of moving things with the energy that surrounds you."

"Speaking of energy, will I make electronic things go haywire when I'm around them?"

"If that were the case, then I wouldn't be able to use computers, cellphones, and other electronic devices because of my ghostly visitors. I think it's one of those concepts that many in the media and the literary industry latched onto, making viewers and readers believe all the hype. It does sound cool, but it's not true. Well, not in my experience." Moving toward the stairs, she said, "Now, practice moving things. I'll warn you that it takes time."

"I have nothing but time," Astrid pointed out. "I'll get started right away. I'll begin by trying to sit on the couch. What should I do if Nolan shows up and you're in the shower?"

"Nolan doesn't come around unless he needs something, which isn't often. If he does come while I'm upstairs, knock yourself out. I'm his little sister, not his babysitter."

"Thank you for everything. I know I was never very nice to you, but you're helping me in spite of that. I really do appreciate it. Sorry if I'm still a bitch sometimes. I just have to be me."

"At least you're self-aware."

"Mama didn't raise her no fools," Astrid said dramatically, making Rory smirk. "Now, go shower so we can find out who killed me. I may have eternity ahead of me, but I don't want to wait."

"Me neither. No offense, but I'd rather not have roommates. I like my privacy. The sooner you're gone, the easier it'll be for both of us."

2 Caden

"You didn't see the speed limit sign a mile back?"

Caden Brody stifled his urge to snap at the young policeman standing beside his black Chevy Trailblazer. Caden *had* been driving fourteen miles over the posted speed limit. He figured pulling him over would probably be the highlight of the cop's entire Sunday. The man, who looked as though he were in his mid-twenties, seemed extremely tired but maintained a professional attitude. Caden appreciated that and wondered if the policeman saw much action in rural central Florida.

"I accept responsibility for speeding, Officer…?"

"Marsh."

"Officer Marsh. Give me a ticket, and I'll be on my way."

The cop seemed relieved by the admission of guilt. Caden supposed he was used to hearing all sorts of excuses from others pulled over for speeding. Caden never made excuses for anything he did. Regardless, he was worn out and wanted to end his conversation with the policeman. He'd been driving for almost three days straight and was exhausted, stiff, and worried. He needed to get to Nostalgia Road Bed & Breakfast as soon as possible. All that he wanted now was his speeding ticket, which he would definitely pay. Later, he'd have all traces of its existence removed from his record.

Glancing at Caden's driver's license, Marsh ignored the sweat running down his neck and remarked, "Let's see. Thirty years old. Six foot three. One hundred eighty pounds. Green eyes. It says here you have red hair, but it doesn't look red to me."

"It's what a lot of people might call 'ginger.' The lady at the DMV insisted on putting 'red,' and it didn't make a hell of a lot of difference to me."

"If you say so." Darting a glance at Caden's face, he muttered, "Christ, you look like some bad-ass movie star."

"You don't look so bad yourself."

The cop laughed and said, "I was a fullback on the high school football team and still work out, but no stunning good looks here."

"You're wearing a wedding ring, so your wife must think you're hot."

"Are you trying to sweet talk me out of giving you a ticket, Mr. Brody?"

"I wouldn't dream of it. I broke the law and deserve a ticket."

"I see from your license that you're from Louisiana. What brings you to Florida?"

"What brings most people to Florida. I'm here for a vacation."

"In a hurry to get started, are you?"

"I am."

"You mind if I search your vehicle?"

"Not at all," Caden replied casually although he was annoyed by this added delay. "I'll warn you now that it's kind of a dump in here."

"My wife's never used a mop or broom in her life, and I'm not much of a housekeeper myself," Marsh said genially. "Would you step out of the vehicle, Mr. Brody?"

Caden stood in the July heat on the side of the highway and watched as the cop searched the Trailblazer. The thing was packed with weapons, but all of those were hidden and were undetectable by anyone performing a perfunctory search of the interior. The only things Marsh was going to find were empty bottles of sports drinks, cans of nuts, pieces of paper, a computer, an iPad, a bag of recently purchased groceries, and luggage. Caden hoped the man wouldn't ask to go through his suitcases, not because he'd find anything suspicious but because it would slow him down even more.

"All good," the cop said. "Let me write you that ticket. We depend on the revenue from tickets to keep the patrols going. Try not to let it happen again."

"I'll try."

The policeman smiled and said, "Maybe after you get some R&R, then you'll chill and go a little slower."

"Maybe. Thanks for not riding my ass about this. I'm really tired and just want to get where I'm going and catch some sleep."

"Where are you headed?"

"Sage."

Marsh frowned and said, "I live in Sage. People don't vacation there. It's just a little town in Florida."

"I'm staying at a B&B called Nostalgia Road. I guess technically it's not located in Sage."

"Rory Roosevelt's place!" the man exclaimed. "I've known Rory since I was in first grade and she was in kindergarten."

Caden's interest was instantly piqued, and he leaned against the side of his Chevy and asked, "Is Nostalgia Road a good B&B? It looked decent on the website."

"Oh, yeah. The Roosevelts have owned the property for a couple of centuries. Real good folks with old money, but you'd never know they were rich from dealing with any of them."

"What do people out here do to make lots of money? Do they own huge orange groves or something?"

"Nah. The only two families around here who ever had any real money are the Hass family and the Roosevelts. Mr. and Mrs. Hass built their estate about twenty-five years ago, supposedly because Mr. Hass wanted to be centrally located so that he could easily travel around the state because he's an avid golfer. The Hasses have millions of dollars." Suddenly looking pensive, Marsh added, "One of their daughters just died out in Beverly Hills."

"That's too bad," Caden remarked, not really interested but aware of how people in small towns typically liked to gossip. "What about the Roosevelts? If they're so rich, then why is their house and those on their property now being used as a Bed & Breakfast?"

"I don't know where the Roosevelt family money originally came from. I guess whoever settled in Florida brought it with them. From what I know, the family's never been snooty like the Hass family. Rory's parents were both teachers before they died in a small plane crash a few years back. Rory wanted the house and land; Nolan, her brother, wanted the family money. I suppose they worked it out, but Nostalgia Road B&B opened for business not long after the estate was settled. We all figured Rory needed the income to keep things up. She loves that place. She's a real sweetheart."

"Nobody around here's swept her off her feet?" Caden asked, wanting to know if he'd have a potential obstacle in his way when it came to his objective.

"Nope. She just doesn't seem interested in dating. I wish she'd find some nice guy to settle down with, but I imagine there aren't that many guys in Sage who'd appeal to her."

"What makes you say that?"

"She's a web designer. I can't picture her with any of the eligible bachelors who stuck around here after high school graduation. It's too bad. I'd like to see her happy."

Which obviously you don't think she is, thought Caden. *Interesting.*

"Here's your ticket. You're close to Nostalgia Road."

"Thanks, Officer Marsh."

"Call me Harvey. Everyone does."

"Thanks, Harvey. Maybe I'll see you more while I'm in the area on vacation."

"Just don't let me catch you speeding again, okay?"

Caden nodded but made no promises. He climbed back into his Trailblazer and started the engine. He reflected that it had been extremely fortuitous that he'd been stopped for speeding by Harvey Marsh. What he'd initially perceived as a minor inconvenience had turned into an extremely informative exchange. He wondered idly if Marsh had once romantically pursued Rory Roosevelt.

Caden thought of the photos he'd found of Rory online. His assignment had certainly been unexpected, so he'd immediately turned to Google to search for the basics regarding the proprietor of Nostalgia Road. He'd located a reasonable amount of background information and five photos that he'd confirmed were of "his" Rory Roosevelt.

In the first picture he'd viewed, Rory must have been about fourteen. She and several other girls were attending Comic Con, Dragon Con or a similar fan event. All four of the girls were in costume. Rory wore an outfit that included a colorful dress with a short, flared skirt, striped leggings, and black patent leather shoes that looked like they belonged on a five-year-old. She had long, curly, red hair that she wore in pigtails high up on the sides of her head. He supposed she was dressed as some sort of anime character although he had no idea which one. Her outfit was in no way provocative, and she and her friends appeared to be geeky teens having a great time at a convention for fans. Her blue eyes were alight with excitement. Caden had actually smiled when he'd studied the girl. She'd looked so joyful and innocent.

The second photo he'd found was of her in her high school cap and gown for graduation. Rory's curly, red hair was shoulder-length, and she was smiling. However, her smile seemed forced.

The sparkle he'd seen in her indigo eyes in the earlier photo was gone. That had made him frown, and he'd wondered what had happened to her during the years in-between the shots.

The third photo had been attached to a newspaper article about her parents' deaths in the small plane crash. It showed Rory and a man with curly, red hair standing in the midst of mourners outside a church. The man was identified as Nolan Roosevelt, the son of the deceased male high school history teacher and the female middle school computer instructor. Both Roosevelt children looked grim, as would be expected. Yet, there was something about the photo that bothered Caden. It was the fact that, despite their proximity, the siblings didn't appear to be attempting to console one another. It was almost as though they couldn't bear to be close.

Next, Caden had pulled up a headshot Rory must use for business purposes. She looked professional but still projected that same air of innocence he'd noted in the first photo. She'd definitely matured into a beautiful woman, but the sparkle was still absent from her eyes.

The final photo perplexed Caden. Although he deduced that it must have been taken recently, he couldn't think of why anyone would post it on their Facebook page, Instagram, LinkedIn, Pinterest, or any other social media account that might have led to its appearance as a search result on the Internet. In the photo, Rory was standing on a dock in a simple but attractive white dress. She was evidently unaware of the fact that she was being photographed and was not looking toward the camera. Her long, red curls hung down her back, and her face was in profile. Caden had studied her delicate features and fair skin and pondered how a woman who looked as though she'd stepped out of an advertisement designed to attract tourists to Ireland possessed the surname of Roosevelt, which had Dutch origins. As he'd studied the image, he'd vowed to discover who had taken the photo and why and to research the Roosevelt family tree when he had some time.

He wanted to call Elias, his seventy-one-year-old adoptive father. The gray-haired, distinguished-looking man with gun metal gray eyes probably had more connections than the President of the United States. He was a wealth of knowledge, single-minded about his reason for being, and totally ruthless when it came to safeguarding his life, his goals, and his sons. They all respected him and relied on him for guidance when they felt it was needed, despite their bent toward self-reliance.

"There's no shame in asking for help if you're ignorant about something and are aware of it," Elias had told them many times over the years. "The shame is in being ignorant, knowing it, and not asking for help."

Caden would have liked to discuss this case with Elias, but he'd been experiencing a growing sense of unease during the past several months regarding his adoptive father. Caden hadn't shared his concerns with his brothers because he couldn't verbalize what exactly was making him feel so disquieted. All of the Brody sons were close to one another, but he remained uncertain as to how they'd react if he voiced his doubts regarding Elias and his objectives.

To compound the issue, Anderson, one of Caden's adoptive brothers, had been seriously injured the day Caden had accepted his current assignment, and Elias had flown to the Los Angeles hospital where Anderson lay comatose. The other Brody sons knew they couldn't join their father at the medical facility, but the thought of their brother's existing in limbo weighed heavily on them. Caden knew that none of them would rest until they'd received confirmation from Elias that their brother was going to either live or die.

Anderson will make it, Caden thought, as he turned his Trailblazer onto the road that would take him to his current destination. *He's twenty-two, strong, and healthy. He's a fighter, just like the rest of us. He won't surrender to death without a struggle.*

Recalling the last time he'd seen Anderson, which had been four weeks earlier, Caden prayed for his brother's recovery if it were possible. However, if Anderson wasn't able to continue living and doing the work he loved, what they all loved and had been trained to do from childhood, then Caden prayed for God to take him right away. None of them wanted to simply exist. Death would be preferable.

Caden forced his thoughts back to Rory Roosevelt and Nostalgia Road. He still didn't understand why he'd been asked to take this assignment, but he knew there was a reason. He just didn't always know what the reason was.

He heard the siren of the police cruiser and glanced into his rearview mirror. That was when Caden saw the flashing lights. Swearing, he pulled his SUV over to the shoulder of the road, slowed to a stop, and lowered the window. Harvey Marsh got out of his squad car and ambled up beside the Trailblazer's driver's door.

Offering a friendly smile, Harvey said, "I bet your auto insurance company loves you. What's your premium, or are you typically lucky enough not to get caught speeding even though you probably do it most of the time?"

"I may have had a ticket here or there," Caden replied, trying not to sound sarcastic. "How fast was I going this time?"

"*Only* twelve miles over the limit." Sighing, Harvey said, "I don't want to have to write you another ticket, but I do want you to take me seriously."

"I have a lead foot."

"I had a feeling. That's why I tailed you from a distance. I matched my speed to yours so that I could tell how fast you were going."

I must be pretty damn tired not to spot a tail of any kind, reflected Caden. *Man, I really have to sleep. Now.*

"I won't write you another ticket if you *swear* to me that you'll go at or below the speed limit until you're at Nostalgia Road. Or do you need an escort there?"

"No. I'm good. I swear I'll pay attention to how fast I'm going and get to sleep as soon as possible once I arrive. Thanks, Harvey."

"We all make mistakes," the cop said with a wry smile. "Just don't make any more today."

"I think I can manage that much."

"I hope so. Otherwise, I won't hesitate to give you another ticket. Got it?"

"Got it."

"Good. Have a safe and *slow* drive to Nostalgia Road."

"Will do."

"I have a feeling I'll be seeing you again soon."

Not if I see you first, Caden thought, as he grinned at Harvey Marsh and nodded.

3 Rory

"That's a *little* better," Astrid said unconvincingly when Rory came back downstairs forty-five minutes later. "The blue dress does match the indigo color of your eyes, and those gorgeous red curls of yours look perfect spilling over your shoulders like that."

"But…?" she prompted, knowing the ghost would volunteer her opinion whether Rory wanted to hear it or not.

"It's simply so…so…"

"Just spit it out, Astrid."

"You look like a country girl."

"I *am* a country girl. That doesn't mean I'm a hick. The dress is comfortable, pretty, and sweet. It's not like I'm wearing an outfit from the times of *Little House on the Prairie*. The hem falls above my knees."

"But you're not showing any cleavage! Those little buttons run all the way up to that Peter Pan collar. At least you're wearing cute sandals and not Mary Janes."

"Guests don't need to see cleavage, and I don't need to be getting fashion advice from a socialite who died looking like a high-priced call girl!"

Astrid appeared incensed for a few moments and then said, "You never did answer my question earlier about whether or not you'd ever had sex."

"It's none of your business."

"That means you haven't."

"I have," she countered with a small sigh.

"With a person or something that required batteries?"

"A person."

"More than one?"

"God, you are such a witch!"

"I'm not a witch; I'm a ghost," Astrid corrected with a smug little smile. "So, you've only had sex with one person. No wonder you're uptight."

"I'm uptight because I had guests who caused trouble last night and then you showed up this morning."

"What happened with your guests?"

"I ended up having to call Harvey to come deal with them."

"Harvey?"

"You should remember Harvey. He was a year ahead of us in school and was a fullback on the football team. He has brown hair, brown eyes, and a great smile."

"Sorry. I only paid attention to quarterbacks."

"Why am I not surprised?" Rory muttered. Then, louder, "Anyway, Harvey's a cop now."

"What did the guests do that required calling a policeman?"

"They got drunk, opened all the windows of Palmetto House, spilled things, and blared music so loudly that it was keeping me awake here in the main house. I didn't want them to disturb me or the other guests on the property."

"Did Harvey arrest anyone?"

"No, but he told them to turn off the music, shut the windows, and go to bed. I'd already said all that, but it had a lot more impact coming from a cop. They dropped the cottage key in through my mail slot and then skulked out before breakfast this morning. I won't ever have them back as guests."

"But what if they give you a bad review online because you called the cops on them?"

Rory shrugged and said, "I typically have great reviews. Owners of B & Bs always get a few bad ones."

"Is there a slow season for Nostalgia Road?"

"For my B & B, that would be summer. Most people come here on vacation during the period ranging from September through May. I'm usually booked from October through April, since a lot of northerners want to escape the freezing weather and snow and enjoy a more temperate climate here in Florida."

"But it's the middle of summer and you sound like you're booked right now."

"It's the week of July 4th. Things are usually packed around Independence Day. After this, I'll have some guests but will rarely be booked solid until the very end of September. It's the nature of the business."

"I'm glad there won't be as many people around for a few weeks. You can focus all of your attention on helping me."

"I can focus more attention on helping you, but don't forget I also run a web design business."

"Then make the most of your free time and get started!" demanded the ghost.

Anything to shut you up for a while, Rory thought.

She ate a chicken salad sandwich while searching the Internet for information on Astrid and her death. Most of what she found was very illuminating although none of it directed her toward an obvious killer. After two hours of research, Rory leaned back in her chair, stretched, and yawned. Rising, she went to the window and looked out at the lake beside the house. She loved the view of the water, dock, trees, and sky. That was one reason she'd made that particular room her home office. The other reason was that it was located right next to her bedroom. It made things convenient if she woke during the night filled with inspiration regarding a website she was creating.

"Did you find out anything?" Astrid asked from behind Rory. "I'm *dying* to know."

"Ha, ha." Turning around, Rory observed, "At least you have a sense of humor. I never got to see that side of you when we were growing up."

"You're *killing* me!"

Grinning, she returned to her desk chair and began, "You were quite the party girl, weren't you? You liked to have a great time with all the celebrities and other wealthy people in Beverly Hills. Because you inherited your husband's money last year, all sorts of men chased after you."

"That wasn't the only reason."

"I'm sure it wasn't. I don't see how anyone who wanted you for your money or, um, talents could have benefited from your murder. Why not marry you first and *then* kill you? Did you have many enemies?"

"Not anyone I'd think would want to go so far as to shoot me. Have they arrested anybody?"

"People are saying your death was a suicide."

"That's ridiculous!"

"I believe you. The police are still investigating."

"Where did they find my body?"

"In your bathroom. In the articles I read and the newscast I watched it was noted that they found drugs on the counter."

She'd expected Astrid to be indignant. When she wasn't, Rory raised one brow but said nothing.

"I did use drugs for recreational purposes, but I didn't have a daily habit."

"Do you think you might have shot yourself while you were high?"

"No."

"How can you be so sure?"

"Because I didn't own a gun and never learned how to shoot one. Plus, I'm right-handed, and you said I was shot in the left temple."

"Interesting. Still, that kind of shot would have been tricky but not impossible. Your inexperience and lack of a personal weapon are more intriguing. I wonder whose gun was found in your hand. You had gun powder residue on your fingers. I'm guessing you got stoned then someone came in with a gun. He put the grip in your hand, brought the muzzle to your temple, and pulled the trigger. You might have been so out of it that you didn't know what he was doing, which is probably a good thing since what happened killed you. But I would have thought that having a bullet fired into your skull at that range would have done more physical damage. Whoever did this must have been wearing gloves and –"

Rory was interrupted by the chime of the doorbell. Rising, she told Astrid to wait upstairs while the new guest checked in. When Astrid ignored her suggestion, Rory wasn't surprised.

"I want to see what you do when you check in guests," the ghost offered, as they went downstairs. "I've never thought about what the masses did in instances like this."

"The masses?"

"I was part of the elite," Astrid said with a toss of her blonde head. "I never stopped to think about the little people."

"You're *so* arrogant!"

"Guilty as charged," Astrid purred.

Rory hurried to open the door before the doorbell could chime again. A muscular man with ginger-colored hair and pale green eyes stood on the porch with his arms folded across his chest. He had high cheekbones, sensual lips, and a strong jaw. Rory had to fight to keep her own jaw from dropping. Not only was he the most handsome man she'd ever seen, but she also instantly felt an overwhelming attraction to him. The feeling was unexpected and unnerving.

"I wish I were still alive," murmured Astrid from behind her. "What a hottie! Tall, built, and sexy! I *love* the tight black shirt, low-slung jeans, and cowboy boots. Yummy!"

The man laughed and then echoed, "Yummy?"

Rory blinked in surprise. Astrid had been the one talking, but had she accidentally repeated aloud what the ghost had said?

"I – I beg your pardon?" Rory sputtered.

"Your dead friend there thinks I'm hot." Nodding to Astrid, he said, "You're pretty hot yourself, but I prefer the lady with the pulse and not only because she's alive. She's got natural beauty and doesn't dress like a fancy hooker."

"You can see her?" Rory asked in disbelief. She fought the urge to add, "You think I'm prettier than she is?"

"If I couldn't see and hear her, then how would I know what she said and what she's wearing? She is nice-looking, except for that hole in the side of her head."

"But how…?"

"How do *you* do it?"

"I was born that way."

"I was, too."

"How'd you know *I* knew she was there?"

"I possess the ability to recognize others who also have supernatural talents." Hooking his thumbs in his front pockets, he said, "I'd like to get out of this heat and register so I can go to my place and crash."

"Um, sure. Come on in, Mr. Brody."

"How do you know his name?" Astrid asked.

"Because my guests book their stays online or by phone. I only accept people who make reservations. Caden Brody will be staying in Mockingbird Hideaway for the next week."

"Why?"

"I don't require guests to tell me why they want to stay. That's their business." Shutting the door behind the man, she added, "Although I do want to know more about your paranormal ability.

I've never encountered anyone outside my family who admitted that they could see ghosts or could sense others who did."

"What's your extra talent?" Caden Brody asked. "The people I've met who can see ghosts usually have some other unique supernatural ability."

"I...walk in my sleep," she said cautiously.

"Ooooh," Astrid said with mock awe in her voice. "How amazing!"

Caden studied Rory for several moments, nodded in understanding, and then said, "Yes, amazing. We do need to talk more, but I want to get some sleep first."

"Please sign my guest book and the release forms on the little table against the wall across from the stairs. I'll need to see your driver's license and credit card. I'll provide you with an overview of services, get the key to Mockingbird Hideaway, and give you the tour." Once she'd checked his license and Visa card, she said, "I serve a hot breakfast every morning at 8:00. There's a small grocery store in town and a new Publix in Gladeland, which is a larger town about ten miles south of Sage. The Walmart's on the highway in-between if you need more than groceries. There are area maps available for all guests. I provide plates, glasses, silverware, towels, and sheets, and there are a dishwasher and stackable washer/dryer in each cottage. If you leave a mess when you check out, then there'll be an extra twenty-five-dollar charge on your card when I run it through after your stay is over. While you're at Nostalgia Road, you can roam anywhere on the grounds and swim in the lake, but I'm not liable in case of injury or death as stated on my website and in the releases."

"Are you trying to drive people away with that cheery speech?" Astrid asked.

"She's restating her Terms and Conditions and covering her ass," Caden answered. "How long have you been doing this, Miss Roosevelt?"

"It's Rory, and I opened Nostalgia Road three years ago."

Caden allowed his eyes to roam over her from her head to her feet, so Rory gave him a slow once-over herself.

Astrid hit the nail on the head, she thought. *He is yummy. And there's something else about him being here that feels...right. He feels right.*

Feeling flushed, Rory grabbed the keys and left the house with her new guest. When Astrid came out through the wood of the front door, Rory said firmly, "Stay!"

"What am I, a dog?"

"No, but I'm going to treat you like one until you start following directions."

Pouting, the ghost went back inside in a huff.

"She's kind of a bitch, isn't she?" Caden asked, as they walked across the gravel parking area to his Chevy.

"Astrid always was and obviously always will be. She's only been here since this morning, and I already want to kill her. Ironic, since she's a ghost."

"You help ghosts cross over?"

"Yes. My brother doesn't care about that, but I feel like it's an honor to do what I consider to be really good work. You?"

"I get ghosts justice. If that helps them to cross over, then that's great. If they still stick around, then that's their choice. At least I know I've done all I can. I try not to overanalyze what I do and just do what I think is right."

"How do *you* get justice for ghosts? Do you find their killers and help to solve their murders?"

"Yes, but I work outside the law." Before she could comment, he asked, "What's your brother's extra talent?"

"Being able to pick up on people's true emotions. He's like a human lie detector. He says it's why he's still single. People lie more often than you'd think."

"I doubt that. I think people lie most of the time, even if they do it subconsciously."

As they got into the Trailblazer, she directed, "Take the road that leads away from the house and the lake. It'll curve around on the property and bring you back to an area near the water. There's a more direct path you can take on foot to return to the main house."

Rory was uneasy as she rode with Caden to the cottage. There was something about him that felt…different. It was both unnerving and exciting. Once he parked his truck, she hurried out and trotted toward Mockingbird Hideaway.

Hastening to open the front door, she announced brightly, "Here you go!"

"What kind of architecture is this?" Caden asked, as he approached.

"All of the cottages are Cracker houses built in the 1800s. Crackers were English and American pioneers whose descendants mostly live in Florida. These are the types of houses the settlers had."

"Cool."

"*I* think so," she admitted. "There used to be a fifth Cracker house where the main house is located. A century ago, that particular house burned down, and my great-grandparents had the Roosevelt home constructed on the same spot. They maintained the other four cottages on the property that used to house other family members, but nobody lived in them for decades until I made a few necessary renovations, redecorated the interiors, and started renting them out after my parents died. Mockingbird Hideaway is homey and comfortable like the main house. Palmetto House has a Florida coastal feel to it. Orange Blossom Retreat is a bit more girly, and Hurricane House is decorated in a sleek, modern style. Some return guests prefer one house in particular, while others like to rotate from cottage to cottage with each stay. Do you like this house? If not, Palmetto House is also open at the moment."

"This suits me fine. Do I have a good view of the lake?"

"This cottage is the only one that has a direct view of the water. Let's go back outside, and I'll show you."

Moments later, they were standing on the back porch of Mockingbird Hideaway. Caden put both hands on the rail and observed, "I'm in the middle of woods, but I have a perfect view of the water through the clearing. We must be only thirty feet from the edge of the lake. Where's the footpath that you said leads directly to the Roosevelt house?"

"When you go down the steps on the front porch, you'll see two gravel paths that meet at the base. Follow the path that veers right, and you'll end up at the main house."

As they stood on the banks of the lake a few minutes later, Rory pointed and asked, "See the dock and the main home? It's about a half mile walk from here to there. The three other cottages are spread out on the property."

She admired Caden's profile as he scanned the area surrounding the lake. The top of Rory's head was level with the man's shoulder.

She figured that made him a few inches above six feet when he wasn't wearing cowboy boots.

"What *did* bring you here?" she asked suddenly. "Somehow, I don't think you came to Nostalgia Road by chance."

"You're right."

Rory waited for a while, but he didn't elaborate. This should have made her angry. Instead, it simply intrigued her.

"I know you're tired and want to crash. I've got a ghost to help and some web design to work on before I go to bed. Eating something would probably be good for me, too. Will I see you at breakfast tomorrow morning?"

"I wouldn't miss it for the world."

"Do you have favorite breakfast foods?"

"Pancakes and sausage."

"Then I'll make that tomorrow morning. I should go home now," she said, trying to ignore the heat she was experiencing that had nothing to do with the humid July evening.

"I'll drive you back."

"No, thanks. I'll walk around the lake. I'm not in any hurry to return to Astrid."

As she walked along the path toward her large, beautiful, empty house, Rory gathered her mass of red curls and then draped it over the front of her right shoulder. She then absently began to braid it. Experiencing physical desire for the first time in years, she fought to quell a surge of panic. She undeniably wanted Caden Brody, and that scared her more than any ghost who might appear seeking help. After all, she wasn't afraid of the dead. Some of the living were another matter entirely.

4 Caden

Mockingbird Hideaway was unlike any place in which Caden had ever lodged. Since he'd left home after college graduation at age twenty-two, he'd lived in apartments in various cities around the country. His current apartment was in Jackson Hole, Wyoming. He'd been living there for almost a year but knew that he'd probably relocate soon. He didn't like to stay in one place for too long. That wouldn't be wise for someone who did what he did for a living.

When he was working cases, Caden stayed in all sorts of accommodations, including posh hotels, seedy motels, mountain cabins, beach houses, RVs, and mobile homes. He'd slept in his SUV, in cars, in the outdoors, and in tents. Once, he'd stayed in a shallow cave. Normally, he didn't consider how he *felt* about his temporary lodgings, but Caden found the atmosphere of the Cracker House on the rural property in Florida more relaxing than any other place he'd stayed while on a job.

Speculating that this response was the result of extreme exhaustion, Caden decided to unload his Trailblazer. He left some of his weapons hidden in the vehicle but brought others in and hid them in various locations around the cottage. Once that task had been accomplished, he returned to his vehicle for his electronics and luggage. Placing his iPad and laptop on the kitchen table, he took his bags to the master bedroom before returning outside.

The sounds of the crickets and frogs and the movement of the leaves in the trees soothed Caden, and he sat on the porch swing for a while before returning inside in order to fix himself something to eat. Deciding he wanted to remain outdoors for as long as possible, he assembled a peanut butter and jelly sandwich and then took it and a bottle of water with him back out to the swing. He ate slowly, savoring the first extended period of time spent out of his SUV in over seventy hours.

After the sun had set, Caden went inside, stripped off the clothes he'd lived in for the past three days, and then showered. He remained under the spray of the showerhead until the hot water began to cool. Once he'd toweled dry, he didn't bother to dress.

Instead, he wrapped a dry towel around his hips and tucked one corner into the edge at his waist in order to hold it together. He slept in the nude and planned on going to bed soon. However, before he did that, he wanted to perform a more thorough walk-through of Mockingbird Hideaway. He had no idea what to expect when it came to his time spent at Nostalgia Road. If things got dicey, he needed to know the exact layout of the place and what his advantages and disadvantages might be if he was ever cornered in the cottage. Caden strived never to be caught unawares.

The interior of Mockingbird Hideaway did have a decidedly "homey" feel to it. It reminded him of what little he'd seen of the interior of the main house. The living room sofa was comfortable and covered in neutral fabric. The end tables and coffee table were sturdy but looked as though they'd been salvaged from an old house and then sealed with a clear varnish to protect the wood. Framed photographs of nature scenes decorated the walls, and Caden suspected the pictures had been taken on the property owned by Rory Roosevelt. He wondered whether or not she'd taken them herself.

The small kitchen had a rooster theme to it that made him smile. He'd never understood the appeal of poultry-themed kitchens, but it seemed as if many people liked them. He suspected that was the reason behind Rory's choice of motif. After all, she'd want to make her cottages attractive to clients. Or perhaps she actually liked roosters. Although the appliances were fairly new, they weren't stainless and blended in well with the older feel of the home. The four-person dining table with chairs was in good shape but had obviously seen much use before it had been preserved.

The first bedroom contained an oak bedroom set that might have been bought from the same place as the tables in the living room and kitchen. Caden considered that maybe Rory had attended an estate sale and purchased all the pieces at once. It would make sense, both logistically and financially. Framed photos of each Cracker house on the Roosevelt property were displayed on the walls. The quilt on the bed reminded him of ones he'd seen in older homes.

The bathroom wasn't anything special, but the walls had been painted a pale green that made it seem brighter and larger than it truly was. Caden smiled self-deprecatingly as he approached the main bedroom at the back of the home. Although he was checking out everything from the placement of the furniture to the location of the kitchen knives that could be used as weapons either by him or an attacker, he was also observing and appreciating the style of the cottage. Since that was irrelevant in regards to his mission, he was both amused and perplexed by his notice of it.

The master bedroom furniture included a queen-sized bed with a distressed wooden headboard, a dresser, and nightstands. The comforter on the bed was white. There were no photographs in that room, but floating black shelves had been installed that held candles and tchotchkes. Caden fought the urge to examine the baubles on the shelves, reminding himself that there was no point to that exercise.

Do I really think I'll find answers in the knickknacks in this bedroom? he wondered. *If any item is going to help or hurt my mission, then it's likely going to be found in the main house. Face it. It's Rory Roosevelt who's doing this to me. She's so damn beautiful in a wholesome, cute way. I wouldn't give a crap about how the inside of this cottage looked if I hadn't known she'd decorated it. The feeling of attraction I experienced when I first saw her was immediate and unusually compelling. What is it about her that's got me so interested? She's not my type at all.*

Caden paused, both literally and figuratively, as he realized he'd never had a "type" because he'd never made time to get romantically involved with anyone. He'd dated women; he'd taken women to bed; but he'd never *felt* anything toward them outside of casual interest or simple lust. Therefore, the way he was reacting to Rory was unnerving. He was attracted to her, and it wasn't purely a sexual attraction. Admittedly, she did turn him on, but she also made him want to get to know her. Caden felt as if he were practically enthralled by Rory, and that feeling both intrigued and confounded him.

Elias Brody's sons didn't become romantically involved with anyone. Caden couldn't think of a single brother who'd had a serious relationship with any woman – or man, if the brother happened to be gay. They were dedicated to their work, their father, and their reason for being. Not one of them had left Elias's organization in order to marry and settle down.

Admittedly, the mortality rate of the Brody sons was high. They performed extremely dangerous work. Elias had started his "family" enterprise when he'd been thirty-one. That had been four decades earlier. Only one surviving Brody brother was older than thirty-year-old Caden, and that brother was thirty-three.

We've lost six Brody brothers since I was officially adopted by Elias when I was a child. At least a dozen boys never made it through training to the adoption phase. I'm sure some died before I was born and was taken to the Brody house. There are six Brody brothers at the moment but no boys in training. Who will take over when Elias dies? Or will everything he's worked for simply stop? How can it?

Caden shook his head and returned to the bathroom in order to brush his teeth. People had been fighting evil long before Elias had begun his campaign, and others would continue to do so once he was gone. The Brody brothers worked daily in an effort to stop those who did unimaginable things to innocent men, women, and children. Others were out there waging war on evil, too. Caden was certain the battle between good and evil wouldn't end until the end of the world itself.

Rory Roosevelt was an innocent with some sort of enormous evil looming in her future. Caden was used to killing people who had either already killed or were in the process of killing others. In this instance, nothing had happened to the innocent, yet. She wasn't even aware that she was in danger. But she did have one advantage other victims didn't: She had supernatural abilities that permitted her to see ghosts and to assume an astral form while she slept. Well, she hadn't exactly told him she took on an astral form, otherwise known as an ethereal body that allowed her to move within the real world or perhaps other planes of existence, but she'd certainly intimated it. He decided it wasn't something she wanted her current resident ghost to know and wondered whether or not Rory's astral form wore clothing.

Caden glanced down and sighed at the physical evidence of his desire. Leaving the bathroom, he went to the kitchen table and opened his laptop. Then he pulled up the photo of Rory standing in the white dress on a dock. He knew now that the dock in the photo was the dock he could see from the banks of the lake near his cottage. He allowed his eyes to study every detail of the picture, from the quaint, old-fashioned cotton dress Rory wore to the mass of dark, red curls hanging down her back. The sight of her delicate bone structure and toned body made his balls hurt, and he found himself unconsciously holding his breath when he examined the curve of one breast that was visible in the picture and the roundness of her backside. He wished that he could see her blue eyes again.

Caden decided it was time for bed. Perhaps he'd find peace as well as rest while he slept. He knew that he probably had a long and stressful day ahead of him tomorrow. Longing for someone he couldn't have was a waste of time. Frustrated, he roughly pulled off the towel and tossed it into a clothing hamper in the master bedroom.

Is Anderson still alive? Caden wondered, as he stretched out on the mattress. *If he is, has he woken up from his coma? If he won't recover, then will Elias end his life right away? I can't imagine he'd let him linger for long in some vegetative state. Why hasn't Elias let us know what his status is? He's aware that we're all waiting for news. The last time we lost a brother, we were notified right away. What's keeping Elias from calling? Is it a bad sign or a good one that we haven't heard from him?*

Caden stared up at the ceiling and thought about his father. According to Elias, he'd been born in Hungary seventy-one years ago. His parents had immigrated to the United States when he'd been a baby and had settled in New Orleans, Louisiana. When he'd manifested supernatural powers at a young age, his father and mother had decided he'd been blessed by God and had encouraged him to master his abilities.

One day when Elias was seventeen, he'd come home and found his parents stabbed to death in their kitchen. The sight had been horrific, but the couple had appeared to him as ghosts and told him to stop screaming, that they felt no more pain. However, they also shared their killer's identity with him and instructed him to get them justice. That request had set their son on a course that would alter so many lives.

It had taken Elias eleven years to get justice for his parents. He'd lived in various parts of New Orleans, learning from the criminal organizations that dominated the dark underbelly of the city. The men who ran the crime syndicates recognized his sharp mind, determination, and the supernatural talents that continued to evolve as he matured. He'd gained a place in their world and was granted the privilege of starting his own enterprise when he'd been in his twenties.

Examining his life and success at fighting evil, Elias vowed to use his personal experiences to develop a network of orphaned boys with supernatural talents who would be trained from birth to fight and kill those who harmed innocents. However, only the strong would survive. In the following years, some of the boys he took in were too weak to endure the rigors of training. Only physically superior, highly intelligent, and completely dedicated boys would be fully accepted by Elias.

Once he'd determined that a boy was worthy, Elias adopted him. It was an honor all boys longed to achieve. They wanted his blessing and paternal love. After all, none of them had had parents in their lives, and what child didn't want at least one parent around? For those who were adopted, Elias was both mentor and father.

Rory had two parents who may not have asked her to kill, but I'll bet they asked her to do something important. It's the only explanation as to why she's supposedly in so much danger. Turning onto one side and staring out of the window in front of him, Caden told himself, *I need to stop thinking about Rory and think about whatever's after her.*

His mind evidently didn't agree. Tossing and turning, Caden thought back to his arrival and check-in at Nostalgia Road. He recalled the moment he'd seen Rory in the flesh and of how difficult it had been for him to act casually but in control. The woman projected an aura that was a juxtaposition of self-confidence and uncertainty, which made no sense to Caden. She was a natural beauty, and he'd loved the modest little blue dress she'd worn that had tiny buttons running up to its collar. He'd had to fight the urge to adjust his pants so as not to draw attention to his erection. Seeing the ghost had distracted him enough to take care of that situation, and he'd been able to regain his senses and focus again.

Caden's initial contact with Rory had gone exceedingly well. It was rare for those with supernatural talents to find one another and talk openly about them, and it had felt good. She also seemed to appreciate it. He'd enjoyed the tour Rory had given him and had watched her retreating back while she'd walked toward the main house. He'd been filled with such unexpected longing when she'd absently begun to braid her hair on her walk home that he'd had to turn away.

Caden finally slept, but he found that even his dreams involved Rory. In one, the woman made pancakes and sausage for breakfast while he sat at a table and watched her cook. Neither of them spoke. He liked the way she moved as she flipped the pancakes and turned the sausage. He also liked the pink-and-purple plaid flannel pajamas she wore. When he looked at her feet, he noticed her toenails were painted the same purple color that was on her pajamas. Her red curls were pulled up in a haphazard knot at the back of her head. She looked comfortable, adorable, and sexy.

Caden woke, groaning, and mentally ordered himself to stop thinking about Rory in that way. He was here to help her, not to have sex with her. He wondered what was wrong with him.

Caden sat up, attempting to think of anything except the woman who slept in the main house. His efforts proved futile, and he eventually rose, went to the bathroom, and took a cold shower, something he hadn't had to do since he'd been a teenager. Once he was dry, he returned to bed but remained wide awake.

He finally slept again. This time, Caden dreamed of Rory standing naked on the dock. It was nighttime, and a full moon illuminated the sky, Rory, the dock, the surface of the lake, and the surrounding trees. As Caden watched, she dived into the lake and swam to where he stood on the bank near Mockingbird Hideaway.

When she reached him, Rory emerged from the water, droplets falling from her skin and hair. Caden wanted to touch her but found that he couldn't move. She came to stand in front of him, but neither of them spoke. Caden experienced an overwhelming desire to have sex with Rory Roosevelt.

No, he thought in the dream. *I want more. Damn it! What have I gotten myself into, and will I be able to get myself out of this and save Rory, too?*

5 Rory

Rory climbed out of bed and walked to the window, glancing up at the full moon before turning her attention to the lake. She loved the way the moonlight reflected off its surface and decided to head for the dock. Wearing her little pink pajama shorts and white tank top, she moved silently through the darkened house, went through the back door, descended the porch steps, and took her time walking across the grass. Crickets chirped; frogs croaked; and mosquitoes buzzed. A breeze pushed at the branches of nearby pine trees and palms. As she took in the night's sights and sounds, Rory sighed with contentment.

Once she'd reached the end of the dock, Rory sat, swinging her feet while continuing to scan her surroundings. She'd always loved to be outside in the dark, which had worried her mother. Her father and Nolan had understood. Whatever had set them apart and allowed them to have their own special supernatural gifts had also made them crave the peace that seemed to be greater between sunset and sunrise.

She lay back on the dock and thought of Caden Brody. He radiated unapologetic masculine sensuality. Rory found him unbelievably attractive and liked his straightforward attitude but suspected that he was hiding something. True, she'd only met him the previous day and hadn't been able to spend much time with him. His vagueness regarding certain parts of his past and present still bothered her.

Feeling guilty, Rory stood and decided to take the path that led around the lake to Mockingbird Hideaway. Ignoring the small voice in her head that was telling her that she'd never spied on guests and shouldn't start, she kept walking until the cottage was in sight. She half-expected the man to be sitting on the swing, looking out across the water. Then, she recalled how tired he'd said he was and noted that there were no lights on in the cottage. Mounting the steps, Rory moved to the end of the porch near the master bedroom. Caden hadn't drawn the curtains, and she peered inside then bit her lip, her face burning with a combination of embarrassment and excitement.

Caden was lying on the side of the mattress closest to where Rory stood. He slept on his side, facing her direction. The comforter, blanket, and top sheet had all been pushed away, and he was gloriously nude. She knew she should turn her head but couldn't seem to move. He was too beautiful, if one could use the term "beautiful" to describe someone who radiated machismo even in sleep. His powerful body was a masterpiece of sculpted muscle decorated with some scars, while his face commanded attention with its well-defined cheekbones, straight nose, full lips, and the stubble that shadowed his chin and jaw. It appeared that something was different about the skin atop his left shoulder, but Rory couldn't make out what it was.

Caden's ginger-colored hair was mussed with sleep. He had a sprinkling of it on his chest and a line of it running from his bellybutton down to the hair that surrounded his –

Oh, my God. He must be dreaming. Shaking her head, Rory thought, *I have to stop with the voyeurism and go back to the main house. I need to not dwell on what I can't have with him or any other man.*

Feeling anxious, sad, and lonely, Rory left the porch but didn't go home. Instead, she continued around the lake for another half mile and then veered right. When she reached the gate of the small Roosevelt family cemetery, Rory paused before walking through it and meandering around the graveyard. She knew each headstone and marker without having to read the inscriptions. After all, she'd grown up on the property and had explored every bit of it in the course of her twenty-five years.

She silently greeted each member of her family as she passed. Out of all of those buried in the cemetery, the only people she'd ever personally known had been her parents. Everyone else had died before she'd been born. Although she hadn't actually met any of them, Rory felt as though she owed it to each one to acknowledge them when she occasionally came to visit. After all, they were her family. As it was, she and Nolan were the only Roosevelts left.

"You come here often?"

Rory whirled around. Caden stood near the gate. He was shirtless but wore his jeans and cowboy boots. She couldn't see his face clearly in the darkness of the graveyard, but he didn't sound upset. In fact, he sounded amused.

"You can *see* me?" Rory squeaked. "Even Nolan can't see me when I walk in my sleep in my astral form."

"Well, I can. It's not like when I see a ghost. You don't look like your normal self. You kind of shimmer."

"I *shimmer*? Really?"

"Really. Ghosts look like regular people to us, although we can sense that they're dead even if they don't have gaping wounds or crushed bodies. But you look like your normal self, and I can feel that you're alive somewhere. It's like there's a sheen of iridescent glitter covering your skin. It makes you look even more beautiful."

"I wonder if anyone else can see my astral body. Of course, I'm still sleeping back at the house, so no one would suspect my conscious mind took a hike in a different form." Chewing on her lower lip, Rory asked, "You think I'm beautiful?"

"I don't say things I don't mean."

"How'd you know I was sleepwalking?"

"I told you I can sense others like me who can see ghosts. I woke a little while ago and felt as if you were nearby. I pulled on my pants and boots and left my cottage just in time to see you walking away on the path around the lake. I was pretty shocked at being able to view someone in astral form, and I wasn't sure if I should stay where I was or follow you. Curiosity got the better of me."

At least he didn't wake up and see me gawking at him sleeping naked in his bed, Rory thought. *Thank goodness for small favors.*

Caden looked around the cemetery and asked, "*Do* you come here often? I really want to know."

"Nolan and I meet here twice a year to clean things up. I walk out in my astral form about once a month."

"Why?"

"I'm not sure. I just do."

"I'd like to escort you home."

"That's very nice of you, but it's not as if I'm in any danger. No one can touch me when I'm like this."

"How do you know? If you've never known someone could see you like this, then no one's ever tried."

"I guess I never thought of it that way. I can't touch anything, so I assumed nothing could touch me when I'm wandering in my sleep."

"Let me walk you home and try to touch you."

"Excuse me?"

Caden raised his hands, palms facing her, and insisted, "I'll be a perfect gentleman."

She shrugged and said, "I should be getting back anyway. You don't have to walk me all the way home, though."

"But I will." As they returned to the path, Caden said, "I'd still like to try to touch your astral body."

Admitting that she was curious as well, Rory encouraged him to take her hand. He reached for it. To their astonishment, he was able to wrap his hand around hers. Instant heat seemed to flare throughout Rory's astral self, and Caden shuddered for a second, prompting her to ask, "Do I make you feel cold like when ghosts come into contact with humans?"

"No. It's like touching something hot that's…vibrating. Do you feel anything?"

"Like my body was flooded with heat. There isn't any sense of vibration though."

Caden shuddered for a second time and murmured, "Amazing."

"Caden?"

"Hm?"

"What do you do exactly?"

"Get rid of human filth."

"Somehow I don't picture you up to your butt in poop shoveling away."

"Not that kind of cleaning up and not that kind of filth."

"I don't understand."

"I know." Pausing for a few seconds, he volunteered, "Talking to you when you're dressed in those cute little pajama bottoms and that tank top with your glittering skin is even more distracting than talking to you when you're awake and wearing a sweet, sexy dress. I promise I'll explain after breakfast tomorrow."

So there, Astrid, Rory thought smugly. *Not all men find skanky attractive. I'd much rather be sweet and alluring. Too bad it can't go any further than that.*

"Do you swear you'll tell me everything? Cross your heart?"

He nodded but finished, "And hope *not* to die."

They continued on in silence for several minutes before she asked, "Are you from Florida, too? Does your family live anywhere around here?"

"No and no. I was told my parents were good, hard-working people."

"You were told? By whom? It sounds like you don't know your own parents."

"That's right. It's part of my story. After breakfast, I'll share. I'd rather not talk about it now."

"What if you skip out on me after you walk me home?"

He stopped walking, his handsome features suddenly distorted with what appeared to be fury as he growled, "I don't break my word, and I don't skip out on people! Never!"

"Okay," Rory said soothingly, giving his hand a reassuring squeeze. "I'm sorry. I didn't mean to make you mad."

"It's not your fault," he grunted.

Wait until tomorrow, she told herself. *Don't push him any further. He swore he'd tell you everything after breakfast. It's not that much longer. Be patient.*

"Thanks for walking me home," Rory said when they reached the main house.

"Enjoy the rest of the night."

"You, too. Sorry I inadvertently woke you."

"S'okay. I hope you liked what you saw before I came awake. I was dreaming about you."

"Wh-what?"

"I may wake several times during the night, but I sleep pretty deeply when I am asleep. You had to have been standing on my porch for a while for me to sense your presence. I can guess what you saw while you were lingering outside my window." Grinning, he said, "It makes me hard again just thinking about it." Before she could formulate an appropriate response, he nodded to her and said, "See you soon."

Oh...my...God.

Mortified, Rory went upstairs and returned to where she was lying in bed. Her astral self settled back into her physical body. Seconds later, her eyes snapped open.

"Oh...my...Lord."

"What?"

Rory yelped in surprise then ground out, "Astrid, I told you not to invade my privacy! You scared me half to death!"

"And someone shot me all the way to death! I need to be near you. You're my only hope for getting justice so that I can move on."

"Haunting me is not going to help my disposition."

"But you have to do something concrete to find my killer!"

"Your body was only found a few days ago. After the autopsy –"

"Autopsy?!? They're going to cut up my beautiful body?"

"Your beautiful body has an ugly hole in the side of its head. They have to do an autopsy. Then, your parents will have your remains flown back here for the funeral and burial. Just out of curiosity, who inherits your millions now that you're gone?"

"My parents and two sisters will get equal shares of half of my estate. The rest will go to charitable trusts and foundations my husband supported."

"That was very honorable of you."

Astrid tried to look as if her comment didn't matter, but Rory saw through her façade. The woman might be a nasty person in general, but Rory realized she did have more depth than she'd given her credit for. Rory wondered if Astrid had been like that all along or if her older husband had impacted her more than she'd anticipated when they'd married.

Yawning, Rory said, "It's almost 6:00. I doubt if I'll be able to sleep any longer. I'm going to shower, dress, and take care of a few things before I start cooking breakfast."

"You'd better watch out for Caden Brody," Astrid warned. "I don't trust him. Not long before you woke up, he came all the way to the house talking to himself. I think he might be crazy."

She laughed and said, "I doubt that he's crazy. Maybe he was talking to a ghost."

"Wouldn't *I* see another ghost?"

"Not necessarily. Some ghosts interact with each other, while some think they're the only ghosts around. As for Caden, don't worry. I'll be careful. I don't completely trust him myself."

"I never completely trusted anyone when I was alive."

"Not even your parents or sisters?"

"Especially not my parents or sisters. You wouldn't believe the scheming that goes on in my family."

"Some days I'm extra-thankful for my mostly unexciting life. It didn't bother you to be so shallow and manipulative when you were alive?"

"I am my mother's daughter. Speaking of my mother, you said something about my funeral."

"It should be within the next week. I'll attend and see what I can find out if I haven't managed to figure out who your killer is before then." Standing and stretching, Rory admitted, "I'll go anyway. I may still not like you very much, but I see now that you aren't all bad. I believe in remembering the good in people after they pass."

"What if they don't have any good in them?"

"I haven't come across anyone like that, yet, but if I do, they won't get anything from me but pity and scorn."

"Pity?"

"If the person was that bad, then I'd pity him. He'd obviously be so warped that he would've missed out on the goodness in the world. That's tragic."

"Your way of thinking is so foreign to me."

"Right back atcha."

Caden Brody arrived at 7:45 wearing a snug-fitting red shirt, black jeans, and black cowboy boots. Rory hated to admit that the sight of him thrilled her so much, but she was glad she'd chosen to don a deep-green, sleeveless dress that had a scoop neck and fell just above her knees but was in no way revealing. Caden had said he preferred sweet and natural, and she'd been relieved. That was what Rory preferred, and she wasn't about to pretend to be someone she was not.

The five other current guests arrived at the Roosevelt house for breakfast at 8:00 a.m. Rory served pancakes, sausage, coffee, orange juice, milk, and also provided syrup, preserves, and butter. The five guests besides Caden were members of the same family who were at Nostalgia Road for an impromptu mini-reunion and would be leaving that afternoon. They were pleasant and made it a point to include the newcomer in their breakfast conversation about the summer heat, how it compared to heat in other states, and how lovely it was to stay at such a charming B & B in a wonderful rural setting. They also discussed various dates for a return visit to

Nostalgia Road with more relatives and promised Rory they'd be booking said trip in the very near future.

Once the other guests had gone, Caden insisted on helping Rory clear the dining room table. They brought the dishes to the farm sink in the kitchen, and she filled one side with hot, soapy water while she began to rinse off the plates, glasses, and utensils in the other.

"I'm going to put these in to soak while we talk. Have a seat at the kitchen table, and I'll be with you in a second."

"Mind if I get another cup of coffee?"

"Be my guest."

His mouth twitching, he said, "I *am* your guest. You want any coffee?"

"No, thanks. Neither Nolan nor I like coffee. I will take a root beer, if you don't mind grabbing me one out of the fridge."

As he moved toward the refrigerator, he asked, "Does your brother ever come around besides when it's time to clean up the cemetery?"

"Not really. He owns a local bar and says that keeps him pretty busy."

"He could make time to come out here."

Focusing on the knife in her hand, Rory agreed and then confided, "He says it makes him too sad to be here for long because it hurts too much to think about Mom and Dad."

"You obviously don't feel the same way."

"Nolan and our father were both into flying small planes. Mom and Dad had decided to take a quick trip to Miami for their anniversary. Dad was in the process of building a new plane, and he'd sold his old one. He and Mom were going to drive even though it would take them a lot longer than flying. Nolan offered them his plane instead. They crashed about forty miles from Miami. The plane exploded, and there wasn't much left, so the Federal Aviation Administration couldn't determine if it was mechanical failure or pilot error. Dad was a great pilot, but who knows if he had a heart attack or something? Even though no one said it was Nolan's fault, he has blamed himself. After all, they were in *his* plane. He never piloted a plane again."

"Do you blame him?"

"Of course not. Even if something did go wrong with the plane, it wasn't Nolan's fault. He and Dad were meticulous about safety. Sometimes, things just happen."

"Do you go to see your brother when you're in town?"

"No. We haven't been close in years. Frankly, I'm surprised he agreed to come out twice a year to help me with the cemetery maintenance, but I suppose it assuages his guilt somewhat by making him feel like he's doing right by Mom and Dad and our other relatives when we tend to their graves. Either that or he just feels guilty because I'd be doing it all alone if he didn't help. I know he wishes I'd sold the family property instead of buying him out and staying. He has to admit that it gave him what he wanted and got me what I wanted."

"Did you ever move away from home before your parents died?"

"Sure. I went to the University of Central Florida and got my degree in computer science. I didn't care for living in Orlando, but I knew what the degree from UCF would mean and wanted to have a rewarding career in web design. I'd graduated six months before Mom and Dad were killed and had moved back home so that I could work on building my business. I was living in what I now call Mockingbird Hideaway when it happened. My customer base was already pretty solid, and I knew I could do my job from any location. I couldn't stand the thought of seeing a couple of hundred years of Roosevelt history being ignored or forgotten. I figured out how to save this place."

"Except if neither of you marries or has kids when the two of you die, your family's history will still be forgotten."

Rory nodded but said nothing. She'd thought of the same thing many times, but she didn't allow herself to dwell on it for long. It wouldn't do any good. She had no plans to marry or have children. Nolan had vowed that he never wanted a wife or kids although for different reasons than his sister's. Unless something changed their minds, the Roosevelt legacy would die along with its last two descendants.

"Enough about me," Rory said, as she rinsed her hands and reached for a dishtowel. "You promised you'd come clean after breakfast this morning."

"And I always keep my word," Caden assured her. Once she'd accepted the bottle of root beer from him, he said, "You may not believe a lot of this. You may even kick me out or call the cops to haul me away to an asylum, not that I'd let them take me."

"My capacity for believing things most people only dream about is almost unlimited."

"We'll see about that," Caden muttered. "Just remember you asked for the explanation."

Taking a seat across from him at the square kitchen table, she said, "I'll remember. Don't worry."

"Astrid needs to leave first."

The dead woman *harrumphed* from where she stood in the doorway, so Rory ordered, "Upstairs, Astrid! I'll get you after we're done. Practice moving things while you wait. Don't argue with me."

"But –"

"Go to your room right this minute or else!"

The ghost flounced off, and Caden flashed Rory a grin before saying, "Damn, you're good. What'd you threaten her with if she doesn't listen to you?"

"That I'd stop helping her." Lowering her voice, she whispered, "I wouldn't, but she doesn't know that."

"And what she doesn't know…."

"Exactly. Now, where were we?"

6 Caden

"You can't share what I'm about to tell you with anyone else. I mean *never*, Rory."

"I'm good at keeping things to myself," she assured him. "I want to hear whatever you have to say."

Nodding, Caden began, "I was raised in the New Orleans French Quarter as the son of Elias Brody," Caden began. "I wasn't his biological child, and neither was any of his other sons."

"You don't sound like the Cajun people I see on TV or in movies."

"Not all Louisiana residents are Cajuns. I grew up hearing such a variety of accents because of the diversity of residents and visitors to New Orleans, plus we traveled a lot. I've moved all over the country since I left home eight years ago. My father doesn't have any discernable accent, so I wouldn't have picked it up from him before I set off on my own."

"Where were your biological father and mother?"

"None of the Brody brothers know our birthparents. All we have is Elias."

"How many sons does your father have?"

"Over the years? He's had a lot."

Rory narrowed her eyes and repeated, "A lot. What kind of an answer is that?"

"I'm already sharing more with you than I typically share with anyone outside the family, but I need to put my trust in you so that you'll reciprocate in kind. Knowing that, do you want me to go on?"

Caden watched her ponder his question for a few moments before she nodded.

"The Brody sons weren't raised to be one, big, normal family," he began. "Elias had a master plan that involved using boys born with supernatural abilities to locate and kill those who took the lives of innocents. We were only granted the privilege of legally taking Elias's last name as ours if we survived his training."

"*Survived?* What kind of training did you have as children?"

"You name it; we had it."

44

"Oh, I so don't want to start naming things at this moment." Obviously trying to absorb what he was saying, Rory asked, "If you didn't have mothers, then did you have nannies?"

"Yes. Elias made the determination as to when each boy was ready to start training. It was something the younger boys both dreamed of and dreaded. We had no families to speak of and desperately wanted to be part of one."

"What made *you* an outcast? Do you even know how you came to live with Elias?"

"He keeps files on each of the boys he takes in. According to mine, my parents were good, hard-working people who already had six kids when my mother got pregnant with me. She had problems from the very beginning of the pregnancy and went to a *traiteur* for healing."

"What's a *traiteur*?"

"A faith healer who believes his or her healing power comes directly from God. *Traiteurs* don't take money in exchange for their services. They believe they're performing God's work, so they don't accept payment for what they do when they heal. In my mother's case, the *traiteur* prayed over her and told her something was wrong with her baby and that it couldn't be fixed. She also remarked that God might take me to Jesus early since I was fundamentally flawed. She said evil would try to claim me and that I should be taken away after birth and hidden with someone who could teach me to protect myself."

"What a terrible thing to tell someone!"

"I'd like to imagine my birthparents were sad to lose me, but they might have been relieved. I don't know anything else about them. Elias said the *traiteur* brought me to him wrapped in a worn blanket within an hour of my birth."

"How old were you when you started your...training?"

"My ability to see ghosts and sense others with supernatural abilities was nurtured from the time Elias accepted me into his home. I began to learn how to fight when I was five. That training continued as I grew and expanded to include tracking, catching, and killing murderers."

"So, you're like a mercenary?"

"Mercenaries take part in hostile activities, but it's typically for personal gain. I do what has to be done, but it has nothing to do with money. It has to do with good versus evil. If I have to use violence or kill in order to stop a murderer, then so be it. Does that horrify you?"

Rory considered before answering, "No. The average person would be horrified, but I've seen too many ghosts who had been slaughtered when they were alive by evil men and women not to understand. If the person can be legally punished, then I think that's the best solution. However, if they can't be brought to justice...."

Caden fought the urge to sag with relief. He hadn't known exactly what he would tell Rory that morning or how she'd react. Those raised in the Brody household were warned by Elias about sharing the stories surrounding their births and other details regarding him and their lives, but Caden had sensed that he'd have to take the chance in order to reach Rory Roosevelt. He was immensely grateful that his gamble had paid off.

"How do you have any income?" Rory suddenly asked. "Ghosts can't pay you for helping them."

"I wouldn't take their money even if they could."

"Then how?"

"Most of the whack jobs I stop are much smarter than the typical murderer. This means they often have a lot more money, too. When that's the case, I not only end their lives; I also take their money, although I never secure any of their property for myself. This means I can do what I was born to do."

"Elias taught you that, too?"

"Yes. All of his sons are self-sufficient, not caring about wealth or notoriety. We have other goals."

"Total vengeance for innocent victims."

"Yes. We end the lives of warped men and women and then take any monies they've worked hard to accumulate. It gives me and my brothers satisfaction. We sacrifice our personal lives in order to help those who couldn't save themselves and those they left behind. At least half of anything we take from the killers goes to the victims' families or to charities if they had no living relatives. We use the rest to support ourselves and fund our work."

Once she'd drained what remained of her soda, Rory asked, "What kind of fighting do you do?"

"Hand-to-hand. Mixed martial arts. Guns. Knives. Elias uses magic as well. We do whatever it takes."

"Magic?"

"That's all that stuck out after everything I just told you? You sound like you don't believe in magic, yet you can see ghosts and walk around in an astral body."

"I've just never met anyone who actually said they knew how to use magic or knew others who did. I'm not discounting that it exists."

"Magic can be tricky, so I try to avoid it."

"Okay, so tell me what happens after these bad people are dead?"

"I utilize available technology to disperse assets to untraceable accounts. We Brodys are taught to be versatile."

"So, what really brought you to Nostalgia Road?"

The corners of Caden's mouth turned down and the muscles in his belly tightened before he admitted, "A ghost came to me a few days ago and said an old evil was threatening to return to a place that contained enormous supernatural energy. He said this place was located in Sage, Florida and had been protected by the Roosevelt family for generations. He pleaded with me to intercede, because the last two Roosevelt descendants might be in grave danger. So, here I am."

"I've never had ghosts warn me about anything. All they want is for someone to help them."

"That's why I took him seriously. He wasn't asking for my help to get justice. He was pleading for me to save his children."

Rory stiffened before asking hoarsely, "You saw my dad? But how? Why? It's been three years. Neither Nolan nor I ever saw our parents after they died."

"Your father said he'd tried to contact you and your brother, but neither of you could see him. Your mother crossed over after the plane crash because she didn't have the gift and thought it was simply a horrible accident. Your father knew better and decided he had to find some way to reach you. Somehow, his efforts eventually led him to me."

"Is he with you now?"

Caden hated to hear the hopeful tone in her voice because he had to tell her, "No. I could sense that he was barely holding on. Once he'd imparted his warnings and pleas, I vowed to do whatever

I could to help you and his son. Your dad thanked me, told me to tell you he loved you and your brother, and then crossed over."

Rory blinked back tears, making Caden want to put his arms around her. He knew he was overloading her with information, but he felt as though every moment might be crucial in their fight against an evil they didn't understand. His feelings of protectiveness toward the woman mingled with his desire for her, and his body reacted accordingly.

"How do I know you're not crazy?" Rory asked. "How can I be certain you're not making all this up? Can you prove to me that my father was really the one to contact you?"

"He said you'd be suspicious and to ask you if you still kept the paths to the elements clear, whatever that means. He also wanted Nolan to know it wasn't his fault that the plane crashed. It wasn't due to mechanical failure or pilot error. Your father told me evil was what had brought down that plane and that it could destroy his children, just as it had killed him and their mother."

Rory gaped at Caden before saying, "This could be a trick. You said you could sense others who see ghosts. What if you're really telepathic and can read minds? Or what if you do know how to use magic and are using it against me? That could explain everything you've said and done since you arrived. You could be manipulating me for personal gain."

"I could, if I were telepathic or did use magic with bad intent. I'm not and I didn't, but I don't know how to prove it to you."

Raking her fingers through her red curls, Rory said with more than a hint of frustration, "I need to know if you're at Nostalgia Road to help or harm."

"To help, of course. Still, you're going to be wary of my motives no matter what I do."

"You're right." Pressing her fingers against her temples as if she had a headache, Rory asked, "When did my father appear to you?"

"Four days ago. Luckily, I was in-between cases. I located this place on the Internet, made my reservations, got in my Trailblazer, and started driving. I wasn't sure what to expect. I'm still not sure. The thing is, I don't quite know what this big, bad evil is supposed to be. I take down living bad guys. What if your dad was talking about fighting dead ones?"

"I don't know. I don't know how to fight, period."

"Your father talked about this property's being a center for supernatural energy. Had he ever told you that?" When she didn't answer, Caden pointed out, "You have to work with me on this. I've told you a lot more than I probably should have, but I'm not leaving knowing you might be a target for some living or dead killer. I trusted you with my story. Trust me now."

"You could have made all that up."

"For what purpose?"

"Maybe you're working for the bad guys."

"If I were, then wouldn't I simply skip the pleasantries and just kill you?"

"Not if you needed me alive in order for your scheme to work."

"Damn it, Rory!" he shouted, causing her to jump visibly. Forcing himself to calm down, he went on, "I'm only trying to help! I'm not telepathic, and neither are you! So, we're going to stay in a stalemate unless you agree to trust me." When she hesitated, he continued, "Look, you can ask me anything, and I promise to answer truthfully."

"All right. What's your greatest fear?"

"Man. You don't pull any punches, do you?" When she colored with embarrassment, he decided to forge ahead and confided, "Losing my humanity because of what I do to protect and avenge others. What's yours?"

Averting her gaze, Rory said in a small voice, "Being used by someone for his own ulterior motives."

Caden sat back in his chair and said, "Well, doesn't that just take the cake? You suspect me of wanting to do exactly that. God certainly has a sense of humor. He must believe I don't have enough challenges in my life already." Before she could comment, he went on, "I get that I'll have to earn your trust. How about if I start by helping you find Astrid's killer?"

"But you're only here for a week."

"That's how long my reservation's for. I don't intend to leave until things at Nostalgia Road are settled. I'll keep renting one of your cottages until this is over."

"What if it drags on for months? I already have all cottages booked starting at the end of September."

Caden glanced around and asked, "How many bedrooms do you have in the main house?"

"Nobody stays here but me," she said firmly. "Well, me and my ghostly visitors. I like the solitude."

"Screw solitude. What if your life's really in danger?" he demanded.

"What if you're really the threat?" Rory shot back.

"I'm not!" Clenching his jaw, Caden insisted, "I'm staying until I know you're safe from whatever evil is trying to harm you. I made a promise to your father and accepted the assignment he gave me. Elias raised me to keep my promises."

"And to fight and kill. Somehow, I don't trust your adoptive father when it comes to –"

A shriek from upstairs startled both of them. Caden was bigger and bulkier than Rory, but he was also in top physical shape and was, therefore, faster. She darted behind him up the stairs. His main concern was protecting her, and he wasn't about to let her pass him in case danger was imminent.

He wondered whether or not Astrid was crossing over. Ghosts sometimes did that even if they'd been hanging on, waiting for their murderers to be brought to justice. However, they didn't usually shriek when they went. They were silent as the image of their corporeal form began to blur then fade until they simply disappeared.

Caden stopped so suddenly when he reached the door of what was currently Astrid's room that Rory slammed into his back and tumbled to the floor. He whirled around, asking if she was all right. She nodded and accepted the hand he offered her, effortlessly pulling her to her feet. She stared up at him with what looked like expectation, and he felt goosebumps skitter across his skin and warmth spread deep within him.

"I did it!" Astrid cried, breaking the spell of the moment.

"What did you do?" Rory asked while maintaining eye contact with Caden.

"I moved a pencil off the desk! I never thought I'd get excited about something as mundane as that, but it was fabulous after not being solid for…for however long I've been a ghost." Her brow furrowing, she admitted, "I can't remember how long you said I'd been dead."

"Just a few days," Rory told her. "Ghosts don't keep track of time like living people do." She looked down, saw the pencil on the floor, and said, "That's great. Keep practicing but no moving things around in front of my guests. I don't market this place as a haunted B&B and don't want to start."

"You're no fun!" Astrid huffed.

"There's no time for fun. Caden and I are going to look for your killer."

"This is a test," Astrid said, imitating an announcer's voice. "This is only a test. Do not turn off your extrasensory powers."

"At least she has a sense of humor," Caden observed.

"It's one of the few things I appreciate about her."

"Hey! You have your own issues, Rory Roosevelt! I may not be Miss Selfless, but neither are you! You live out here in Nowheresville like a hermit and have only been with one man in your life!"

Her face instantly coloring, Rory snapped, "TMI in front of our guest!"

"I don't care if it's too much information! I'm dead. I have no future! You do, and you're wasting it by hiding out here where no one can hurt you! That also means no one can love you! You need to *live*!"

Rory turned and marched down the stairs. Caden listened as she returned to the kitchen before saying, "Not cool, Astrid."

"I'm only trying to help! I used to be mean to her and her geeky friends because…well, because I could. It was wrong, and I want to make amends. Rory is different than the way she used to be. She was a girly-girl nerd, but she was really social. She changed at the end of our senior year."

"People change," Caden pointed out.

"Not that drastically that quickly. Something happened, but I'm not sure what it was. All of us in the senior class noticed, but nobody seemed to know what was wrong. Plus, she and her brother used to be so close, but we could tell that they acted different toward each other that summer before we graduates went away to college. I guess they've stayed estranged. She's not herself anymore, and I find it sad. I may have been a bitch, but I was always true to myself. That's the way it should be."

"I have a feeling you were nicer than you thought you were."

Astrid shrugged, her blonde hair swaying with the movement and once again revealing the hole in the side of her head. Caden told her to remain in her room and then went downstairs.

Rory stood in front of the farm sink, unenthusiastically washing and rinsing the dishes that had been soaking in the soapy water. As Caden crossed the kitchen, she didn't turn or acknowledge him, even though she had to have heard the sound of his cowboy boots as he approached.

"Astrid may be a bitch, but she's right. You *are* hiding out here. What scared you into isolation?"

"I run a B&B and deal with customers all the time. I'm not isolated."

"Having some human interaction and having meaningful interaction with family and friends are two different things."

"And you know this how?" she snapped. "How many meaningful relationships do *you* currently have?"

Moving to stand behind her, Caden admitted, "None outside of my family circle, but I do have close relationships with my brothers. Would you say the same about you and *your* brother?"

Rory had to be aware of his proximity but didn't stop rubbing the sponge over the plate that she held in her left hand. A part of Caden wanted to touch her so badly that he felt as if he might die if he didn't. Another part of him worried about the repercussions if he followed his instincts. Torn, Caden wetted his lips with his tongue and weighed his options. After hesitating for a moment, he placed his hands on Rory's shoulders and bent his head, his hot breath gently stirring some hair near her right ear. She stiffened but didn't push him away.

"I won't be hurt again by any man," Rory said softly but with resolve.

"I have no intention of hurting you. Quite the opposite. Let me hold you."

"No. I don't need any man to hold me." Pausing, she added, "Besides, Astrid could come in at any moment."

"She's a ghost. Who's she going to tell?"

"Me. She's already a pain in the butt. I don't want to add fuel to the fire."

Slowly slipping his arms around her waist, Caden murmured, "I do." When she didn't protest the embrace, he continued, "Christ,

Rory. You're so alluring without even trying. I love these little dresses you wear, and I can't stop thinking about you no matter what else I'm doing. You were even in my dreams, remember? Don't push me away."

"I...don't want to," she admitted. Her hands stilling in the warm water, Rory asked, "What *was* I doing in your dreams?"

"In the last one I had before I woke and followed you to the cemetery, you were standing naked on the dock, looking up at the moon." Pulling her closer, aware that she'd feel the bulge at the front of his pants against her back, Caden went on, "And then you dived into the lake. I was standing on the bank near Mockingbird Hideaway and was naked, too. You were dripping wet as you emerged from the water and approached me. I wanted to touch you so badly, but I couldn't move. Neither of us spoke. I was about to reach forward in my dream when I woke and sensed you nearby." Caressing the flesh beneath her ear with his lips, Caden murmured, "I hated to wake. I wanted to feel you in my dream. I want to feel you now."

"I – I *do* want you to touch me even though I barely know you," she confided in a shaky voice. "But I'm scared."

"You never have to be afraid of me," he insisted.

"Earlier, you told me that Elias taught you not to break promises."

"Yes."

"So...."

Caden waited, sensing that Rory was grappling with some sort of inner demon. Having plenty of those himself, he remained still and quiet. She was evidently at an emotional crossroads, and he felt that he shouldn't try to sway her decision in his favor, no matter how much he wanted to do exactly that.

"Promise me you'll only touch me with your hands and mouth and will stop if I tell you to," she eventually said in a small voice. "Promise me you won't try to have sex with me."

"No sex and I'll stop whenever you want. I promise. There's something about you that makes me forget that I'm not supposed to become emotionally involved with any woman. This – whatever *this* is – seems to be different for both of us. Give me a chance. Okay?"

Offering no verbal response, Rory did give an almost imperceptible nod. Caden's hands skimmed her arms and hips. Her hands remained in the now-tepid water, but Caden could almost hear her pulse rate racing with fear and longing. He wondered why she was so afraid and was determined to help her relax and trust him. She'd obviously never been touched the way that he was touching her and wasn't certain how to react.

In a bold move that Caden suspected surprised her as much as it did him, Rory pushed back against him. That was when Caden's mind temporarily surrendered to his lust. His hands found their way under her short skirt, and Rory gasped, beginning to take in little gulps of air. As his fingers trailed up her outer thighs to her hips, Rory tensed and held her breath. Caden moved to stand on her right side. When he fingered the elastic at the front of her bikini underwear, she withdrew her hands from the water and drove them up into his ginger-colored hair. The raw need emanating from her was almost palpable, but Caden still sensed fear. When Rory lifted her face in order to offer him her lips, he lightly brushed them with his.

"Only touch me through my clothing," she breathed.

"Okay," he said hoarsely.

"What you're doing feels so good, but I may have to tell you to stop soon."

His heart hurt when he heard the slight quaver in her voice, but Caden said firmly, "I remember my promise. You're safe with me."

Rory didn't tell Caden to stop when he lightly nipped at the side of her neck as he slowly slid his hands downward. Releasing a little cry, she attempted to turn in order to face him.

"Don't," he ordered gently. "I'm going to take care of you, remember?"

Rory mutely nodded, her cheek rubbing against the side of his head. The languid strokes of Caden's fingers were certainly eliciting a positive reaction from her. As scared as she was, he could tell that Rory longed for more. He gave it to her, feeling as if *he* were going to explode at any moment. As for her, he had no doubts as to how she felt regarding his actions.

Caden savored the feel of her arousal and added pressure from his thumb to the sensitive spot above the area he was already stroking. Rory suddenly shuddered and cried out with her release. Caden didn't still his fingers as she clutched at him, trembling in his embrace. He delighted in the fact that she'd climaxed so readily.

"Oh, my God," Rory gasped, as she sagged in his arms. "That was so much more than what I'd expected."

Caden stiffened but didn't ask the obvious question. He didn't have to. He simply knew that this had been Rory's first orgasm. He carefully withdrew his hand from underneath her dress, telling her truthfully, "I'm thrilled to know that I gave you such pleasure."

"What can *I* do for *you*?" she asked earnestly, but he could hear the anxiety in her voice.

"Nothing for now. If you want to go further with me someday, I'll gladly make love with you. Until then, I'll get myself off by just remembering what happened here." Caden grinned and then said, "I think I need to return to my cottage and take care of that now. Then I'll shower and come back. We can get started on finding Astrid's killer and figuring out what your father was worried about." Moving to stand in front of Rory, Caden took her in his arms, kissed her tenderly, and then announced, "I'll be back as soon as I can."

"You promise?"

He grinned and said, "Oh, yeah. I definitely promise."

7 Rory

Rory blushed as she thought about what Caden was doing in his cottage. She was both embarrassed and aroused. Her panties were still damp as a result of what he'd done, and she decided she should go upstairs and change them before he returned. Astrid was seated on the edge of the mattress when she entered the master bedroom.

"I don't know if I should congratulate you or him," the ghost said. "Bravo to both of you. It sounded like you enjoyed yourself. Aren't you proud of me? I didn't look even though I really wanted to, and I'm not hanging out at Mockingbird Hideaway watching that magnificent man jerk off." Sighing, she confided, "Being dead means I have absolutely no sex drive. What a bummer."

Trying not to think of Caden's coming while fantasizing about her earlier climax proved futile, and Rory didn't want to change her underwear in front of Astrid. She was about to ask the woman to leave the room for a few minutes when she heard a truck that had a familiar rattle in the engine pull into the parking area.

"My brother's here," she told Astrid. "I wonder why? He's not what I'd call a frequent visitor."

"Go see what he wants," the dead woman encouraged. "I'll come with you. I want to know how he's held up as he's aged."

"For cryin' out loud! He's only two years older than we are. Well, then I am and you were. Besides, I thought your libido had flat-lined along with your heart."

"It did. That doesn't mean I'm not curious and can't still appreciate a great body when I see one."

Rory heard Nolan knocking. It made her uncomfortable each time he did it. The main house was his family home, too. He had a key. Still, he never used it. She was glad he respected her privacy but didn't want him to feel like a guest in the old Roosevelt home.

"Who is it?" she called out through the front door once she reached it.

"As if, Rory!"

She opened the door, took one look at her big brother, and then asked, "What was it this time? Drunks fighting over a pool game?

A customer who didn't pay his tab? A lovers' quarrel you had to break up?"

"Two jackasses wailing on each other over a woman who wasn't worth fighting for. Is the black eye really that bad?"

"No, but the split lip is. I see you got a few stitches."

"Yeah, I –" Noticing Astrid, Nolan blinked in surprise and cried, "Holy shit! Astrid Hass? What the hell are you-?" Then he noticed the hole in the side of her head and said more evenly, "Oh. Sorry. Tough break."

"Tough *break*!" Astrid echoed in disbelief. "I friggin' got shot in the head!"

Nolan shrugged and said, "Yeah, I kind of noticed that. Do you know who did it?"

"She doesn't," Rory said, not wanting to talk about the dead woman while standing in the open doorway. "Get in here. We have to talk. There's a lot going on."

He frowned down at his sister and nodded, which told her he already knew something was wrong. Nolan was several inches taller than she, but they had the same curly, red hair and deep blue eyes. Although he wasn't as muscular and lean as Caden, he was in good shape. He *had* to be if he was going to maintain order in his bar. The way he sauntered into the house belied the air of tension emanating from him.

"Even with that black eye and stitched lip, you're still a looker," Astrid cooed once Rory had closed the front door behind her brother. "The torn jeans and faded Bob Marley t-shirt make you even sexier."

"Thanks for the compliment. You look...were looking good yourself when you died."

"You two can inflate each other's egos later," Rory said irritably. "And why are you talking to her, Nolan? You never speak to ghosts."

"I never have known the ghosts who reveal themselves to me, so they've been easy to ignore. I knew Astrid. It'd be weird if I just ignored her like I do my usual visitors." Walking toward the kitchen, he asked, "Got any beer?"

"Isn't it a bit early to be drinking? It's the middle of the morning."

Nolan stopped, turned, and said, "Cut me some slack. I was up all night dealing with the assholes who drew me into their shit. I finally had to call the police station so that Harvey could haul their butts to jail when they wouldn't stop fighting. He told me *you* had some assholes out here night before last and had to call him to scare the guys into towing the line."

"It worked. The men left without causing more problems."

"I wish you wouldn't insist on running the B&B. What if you had a criminal check into one of your cottages? Hell, some regular idiot who had too much to drink or got stoned could hurt you. You might have a killer on the property and not even know it."

"I've been handling things fine ever since I opened Nostalgia Road. I need the income to keep the property up. I do have problem guests once in a while. That's the nature of the business. Most people are fine. However, I'll tell you now that I do have a killer on the premises at the moment. He can see ghosts like we can and has the ability to sense others who have the same gift. He was sent here by Dad to help us."

"You're serious," Nolan said flatly.

"You can tell when people are lying. Have I ever tried to lie to you?"

Nolan looked to Astrid and asked, "This guy saw you when he arrived?"

"Immediately. He's hot! I really wish I weren't dead."

"You trust him, Rory?"

"I do, but I want you to use your human lie detector abilities to confirm that he's being truthful. If he is, then we're in some sort of supernatural danger."

"Why would Dad go to him and not come to us? This bastard sounds like he's pulling your chain. You should know better after what happened to you."

Rory flinched. It had been seven years, but time hadn't dulled the sting of hurt and humiliation. She knew that Nolan loved her. She also knew he wasn't capable of understanding how she felt when reminded about the incident that had stolen her willingness to trust men.

"Don't you *dare* talk to her like that!" Caden growled, venom practically dripping from each word. Rory hadn't heard him enter the house. Coming further into the room, he said, "Show your sister some respect."

"What makes you think you have the right to tell me how to talk to my sister?" snapped Nolan. "You tell me everything you told her, and then we'll see if you're being straight with her or if your ass is mine!"

"Oh, he's being *straight* with her," Astrid said with a devilish grin. "I can vouch for that."

Oblivious to the innuendo behind her words, Nolan said, "I reserve the right to make up my own mind."

Caden smiled, but Rory saw the thinly veiled rage and the resolve in the man's eyes.

"I'm getting a beer," Nolan remarked before heading for the kitchen. "We'll talk on the back porch."

"Let's do it," Caden said smoothly, sounding threatening although his tone was casual.

"Not without me," Rory protested. "I want to hear everything you say to make certain I'm satisfied with whatever my brother's abilities tell him about your honesty. Once the results are in, then we can decide how to proceed."

"I wouldn't dream of excluding you," Caden told her. "I think I'll get a beer myself. You want one?"

"It's too early in the day. Besides, I'd rather be completely sober so that I can better enjoy the pissing contest the two of you are about to have."

Nolan sat sullenly in one of the rockers on the back porch and then opened the beer bottle in his hand. Rory had intended to sit between the two men, but Caden didn't give her the chance. Instead, he occupied the seat next to her brother and asked if she'd take the seat beside his. For an instant, she imagined she was back in front of the kitchen sink with her fingers in the man's hair. Her response to him had shocked and confused her, but she couldn't truthfully say that she didn't want him to touch her in such an intimate way again. Startled, she realized she longed for him to do more.

"You all right?" asked Caden.

"I won't know the answer to that until you talk to my brother."

Nolan listened as Caden shared his story. Rory noted that Caden left out the parts relating to his family origins. By the time Caden finished, both men had drained their bottles and Rory's stomach muscles were knotted with anticipation.

What if Caden lied to me about everything? she wondered. *What if I allowed him to touch me, and he only did it because he had ulterior motives?*

"He's telling the truth," Nolan said grimly. "Shit. I'm glad to know after all these years that I can stop blaming myself for Mom's and Dad's deaths, but what the hell happened to them? Rory, what was Dad talking about when he mentioned elements?"

She was about to answer when the five family members who'd been staying in Hurricane House and Orange Blossom Retreat walked around from the front of the Roosevelt home in order to turn in their keys. Rory ushered them inside through the back door, thanked them for their business, and happily booked their stay that included other relatives and all four cottages for a week the following April. Once the guests had departed via the front door, she returned to the back.

Just as she was about to push open the screen door, Nolan said, "I see the way you look at my little sister. Stay the hell away from her. She's been hurt enough. If anyone hurts her again, I'll kill him."

"Hurting her is the furthest thing from my mind. Even if it weren't, you don't have the balls to actually kill me. You might be good at brawling and breaking up bar fights, but you're no killer."

"And you are."

"I've already told you what I've been doing for years. I take down evil people who hurt and kill innocents in terrible ways. Rory is an innocent."

A long period of silence followed. Rory waited where she stood, trying not to make a sound. She wanted to see what each man was going to say and do. Now that she knew Caden wasn't lying, she needed to know how he really felt about her. Since he was talking to her brother, he had to be completely honest. Nolan would "out" him if he lied about anything.

"What makes Rory so special to you? You only met her yesterday. I love her because she's my baby sister and is…well, my baby sister. But she's not exactly a social butterfly."

"Is that what you expect from women?" Caden ground out. "You want some eye candy who'll impress others? I may not have known your sister long, but she's already made a real impression on me. I *feel* her beauty and strength almost the same way that I can sense when someone around me can also see ghosts. From the moment I saw Rory, I felt the overwhelming urge to know her as well as to protect her."

"What if I tell you to fuck off or else?"

"Then I'll beat the shit out of you. I intend to do what it seems like no one else has done for Rory in a long time, which is to take care of her."

"I love Rory!" Nolan insisted. "I take care of her!"

"You might love her because you're her brother, but you're clueless about what she needs. You stay away from this place because it makes you sad. Hell, it probably makes you sad to see Rory because you remember what she was like as a girl. It makes you feel impotent. Instead of trying to deal with whatever happened and help her in the process, you deflect blame by putting it right back on her. That's really messed up."

Rory closed her eyes. Caden was telling her brother all of the things she'd longed to say for the past seven years, but she hadn't wanted to take the chance she might sever the fragile remnants of their previously close sibling bond. Nothing had been the same since that fateful night when she'd been eighteen, and things had become more strained three years ago after the plane crash.

"I don't have to listen to this," Nolan declared. "I'm going back to my bar. At least *there* I know what's expected from me. I have no place or purpose at Nostalgia Road. All I'm good for is helping Rory clean up the family cemetery twice a year."

"You can't deal with the unknown, so you're going to turn tail and run. I think I see a pattern here. What a coward!"

Rory rushed out onto the back porch in time to see Nolan swing his empty beer bottle at Caden's head. The man easily dodged the bottle and punched her brother in the nose. Nolan stumbled and landed unceremoniously on his butt. He struggled to his feet, blood running over his stitched lip and his chin. He scrambled up and then rushed Caden, obviously intent on landing a blow to the other man's gut. Again, Caden moved quickly out of the way, this time simultaneously elbowing Nolan between his shoulder blades. The younger man fell to his hands and knees. That time, he didn't immediately try to rise.

"Give it up," Caden advised. "I have way more experience when it comes to fighting and killing."

"You bastard," Nolan spat. "You'd kill me?"

"Not unless I had to. I don't kill people because they're ignorant cowards; I kill them because they like to hurt and kill others."

"I could learn to do what you do," Nolan said defiantly. "I could be just as good or better at it than you."

Caden laughed. His reaction caught Rory off-guard. From the looks of it, neither Nolan nor Astrid had expected it either.

"What's so funny?" Nolan asked gruffly, as he stood and wiped at the blood on his face.

"I was raised from birth to do what I do. At twenty-two, I was deemed one of the best and began working solo. Even if you learned everything I know, you couldn't face the evil I see on a regular basis and continue fighting."

"I could!"

"Grow up," Caden said soberly. "I've killed men and women who enjoy doing things like imprisoning, torturing, poisoning, raping, mutilating, and then murdering their victims. So far, those victims have ranged in age from newborn to ninety-eight. Sometimes, I catch the murderers in the act of hurting or killing another victim. I live with those images every day and wonder whether or not the people I'm able to save wish I'd let them be killed. You could never handle any of it."

"That doesn't make me a coward," Nolan said.

"No. Running away from helping your sister and not aiding her in her efforts to preserve your family's legacy is what makes you a coward."

Nolan rounded on Rory and asked, "When are you going to tell this maniac to leave?"

"I'm not. He's offering to help try to stop whatever evil is threatening us and possibly others. Unlike *you*, I'm willing to admit when I need help."

"Oh, really? You didn't ask for help seven years ago."

Tears stung Rory's eyes. She wanted to tell her older brother that she shouldn't have had to ask, that he should have simply done what was necessary in order to gain justice for her. Instead, he'd instantly withdrawn from her as soon as she'd confided in him. He'd made her realize that she couldn't tell anyone else. If she did, then they might reject her, too. Their parents had died not knowing the truth, assuming that her personality change at age eighteen was due to adjustment issues resulting from the transition from high school to college. She'd been so close to them and hated keeping secrets, but Nolan had made her afraid with the way he'd reacted.

"Just go," she told her brother. "I'll handle whatever this is."

"No! Leave Nostalgia Road. Move into town. You can start over. You'd be safe. This place can rot and be forgotten as it should have been a long time ago."

"How can you say that?" Rory asked in disgust. "We're the last two Roosevelts! This place and our gifts are part of us. We can't just walk away! We shouldn't!"

"Why not?"

"If you have to ask, then you should go now. You obviously don't understand."

Scowling at her, Nolan barked, "*You're* the one who doesn't understand! Nobody asked us if we wanted these 'gifts' we got when we were born. Nobody asked if we wanted to see and hear dead people off and on all the time! When I'm away from here, then I can lead a pretty normal life. I ignore the dead women who pop in and out of my world. Eventually, they go away. Aside from having them hanging around, my life is my own. Yours isn't." Before she could protest, he demanded, "Leave with me!"

"No. I can't pretend as if the ghosts who come to me for help aren't there. Generations of Roosevelts worked hard to safeguard this place. I won't allow it to be compromised. I don't want to deny who or what I am. I may tire of having dead people showing up and hanging around, especially if they're pains in the butt like Astrid. Yet, I remind myself that I'd want someone to help me if I were in his or her place. What if that person ignored me and I couldn't hold on any longer? Would I spend eternity in some sort of limbo? How horrible would that be?"

"Stop trying to guilt me into helping you!"

"I'm not! You make your choices, and I make mine. We each have to live with the consequences."

"Or die with them," Nolan muttered, jogging down the steps and going around the house without so much as a glance in her direction.

Rory swallowed the lump in her throat that appeared when her brother's truck roared to life. Tears blurred her vision as she listened to him drive out of the parking area and turn onto the road. When she couldn't hear it anymore, she blinked away the tears. Caden moved to take Rory in his arms, but she backed away, offering him an apology as she retreated into the house. She was both dismayed and pleased when he followed.

"Wait."

Rory paused at the foot of the stairs, one hand resting on the newel post. Caden stood several feet away, not attempting to come closer. She expected him to tell her that Nolan would be back and that they'd all work things out together. When he did, she'd have to respond that she knew her brother better than he and that Caden and she were on their own when it came to fighting whatever or whoever might be lying in wait.

"It seems like Nolan loves you, but he's a real ass," Caden remarked. "He won't help us."

"No. For the past seven years, all he ever wanted was to get away from this place and from me."

"Why? I'd think he'd want to stick around to protect you and spend time with you, especially after your parents died."

She turned and said, "Then you'd be mistaken."

"What the hell is going on between you and your brother?"

As Rory began to climb the stairs, she said, "I'm sorry, but I can't talk about it now. I want to be alone for a while. I'll come downstairs again soon. Then we can start our investigation into Astrid's death and whatever is going on here at Nostalgia Road. Just give me some time. I promise I won't keep you waiting for long."

8 Caden

Caden forced himself to inhale and exhale slowly and deeply in an effort to quell his anger. He was furious with Nolan Roosevelt for his behavior during their encounter and for the way he'd treated his sister. Perhaps he could uncover the root of the problem between the siblings by researching Rory's background more thoroughly.

What's wrong with me? Caden wondered. *She's known me for one day, and whatever traumatic experience led to the rift between her and Nolan happened a long time ago. I have to give Rory time. She needs to trust me implicitly for both our sakes. Once she feels comfortable enough to tell me her story, then I'll know I've gained her complete confidence. Our lives might depend upon it.*

"I'll talk to her," Astrid announced.

"Let her be," Caden ordered quietly. "I'm going back to Mockingbird Hideaway. If Rory wants to explain, she knows where to find me."

"But –"

"If I don't see her again today, then I'll show up for breakfast tomorrow at 8:00. We'll take it from there."

Astrid planted her hands on her hips and impatiently tapped her foot before declaring, "You don't strike me as the type to tiptoe around unpleasant topics, so why are you doing it with Rory?"

Annoyed, Caden snapped, "I don't know! I think time is of the essence when it comes to what her father told me about this mysterious danger, but I feel as if I can't push her any further than I already have."

He expected Astrid to make a snarky comment, but she merely looked contemplative, nodding before saying, "You've never really cared about any one woman in your life, have you?"

Taken aback, he paused before admitting, "Not in the way you mean."

"But you care about Rory?"

"Maybe. I've never felt like this about any member of the opposite sex before."

"Neither has she."

"How would you know? You two weren't exactly best friends from what I've gathered."

"We weren't, but that doesn't mean I didn't know a lot about her. She dated boys in high school and was popular in her own geeky group, but I never remember hearing that she was in love with anyone. Our school was small, and I made it my business to know everything there was to know about everyone from the time I was in kindergarten."

"Why am I not surprised?"

"Well, it worked. I was always the center of attention." Frowning, she reflected, "I remember someone telling me in high school that Rory had vowed not to have sex before marriage. I only found out she was no longer a virgin after I arrived here and goaded her into telling me. The way she said it led me to believe that she didn't love the guy. I think *that's* at the root of her problems."

"I'm no psychologist and am certainly not going to question her about that." Scrubbing his face with one hand, Caden announced, "I'm going back to my cottage. Don't push Rory to talk. She and I have some really terrible force to stop and need to work as a team. I don't want her to withdraw from me. Don't interfere, Astrid. That would only make things worse."

When she didn't argue, Caden left the Roosevelt House and then walked back to Mockingbird Hideaway. He'd barely closed the front door of the cottage behind him when his iPhone vibrated. He glanced at the screen, saw that it was Elias calling, briefly closed his eyes, and said a silent prayer before answering.

"How's Anderson?" he asked without preamble.

His father paused then said, "Your brother is dead. His heart stopped. The medical people attempted resuscitation, but I finally told them to cease and desist. It was time to let him go."

Caden's stomach dropped. Neither of them spoke for half a minute. Eventually, Elias asked, "Are you all right?"

"No. Are you?"

"No. Will you be able to attend the funeral?"

"I'm on a job and can't leave."

"Funerals are for the benefit of the living. The dead know how we feel about them. Anderson would understand."

"I still wish I could be there."

"As do I. Three of your brothers will be able to come. Remember Anderson in your own fashion two days from now when he's buried in New Orleans."

A brief period of silence followed. Finally, Caden said, "I don't want to burden you right now, but I may need your help later regarding this assignment. It's extremely unusual, and I'm not quite certain what to expect."

"By all means. I watched your youngest brother die today. I need a distraction and have a few minutes to spare. Talk to me about this case."

Without using names, Caden discussed the visit by Rory's dead father, the long drive to Florida, and what had happened after his arrival. He omitted his encounter with Rory in her astral form, the way he'd pleasured her in her kitchen, and the fact that he was emotionally and physically drawn to her. Caden didn't mention Astrid, figuring her presence was irrelevant in light of the situation. He voiced his concern over not knowing what evil might be threatening Rory and Nolan and wondered aloud if it was a threat to others as well.

"I'd say the answer is yes, especially when whatever force is at work was probably responsible for killing the parents in that plane crash. As for the adult daughter of the ghost, you want her, don't you?"

"I *am* finding it difficult to maintain emotional distance."

"I raised you boys not to become seriously involved with any one partner. There's a reason for that. Feelings of intimacy and love might cloud your judgment and lead to your injury or death or that of those you seek to protect."

Caden had known this would be his father's reaction, but he realized that a part of him had hoped that Elias would give him an excuse that would allow him to bend the rules.

"You have a duty to punish murderers and an obligation to me and your brothers," Elias said sternly. "What we do is dangerous. Watch yourself, and don't put this woman in harm's way. I wouldn't want to have to eliminate an innocent because what she knows threatens our work. Am I making myself clear?"

Chills ran up and down Caden's spine. He wondered whether or not Elias had lost his mind. Caden was well aware that the man was ruthless when it came to fighting evil, but it sounded as if he'd just threatened to kill Rory. His sons knew that their father would do anything to protect his cause – anything except harm an innocent.

Has the good fight finally taken its toll? Caden wondered. *Has Elias lost sight of his original purpose? If so, then he may have become our enemy instead of our guide.*

"I need to go, Elias."

"So do I. Call me if you want to talk more about the assignment."

"I will," Caden said, although he had no intention of doing so after Elias's threat.

They ended the call, and Caden stared darkly at the black screen of his phone. He wanted to cry for his dead brother but was still in shock after receiving the news. He knew from experience that the tears would come later. Just then, he was angry with and suspicious of Elias.

In an attempt to redirect his thoughts, Caden decided to call Beck, the eldest of his four remaining brothers. Unfortunately, the call went directly to voicemail. He left a brief message that simply said, "Beck, call me when you can."

Next, he phoned David, the brother who was one year younger than he. Caden was relieved to hear the man answer after the second ring. They greeted one another warmly, but there was no use trying to hide the grim tone in their voices or the sadness that somehow traveled through the smartphones that made their conversation possible.

"I want to be the one who kills this monster," David said angrily after he'd told Caden he was on his way to New Orleans from Ohio, the site of his most recent assignment. "My ride will have me in Louisiana around 4:00 a.m., and the funeral will happen day after tomorrow. I told Elias I'd put off my next case until Anderson's killer has been dealt with."

Caden imagined his African-American brother speeding down the highway in his Lexus. Whereas Beck was careful not to exceed the speed limit in order to avoid unwanted attention, Caden and David loved speed and had long ago given up their half-hearted attempts to drive at or below the recommended limits. Both were excellent drivers and had never been in an accident, but Beck and Elias often chided them for their reputations as the "speed demons" of the Brody family. Neither of them cared, and the others knew it.

"You know Elias is going to ask Beck to handle this," Caden said resignedly. "I'd love to take care of it myself, but I'm tied up indefinitely in Florida."

"You going to Disneyworld while you're there?" David asked in a not-so-subtle attempt to lighten the mood.

"Can you picture any of us at Disneyworld?"

"Nope. I guess not. What are you doing in Florida?"

"What you were doing in Ohio. I'm working a case."

"Beck's in the middle of something, too. He and I talked a few days ago, and he said his assignment was pretty intense and wouldn't even tell me where he was. I know he won't be able to return home for the funeral."

"Will Sawyer and Thorn be there?"

"Sawyer's still on that job in New Orleans, so I'm sure he'll be there."

"And Thorn?"

"He called right before you did. He was heading for Texas but said the matter wasn't as urgent as most of our other cases. He'll be at the house with me and Sawyer when Elias returns and stay for the service and burial. Then, we'll see who gets to take on the bastard who killed our little brother."

"It'll be Beck."

"I told you Beck's indisposed."

"It *will* be Beck," insisted Caden.

"How can you be so certain?"

"Because Beck is the oldest. He'll be offered the assignment out of Elias's sense of honor or duty or both. Elias will do whatever he wants, regardless of what *we* want."

"You sound pissed with Elias."

"I am."

"Why?"

"Because I just got an ominous lecture about what an idiot I am and about what Elias might do regarding my choices and my client."

"I don't understand. We *lived*, Caden. We survived his training. He respects us almost as much as we respect him."

"Does he? I'm starting to wonder. Something's changed. The conversation I had with him when he called to tell me about Anderson's death made me uneasy. It sounded like he was threatening to eliminate me and an innocent woman if we jeopardized his plans, whatever those are."

"You're in love, aren't you?" David said quietly. "You've finally fallen for a woman. Or is it a man?"

"Anderson liked to swing both ways. You know I'm straight."

"So, is this woman questioning everything in your life that's given it purpose?"

"She hasn't questioned any of it. She's the one I was sent to save. The thing is that I want her, and I don't mean only for casual sex. I've felt a deep *need* to be with her from the moment we met, and it's only gotten stronger since yesterday. There's something so right about her that it's got me twisted up in knots. I never expected to feel like this." When David didn't comment, he said, "For now, keep this between us."

"I won't tell any of the brothers if you promise not to tell them that I...connected with a woman in New York while I was working there last year."

"What?!?"

"Yeah. She's an artist. For the first time ever, I considered leaving the family and my work so that I could be with a woman."

"Why didn't you say something?"

"And go against everything Elias has instilled in us since we were kids? I hesitated for the same reason you hesitated to tell me."

"So, what happened with the woman in New York? You left her?"

"She told me she wanted a man who could commit to her with his body and soul, and I was only halfway there. She gave me an ultimatum, and I left. The last time I had contact with her was seven months ago. Not a day goes by that I don't think about getting in my ride and heading for her place, but I never do it. I can't turn my back on Elias and my brothers. Plus, she deserves better than what I can currently give her. However, it makes me crazy. Part of me hopes she'll fall for some other guy and move on so that she can be happy and I can have an excuse to try not to think about her. I keep saying I'm going to go back to see if she's found someone else, but another part of me knows it would slay me to witness her acting happy with another man." Blowing out a breath, he added, "And I worry about what might happen if I left to join her. I've wondered what Elias would do."

"The more I think about all of this, the less I like it," Caden confided. "Elias did save us boys, but he also groomed us to be what we are. He controlled our lives and our destinies. Hell, he determined if we lived or died when we were in training. Beck's thirty-three; I'm thirty; you're twenty-nine; Sawyer's twenty-five; and Thorn is twenty-four. Maybe it's time we started making our own decisions about our own futures."

"As if we have a choice," David grumbled. "If we don't do what we were born to do, then more people will die. I can't live with that on my conscience."

"Even the best soldiers have to retire from the front lines sometime. Others take up the fight. Who says we can't battle evil in a different way or even in the same way and have wives and families?"

"Caden, most soldiers don't have the extrasensory talents we possess. We have to use those talents to stop evil."

"And get killed young in the process."

"Elias is seventy-one."

"Yet, not one of his sons has made it past his thirties. I'm willing to die for the cause if need be. I just don't know if I'm willing to forego having some sort of meaningful personal life in order to do what we do."

"Soldiers in battle are often killed and leave behind widows and children. Would you want that?"

"No. But soldiers know the risks, and so do their spouses. What would be so different if we did the same?"

"Man, this conversation's really bringing me down. Learning about Anderson's death was enough for one day. Let's change the subject. Tell me about your girl."

"She's not my girl."

"Sounds like you want her to be. Give me details."

Caden did, ending with, "If only I knew what we were up against!"

"You said Rory has a dickhead brother who also sees ghosts. What are the Roosevelt siblings' extra abilities?"

"He can tell if people are lying or telling the truth; she can take on an astral form and walk around in the real world while she sleeps."

"I'd *love* to be able to take on an astral form."

"I happen to think your being able to shapeshift into a German shepherd is pretty awesome. *My* only other talent is sensing others who can see ghosts."

"That's not your *only* other talent."

Caden chuckled in spite of himself and said, "You're never going to let me forget the night you and I shared a hotel room, got drunk, and –"

"No, I'm not. Hell, you were nineteen, and I was eighteen. We were two horny young men, and those twins were horny, eighteen-year-old women. It's not like we had an orgy. You and your twin were in one bed, and me and mine were in the other."

"I'm surprised we even remembered it the next morning, but I'm glad we did. It made the horrible hangovers worth it." Shaking his head, Caden admitted, "I'm happy we never did it again, though. It was certainly a night to remember, but afterward I felt like we'd disrespected the women."

"At least we raised our standards."

"We learned a lesson all right, but I have to admit I felt invincible that night. We were so…alive."

"Yeah, we were."

"Do you feel alive now, David? Except for when I'm killing the bad guys, I feel like I'm sort of just going through the motions."

"I know what you mean, Brother. But there's nothing we can do about it at this moment."

"I guess there isn't. If we don't talk again before Anderson's funeral, then call me afterward."

"Count on it."

"Be safe, David."

"You, too. Watch yourself."

Caden next called Sawyer. The twenty-five-year-old was typically arrogant, surly, and fearless. At that moment, he was also unavailable. Caden left him a voicemail similar to the one he'd left their older brother. Thinking about his conversation with David, Caden tried to imagine Sawyer married with children. He couldn't. He doubted any woman would want to have a relationship with Sawyer that was anything except physical, and Sawyer would never want to be tied down.

Thorn Brody answered his phone on the tenth ring. Caden greeted him then asked, "Are you ever going to set up your voicemail on your new phone?"

"Eventually," Thorn grunted. "Why?"

"Because it's frustrating not being able to leave you a message when you're unavailable. I hate having to listen to all that ringing, never knowing whether you're going to answer or not."

"I have Caller I.D. If anyone in the family phones and I don't pick up, then I'll always call back. The only people who phone me at this number are our father and my brothers. It's not as though I don't recognize your numbers."

"Just do it for our sakes, okay? It's annoying."

"Maybe I like pissing people off."

"That's Beck's and Sawyer's department. You're the brown-haired, brown-eyed, brainiac brother."

"Thanks. That's a *great* description."

"I thought so."

"I'm being sarcastic, Caden."

"And I'm ignoring it."

"Fine. My turn. You're the good-natured action hero; Sawyer's the snarky fighting machine; David's the laid-back powerhouse with the mindset of an attack dog; and Beck's the Asian Renaissance Man who kicks ass."

"Asian and whatever other ethnicity he is."

"Does it matter? According to you, I'm the brown-haired, brown-eyed Brainiac brother. Big whoop."

Caden heard the underlying sadness in his younger brother's voice. There was a lull in the conversation, as both men tried to decide how best to approach the topic of Anderson's death. Finally, Caden offered, "I wish I could be there with you, Sawyer, David, and Elias."

"Me, too. I heard you and Beck are in the middle of delicate cases and can't come. It really sucks."

"It really does."

"Elias is going to ask Beck to find Anderson's killer, isn't he?"

"That's what I think."

"Can I tell you something in confidence?"

What is it about today? thought Caden. *Is it because of Anderson's death that we all seem to want to share secrets and misgivings?*

"You can tell me anything, Thorn."

"I think Elias is up to something that's not on the level."

"Elias has worked within the criminal syndicates from the time his parents were murdered. He probably hasn't been 'on the level' since he was seventeen."

"What I mean is that I think he's lying to us." The tiny hairs on the back of Caden's neck stood at attention while Thorn went on, "You know about my love affair with computers. I can hack into anything. Well, I stumbled across a folder labeled 'Actual Histories of Brody Sons' that even *I* can't hack."

Swearing silently, Caden asked, "What were you doing that led you to this file?"

"Trying to fix an issue Elias was having with the database I created for him." Hesitating, he went on, "I've never trusted Elias. I know that sounds bad, but it's the truth. He's our father, but I always felt like he wasn't being honest with us. Every time I work on his computer and system, I do a sweep for anything out of the ordinary. I'm concerned and stumped by this development. Elias is proficient on the computer, but he's not a computer genius. He would have had to hire someone to create this folder and encrypt it so that I couldn't easily open it. But I know how to dig and can dig deeper than just about anyone."

"Did you copy the folder so that you could work on opening it undetected?"

"There wasn't time. I'm going to try soon. Don't tell anyone else, yet. I don't want to lose my advantage and have Elias direct whoever created the folder to remove it."

"I won't say anything, yet. Update me when you can. I have my own concerns about Elias. I suspect we're not alone in our mistrust. I just don't understand why this is all coming to a head today. Maybe we're on edge because of what happened to Anderson."

"Maybe something supernatural killed him."

Caden thought that unlikely but merely said, "Watch yourself, Thorn."

"You take care, Caden. We lost one brother today, and we've lost others in the past. I don't want to lose any more for a long, long time."

Kill or be killed by evil, Caden thought later that night, as he lay awake, staring at the ceiling. *That was always Elias's Golden Rule. He drilled it into the minds of the boys he fostered and trained. Does he really have a secret agenda when it comes to us? Has he betrayed us, or are we jumping to conclusions?* Turning onto his side, Caden groaned and thought, *I need to focus all of my attention on Rory and the problem here. How can I do that if something so monumental is going on in my family? I have to be at my best, or Rory and I could both pay the ultimate price.*

9 Rory

Rory stayed in her room for the remainder of the day after Nolan's disastrous visit. She grappled with her doubts and struggled to decide how to proceed when it came to Caden.

Should I tell him everything? What if I do and he's unsympathetic? Or what if I don't and my withholding of some crucial detail leads to disaster in our battle against evil? And how do I feel about his desire to love and protect me?

Filled with uncertainty, she eventually stripped, put on nightclothes, got into bed, and slept. After a time, her astral body rose. Astral Rory stared down at the bed. She attempted to be objective, as she studied her sleeping self. She was breathing evenly. Her red curls fanned out across the pillow and spilled over onto the sheet below. She hadn't switched off the small lamp on the bedside table, and the dim lamplight made it appear that her pale skin glowed. Her eyes roamed over her face and the delicate features she'd inherited from her mother. Rory thought herself attractive although not a stunning beauty. She reflected that her breasts, which stretched the cotton knit fabric of her white tank top, were just the right size for her body. One arm was draped across her ribcage, while the other was extended beside her. The paisley comforter covered her from the waist down, concealing a little Buddha belly, a rounded backside, and nice legs.

Rory's astral form turned away, determined to study the rooms of the house in the same objective fashion. She wished that she could view her supposedly shimmering astral body in a mirror, but, like ghosts, she was unable to see her own reflection in her current form. So, Rory tried instead to imagine what Caden would think if he was to wander through the entire old Roosevelt home.

The sleigh bed with its queen-sized mattress had belonged to her grandparents. Rory recalled asking her parents whether or not she could have it as a present for her thirteenth birthday. They'd been delighted, expecting a request for more video games or computer equipment.

I don't need to wander around my house, wondering if Caden will like it. I love it, and that's all that matters. Everything in this place was either bought or made by someone in my family, and I never want to live anywhere else but here in this slightly cluttered, eclectic jumble of furniture, linens, dishware, pictures, knickknacks, and books. If Caden doesn't like it, then he doesn't. I won't change for him or anyone else.

The desire to go outside and walk to Mockingbird Hideaway was compelling, but Rory fought it. She went back to bed, forcing herself to settle into her physical body. Opening her eyes once she'd become whole again, Rory wondered whether or not Caden was awake. If he was, then was he having another erotic dream about her?

Stop that! she ordered. *Don't think about it. Concentrate on doing whatever you have to in order to help defeat this terrible evil that Dad mentioned. Then Caden will leave, and you can go back to the way things were.*

Rory didn't want things to go back to the way they'd been before Caden's arrival. She'd been surprised by the realization that she did want him physically. She hadn't considered wanting anyone physically for seven years, but she couldn't deny her body's natural reaction. The truly surprising thing was that she also wanted to know Caden on a much deeper level, despite his odd upbringing and vocation.

Her body burned with desire for the man, and Rory desperately wondered what it would be like to really get to know Caden Brody and to make love to him. Remembering the feeling of her first orgasm that morning made her tingle all over. She wanted to touch herself the way he'd touched her earlier that day but knew she wouldn't get the same results. After all, it would be her fingers there, not his.

Sighing, she rolled onto her belly and closed her eyes. Soon, she slept again. She woke at dawn from a familiar dream that had involved screams, pain, and humiliation.

I have to tell Caden, she reasoned once she'd recovered herself enough to think rationally again. *What if it pushes him away? But I need to trust him. I'll tell him after breakfast. I have no other guests at the moment, so at least we won't be interrupted.*

Removing her top and sleep shorts, Rory went to her bathroom, showered, and put on a purple dress that had three-quarter length sleeves and fell several inches below her knees. She slipped into sandals and pulled her hair into a ponytail before going downstairs to start mixing a batch of orange-cranberry scones. The timer went off just as Caden knocked on her back door at 8:00.

"Come in!" she called, as she reached for an oven mitt.

Rory felt her heart drop into her stomach the moment Caden stepped into her kitchen. Caden looked tense and worried. She suddenly wished she could turn back the clock to the previous day and give him her explanation. Perhaps if she had, he wouldn't currently look so worn out. She suspected that he hadn't slept at all the previous night.

"Your timer's beeping," he noted. "I don't feel like eating, but I'm hungry. Whatever you're baking smells great. Is it ready?"

"What? Oh. Yes. Sorry. Have a seat at the kitchen table, and I'll take the scones out of the oven. They're orange-cranberry. If you don't like them, then I can make something else. I don't have other guests at Nostalgia Road right now. I could freeze these."

"No. I love orange-cranberry anything." He pulled out a chair, turned it around, and straddled it before crossing his arms over the back and asking, "Where's Astrid?"

"I'm not sure. She's left me alone since Nolan's visit and the exchange you and I had after he stormed off yesterday."

"I'm sorry. I didn't –"

Caden's voice cracked, and Rory, who'd been removing the scones from the oven, straightened and glanced over her shoulder at him. Placing the bakeware on a trivet, she put the oven mitt onto the counter and stared at Caden, whose green eyes were shining with tears. Seeing that he was suffering in some way, her heart ached for him, and she longed to put her arms around his shoulders and cradle his head against her chest. Something made her hold back.

"Caden?"

He closed his eyes before shaking his head. After a few moments, he said, "I'm screwing this up."

"No. *I'm* obviously screwing it up. I should have talked to you yesterday. It's my fault."

His eyes snapped open and then narrowed before he said, "I'm not upset because of you. Believe me."

"What then?" she asked, her brow creasing with confusion.

Looking away, he muttered, "Family issues."

"Siblings fight."

"Not those kinds of issues. I can't tell you right now because I'm still piecing things together. The issues are…troubling." Grimacing, he admitted, "But that's not the real reason why I'm so sad this morning."

"Why, then?"

"Our youngest brother died yesterday. He'd been in a coma for a few days. Elias called after I got back to Mockingbird Hideaway and gave me the news."

"Oh, Caden!" Rory cried, tears of empathy filling her own eyes. "I'm so, so sorry."

"Me, too. We're all going to miss him."

"When will you leave for the funeral?"

"I'm not going. My older brother either. We can't leave the jobs we're on to go home for the service. Elias and our other brothers understand."

"Are you sure?"

"One hundred percent."

Resting a hand on the back of the empty chair next to his, Rory asked, "What was your brother's name?"

"Anderson. He was twenty-two." Without waiting for her to ask, he volunteered, "He was injured because of the assignment he was working on. Of course, I don't know any details. Elias only shares what he wants."

Rory sensed anger in Caden's voice and wondered if he was angry with himself, his dead brother, his father, the killer, or even God. She somehow suspected the answer might be all of those possibilities. Unable to think of anything that wasn't clichéd, she got him two scones and a cup of coffee, taking them to the table.

"You didn't eat dinner, did you?" she asked.

"No, but I'm betting you didn't either."

"My reasons were nowhere near as serious as yours. Let me get myself a scone, and then we can both eat. I'd like to talk to you about things afterwards if you're up to it."

"I am. Even if I weren't, I'd want to hear what you have to say. The more I know, the better prepared I'll be."

Once they'd finished breakfast, Rory put their plates and her milk glass in the sink while Caden drained his coffee mug. Then, they moved to the living room, sitting beside one another on the couch. Rory knotted her hands in her lap and then stared at them for a minute before she began to speak.

"I don't really know how to explain."

"Whatever way you choose will be the right way. Take your time."

Shifting slightly, she said, "Um, Nolan and I obviously grew up here. Our parents were great, and we were happy. Mom had no paranormal abilities, but Dad, Nolan, and I did. Nolan tried hard to deny our inherent gifts, but I was always curious about them. Dad knew it and nurtured that part of me. He sensed I was a kindred spirit."

"Pun intended?"

Rory flashed him a quick smile and said, "Definitely. We have to have a quirky sense of humor with the things we see, right?"

"Right. What did he do to nurture your interest?"

"It started out with his telling me stories. As I got older, he gave me books to read and then discuss with him. After I became a teenager, he took my supernatural education a little further."

"How so?"

"He shared family documents with me, gave me a box of Roosevelt heirlooms, took me on walks around the property to discuss the history behind it, and schooled me in family lore. I know everything there is to know about those buried in the Roosevelt graveyard. No one born with the Roosevelt gift has died a natural death."

Caden swore but had no other comments.

"Dad also shared with me that the positioning of the houses on the property wasn't random. The five dwellings are the points of a pentacle, a five-pointed star where all angles are the same length. They typically stand for a balance of elements that brings or maintains peace. They're tangible symbols that protect positive supernatural energy. My father worked diligently to maintain that balance and charged me with doing the same if anything happened to him. The main house where we are now is the top point of the star."

"And the other points are…?"

"Going clockwise, they're Mockingbird Hideaway, Orange Blossom Retreat, Hurricane House, and The Palmetto House. Dad told me to always keep the paths between the points clear in order to maintain the energy connection. He said if the balance is upset, then evil can gain a foothold or worse. When needed, I have fresh gravel laid along the direct paths that connect the points. Nothing has been severed, so I don't understand how that could be part of the problem Dad mentioned to you."

"Did he ever tell you what the evil was or how to stop it if it got loose?"

"He didn't know. His father had been killed in a farming accident before Dad was even born, so everything he'd learned had been gleaned from a lifetime of studying family history and related information. He did say he suspected that if the evil ever got loose, it would come after whoever was the caretaker of the elemental balance."

"Currently you."

"I accepted the risk a long time ago. I consider it my birthright to protect this place. My only concern is what will happen when I die. Nolan certainly won't take on the responsibility and wouldn't really know how to safeguard things even if he did. Neither of us is married or has kids. I've debated about whether or not I should seek out someone who might be interested in becoming the caretaker when I die."

"You might live a long life and die a natural death."

"I might," Rory agreed although she didn't believe it. "Even if I live to be a hundred, there would still be no one to step in after me."

"You have no idea what the future will bring. Look at the prediction of the *traiteur* before I was born. I didn't die before or during birth, and the Devil didn't find and destroy me."

"The Devil could still come for you. Maybe that's why you were led to Nostalgia Road."

"I doubt that. Now, stop stalling, Rory, and tell me the rest."

"The rest. Okay. Um, I was a geek who loved pretty, feminine things. I also adored reading, playing video games, and using computers. My fellow geeks and I did get bullied by people like Astrid, but we tried to be nice to everyone. Usually, we succeeded."

Shaking his head, Caden muttered, "Such a different childhood from mine."

Nodding, Rory admitted, "Yes, but I didn't quite have a normal childhood myself. Having ghosts around all the time can be depressing, as you well know. It's hard to have fun at sleepovers when you've got ghosts with you whom no one else can see, and those dead people might be disfigured as the result of an accident, beating, knifing, or shooting, bloated because they drowned or emaciated due to prolonged illness or starvation. I learned to deal with this and enjoyed my childhood."

"And then?"

"Before I graduated from high school, I received an acceptance letter from UCF, my college of choice. I was so excited and looked forward to college life and then of eventually starting my own web design company. I dreamed of finding the man I'd marry and of someday having a family with him."

Unable to stop herself, Rory began to tremble. Before she realized what was happening, Caden had scooped her up, pulling her onto his lap. His strong arms wrapped around her, and he cradled the back of her neck in the crook of one elbow. She welcomed this change in position, even though he hadn't bothered to ask for permission.

Burying her face against his bicep, Rory said, "I had such beautiful dreams."

"What happened?" Caden asked in a low voice.

"I did graduate from UCF and then started my own company, but Dominic stole my innocence and my ability to trust before I'd even left home for college."

"Dominic?"

"He was the quarterback of our high school football team. He asked me out on a date in the spring of our senior year. He was handsome and smart but obviously wasn't part of my usual social group. Still, I accepted his offer to have a picnic lunch near the pond on his family's land. I didn't think it would lead to a relationship or anything but figured there was no harm in having lunch with a cute guy." Sighing, she confided, "I've never told anyone but Nolan about what happened. I'm afraid to do it now because I don't want you to pull away like he did or to bolt and run."

"I don't bolt," Caden said resolutely. "You don't ever have to worry about that when it comes to me. I'm solid, Rory."

Closing her eyes and fisting some of his red cotton shirt in her hands, she said softly, "Promise?"

"Promise."

Swallowing hard, she began, "That Saturday, Dominic picked me up for our lunch date and drove us out to a lovely spot on his family's property. It was a beautiful spring day. He spread a blanket under a tree so that we could sit in the shade. He'd brought a picnic basket filled with fruit, cheese, crackers, and wine. It made me feel like a true adult, not an eighteen-year-old high school senior. We talked about school and our plans for what we were going to do after graduation. Dominic seemed to be having as much fun as I was. Eventually, he told me I was beautiful and suggested we make out." After biting her lower lip for a moment, Rory said, "I'd kissed on dates before, but I'd never made out with anyone. I told Dominic I'd like to make out but didn't believe in sex before marriage. He said he understood and seemed sincere."

Caden's arms tightened around Rory, making her feel safe. The gesture emboldened her, and she decided that she *had* to tell him exactly what Dominic had done.

"I did enjoy making out as we sat under the tree next to the pond. But then Dominic tried to go further. I reminded him about what I'd said. He told me he knew what I *really* wanted, and then he forced me to the ground. I cried out for him to stop and tried to twist away, but it was impossible. I yelled for him to let me up, and he *laughed*! He yanked off my panties and then…you know." In a tremulous voice, Rory said, "It hurt. I screamed and tried to fight, but he was a big guy. The more I struggled, the rougher he got. So, I stopped fighting and just lay still and cried. I was relieved when he finally finished. Then, he took…he took my panties and used them to wipe my blood off him. He said it was proof to his buddies that he'd taken the virginity of the prettiest geek in school. When I told him I'd call the police, he said if I did, it would be my word against his. He'd tell the authorities I'd seduced him and was crying rape now that he'd rejected me. I shouted that I hated him and demanded that he take me home. He leered at me and told me I should be honored that he'd been my first since most of the other girls in our high school wanted to have sex with him." Once she'd wetted her lips with her tongue, Rory said tightly, "I cried all the way home. Luckily, my parents and Nolan weren't at the house when Dominic dropped me off. I raced for the shower and somehow pulled myself together before they came back."

"Le bâtard est aussi bon que mort!" Caden snarled. Before Rory could ask him what that meant, he prompted, "How did Nolan find out about the rape, and why didn't he do anything about it?"

"You know he can sense when people are lying. The day after my date, Nolan asked me if I was sick or something, sensing that I wasn't myself. I broke down and told him the whole story. I only wanted some comfort. Instead, he looked stunned and asked me how I could have gone with Dominic to such an isolated place and made out with him. He told me I was a fool not to think that Dominic wouldn't want more. I was so shocked. It only got worse when he said that I should never tell anyone, especially not Mom and Dad. Things were never the same between us again."

"Your brother's a real prick! Being date raped wasn't your fault. You and I don't know each other very well, Rory. But envision me in Dominic's place. Do you think I'd ever do what he did to you? Even if you hadn't told me you wanted to save yourself for marriage, can you imagine I'd have forced myself on you? Do you think I would have kept going if you were screaming for me to stop and telling me I was hurting you? Do you think I'd have wiped your blood on your panties to bring to my buddies as some sick souvenir?"

Rory sucked in a breath as a wave of shock hit her. In the seven years since the rape, she'd only considered how *she* could have prevented it. Rory knew Dominic should have stopped, but, thanks to him and Nolan, she'd ultimately placed the blame on herself. All she'd needed was to have someone remind her of what she'd known at the time of the attack, which was that she'd done everything she could to stop the assault. None of it had been her fault.

"Sons of bitches!"

Startled, Rory jerked her head toward Astrid. She'd completely forgotten about the woman, who now stood in the doorway, appearing enraged. Astrid's hands were clenched into fists, and she looked as if she wanted to pummel someone. Rory wondered if she was angry with Caden, Dominic, Nolan, or all three.

"What jerks!" Astrid snapped. "I can't believe that Dominic Ambrose did that to you and that your brother shamed you into thinking it was your fault! What creeps! You never dated anyone after the picnic, did you?" Without waiting for Rory to reply, she said, "All those years of normalcy lost because of Mr. Rapist Quarterback and that dickhead you have for a brother!"

Not knowing what to say in response to Astrid's rant, Rory stayed quiet, still reeling from the fact that she'd shared her story and the renewed certainty that she hadn't been to blame for her rape.

"I'm going to prove to you that you can trust me," Caden declared.

"She obviously trusts you more than anyone else since her attack," Astrid asserted. "After what you did to her in the kitchen yesterday, there's certainly no doubt about that."

"Astrid, you said you didn't look!" Rory exclaimed.

"I didn't, but I listened, remember? I bet you'd never even had an orgasm before yesterday."

"Enough, Astrid!" Caden snapped.

Looking pointedly at Rory, she said, "You need to trust this luscious, honest man, have some mind-blowing sex, and let go of your loneliness! That's what you want, isn't it? Don't wait. Look at me. I didn't expect to be shot in the head. You never know what might happen to you tomorrow. You could be dead, too."

"Thanks for the encouragement – I think," Rory muttered. "Caden, I don't know what to say or where to go from here."

"Then don't say anything and stay where you are. I only want to hold you right now."

Rory believed him. Shutting her eyes, she inhaled the scent of sandalwood and vanilla that seemed to permeate Caden's skin and then sighed contentedly. His and Astrid's reactions to her admission had given her a totally new outlook on her past and the potential for her future.

"I should get off your lap," Rory murmured.

"Why? I like you in my lap."

"I know. I can feel your...um...you know...pressing against my hip."

"I'm a man, and you're a beautiful woman. I can't help but respond to you like this. However, because I'm a *real* man, I can also control myself. Thank you for trusting me with your secret."

"And me!" Astrid said from where she stood. "I'm going to find a way to do some serious damage to Dominic Ambrose. I don't care if I'm not corporeal anymore. I'll make it happen. It's the least I can do to thank you for what you're doing for me."

"I won't ever forget, but I don't want to allow Dominic's actions to control my life any longer. I'm going to try to let that experience go."

"That's a great attitude to have," Caden remarked. "But you're not going to instantaneously be okay."

"I know. But I feel changed. I'm relieved."

"Glad to hear it."

"Maybe we could go through the family things together."

"First, I need to return to Mockingbird Hideaway for a few minutes to get my tablet."

"I want to go, too!" Astrid exclaimed, sounding more like a five-year-old than a twenty-five-year-old.

"Caden, will you keep an eye on her until the two of you get back?"

"I'll do my best. No promises on that, though. We'll be back before you know it."

Their mouths came together. Rory slipped her arms around Caden's neck and pressed her chest against his. One of his arms remained at her back, but he lowered the other and rested one palm on her hip. She moaned softly, and he broke the kiss.

"I can't do this," he admitted. "I don't want to inadvertently traumatize you. I want you to be totally comfortable with me before we go any further, and I'm finding it hard not to go any further."

Rory rested her forehead against his shoulder and said, "I am comfortable with you. You make me feel safe – and special."

"You *are* special. It's too bad that Dominic Ambrose and your brother made you forget that for so long. I'm going to do my damnedest to help you remember just how special you are."

10 Caden

"What is *your* problem?" Astrid asked Caden, as they walked toward Mockingbird Hideaway. "You and Rory just had a life-changing conversation and some steamy moments. But you seem angry now. What's the matter?"

"Lots of things," he replied gruffly. "For starters, I want to kill this Dominic guy and beat Nolan to a pulp."

"I'd be happy to help with that if I could. I never pegged Nolan as such a jerk! And to think that I slept with Dominic on a regular basis for a year, the rapist pig! I wonder if he did that to other girls besides Rory."

"I doubt if it was an isolated incident. When I think of his luring sweet, innocent Rory out to that place, and then forcing himself on her and using her panties to provide him with some bloody trophy, my vision goes red. You can definitely help me by giving me background info."

"Gladly. I heard what you said after Rory told you what Dominic did to her."

"What?"

"*Le bâtard est aussi bon que mort!*" Astrid repeated. "I took French in college and travelled to France many times with my husband, who loved Provence. That translates into, 'The bastard is as good as dead!' Will you really kill him?"

"Not unless he's totally evil like the other people I eliminate. Exactly how I deal with Dominic will be determined in large part by how he's behaved – or not – since high school."

"I wish I could still use a computer. I could be looking things up on him while you and Rory work on my murder and this big evil thing."

They had reached the front door of Mockingbird Hideaway, and Caden paused with his right hand on the doorknob then suggested, "Why don't you try it?"

"Try what?"

"Using my laptop. You've learned how to move things around. My laptop isn't a touchscreen; it has a keyboard. Maybe you can concentrate your energy on depressing the keys. Perhaps you can do some searches and bookmark links or even create a Word document."

"I'll try. I'd like to help you while you help me. We'd both be helping Rory."

"I also want to know more about Nolan. I don't intend to kill the idiot, but I may rough him up a bit or play on his guilt. He deserves it after what he did to his sister." Balling his hands into fists, Caden asked rhetorically, "How freakin' ignorant can one guy be?"

"Oh, the stories I could tell you about men and ignorance," the ghost said dramatically. "If I were still alive, I could write a book!"

Caden, who had been walking toward the kitchen table of his cottage, paused and asked, "Why did you do it?"

"I didn't kill myself!"

"I'm not talking about your death. You're a stunner, and you certainly know how to hold yourself and show off your assets to their best advantage. That red dress you're wearing leaves little to the imagination. But your appeal isn't only physical. You may be bitchy sometimes, but you have style and smarts. Why subject yourself to the carousel of men you were obviously riding? You probably could have had a high-level corporate job. What gives?"

Astrid looked uncharacteristically subdued as she sat on the couch. After ostensibly studying her stilettos for a few moments, she admitted quietly, "I did want more out of life, but my mother raised us girls to be just like her. The only way we seemed to be able to please Mother was by behaving exactly as she told us. Father never paid much attention to me or my sisters. The only times he did was when we were acting like miniature versions of our mother. The three of us wanted our parents' affection, so we did as we were told and were rewarded with their version of love. By marrying rich men, we gained Mother's and Father's respect." Combing her blonde hair away from her face, Astrid said, "I did consider making a change after my husband died, but I felt as if I was betraying my parents every time I allowed my thoughts to wander down that road. I started to party harder and use drugs in an attempt to make myself feel better. I knew I was capable of more but couldn't seem to deviate from the path my parents set me on the day I was born." A puzzled look crossed Astrid's face, then she added, "Something changed before I died, but I can't remember what it was for the life of me!" Laughing bitterly, she said, "How ironic that I'd pick that expression to use."

"You may recall the details of your death someday," Caden proposed.

"It doesn't matter. It won't alter anything."

"You don't know that. It might make all the difference in the world."

"I'm sure you tell that to each pretty girl you meet who has a hole in her head."

"Nope. You're the first."

Astrid seemed to relax and smiled slightly before asking, "Speaking of firsts, who was yours? How old were you?"

"There's the Astrid we all know and love," Caden grumbled, but he was grinning. "Do you ask everyone about their sex lives, or are Rory and I simply lucky?"

"I ask whomever I please whatever I please." As Caden typed his password, she prodded, "So, tell me about your first time."

"No."

"Why not? Do you still love her?"

"I never loved any of my previous sexual partners."

"So, what difference does it make? You can tell me."

"I can. I choose not to." Straightening, Caden gestured toward the laptop and said, "Have at it. I hope you're able to make it work. I'll expect a full report when I return."

"Which will be when?"

"When I walk through the front door to Mockingbird Hideaway." Lifting his iPad from the table, he said, "Behave."

"I can't do much else," Astrid said irritably.

As Caden walked through the heat of the early July morning, he thought about Astrid's query regarding his first sexual encounter. He wasn't about to tell Astrid Hass about an experience that had been humiliating on more than one level. He thought of young Rory and her desire not to have sex until after marriage, a belief that had probably been instilled in her by her parents. His adoptive father had done exactly the opposite. He'd taken Caden to a high-class brothel as a present for the boy's eighteenth birthday, insisting that sex and love were never to be connected. Caden had lost his virginity to a beautiful young woman he'd never seen before or since. Although his body had responded, Caden had felt empty afterward.

Elias did that for each of his sons when they turned eighteen, Caden mused. *I wonder if his first experience was with a prostitute. Why did we all go along with it? Were we that desperate for our father's approval and love?* Frowning, he thought, *Of course we were, just as Astrid was desperate for her parents' love and respect.*

When Caden entered the Roosevelt house through the back door, he heard Rory talking on the phone with someone who was obviously a potential guest. He prayed that person wouldn't want to stay at Nostalgia Road anytime in the near future. The fewer people around, the fewer people he'd have to protect from danger. Rory must have already had the same thought, because he heard her say, "I'm sorry. I don't have anything available. Could you give me your name and number? If I have a cancellation, then I can call you. Great."

Once she'd hung up, Caden asked, "Can you afford to take the financial hit you'll feel if you can't rent out cottages until this is over?"

"I'll have to. I won't have people staying here and possibly getting hurt. While you were gone, I went on my website and blocked out every date as booked until Labor Day weekend. That's two months away. If we still don't have answers by the end of August, then I'll have to make a decision."

"What kind of decision?"

"Whether or not to let guests who've made their reservations keep them or call and cancel. I've already made up my mind to call the guests who are supposed to visit in July and August and explain that they won't be able to stay here due to unforeseen circumstances."

"But you depend on the revenue you get from guests to keep this place going."

"I'd rather wipe out my savings than see anyone harmed."

"I have the money. Let me help."

"No. Thanks though."

"You can't lose the Roosevelt home, cottages, and property, not with evil waiting to strike. If you don't have the money, then you have to let me help financially."

"We'll see," she said noncommittally. "Come upstairs so that we can go through the documents and heirlooms I mentioned earlier."

He wanted to argue but saw that, for now, arguing would get him nowhere. After agreeing to examine whatever she had to show him, Caden followed Rory up to the second floor. She led him to a door that was centrally located on that level and said with a slight smile, "The Roosevelt Library and Museum. Please don't touch anything without asking first."

"If I do, then will I be refused future admission?" he teased.

She smiled and said with flushed cheeks, "Maybe, Mister Brody."

God, don't let her look at the front of my jeans, Caden prayed. Forcing himself to glance around the room, he admonished, *Stop thinking with your dick. Rory's a date rape victim. I need to go slowly if I want her to be a permanent part of my life.*

"Caden? Are you okay? You look a little stunned."

He nodded, cleared his throat, and admitted, "I am."

"By what?" she asked innocently. "There's nothing outstanding in this room."

"You're wrong." When her brows drew together in confusion, he ignored the pounding of his heart and said, "There's you."

"Me? But I'm so ordinary."

"Ordinary?" he echoed, flummoxed by her description.

"Yes. *You're* like a superhero or something. You're nice, honest, smart, and driven. You're also tall, muscular, and badass. You kill evil people for a living and know about fighting and weapons. When you were talking to Nolan, you said you'd seen people doing terrible things to babies, children, men, and women, yet you manage to keep fighting to stop the murderers, to get vengeance." Seemingly uncomfortable, she continued, "*I*, on the other hand, am a web designer who runs a bed and breakfast. I help ghosts cross over but by doing things like investigating online or by phone and then by contacting people who can help to stop those responsible for preventing their transition. I look all right, but the only workouts I get are when I pull weeds, trim trees and bushes, clean the house and cottages, swim in the lake, and walk the property to make sure everything's in order. I've got a little belly; my butt's kind of big; and —"

"Oh, to Hell with it!" Caden exclaimed. Stepping forward, he put his arms around Rory's waist and pulled her against him so that she could feel the bulge at the front of his pants before saying, "*That's* how ordinary I think you are. You're gorgeous. If that asshole Dominic Ambrose hadn't hurt you like he did, then I'd be all over you with my hands and mouth right this minute. You're so fucking sweet, giving, and sexy. What stunned me a few moments ago was that I realized I want to have you with me forever. For someone who was raised by a megalomaniac who instructed his sons to focus only on their work and never fall in love, that was a pretty big light bulb moment. I'm only worried that you won't think I'm worthy of you."

Rory, whose cheeks flamed red with what he assumed was embarrassment, stared open-mouthed at him. Caden wondered if it was because of his frankness, his compliments, or because she truly didn't think he was worthy of her. She closed her mouth then worried at her lower lip with her teeth for a while. Her hands rested on his chest, and he tensed and waited for her to push him away.

Instead, she raised herself up onto the balls of her feet, hooked her left arm around his neck, and asked, "Why me?"

"Because when I'm with you, I feel as though I'm home. Jesus, I know that doesn't make any freakin' sense but –"

She cut him off with a kiss. Caden's body screamed at him to pick Rory up, carry her to her bedroom, and make love to her until neither of them was capable of rational thought. His brain told his body that those urges would lead him into trouble and would leave Rory feeling regret later. He didn't want her to regret anything. He wanted her to be sure of him – of *them* – as they moved toward…what?

Breaking their kiss, he said hoarsely, "Wait."

"Why should we? I like having you kiss and touch me. I'm not scared when you do it, and *I'm* obviously able to do it to *you* now. I'm ready."

Reluctantly releasing her, Caden said, "You can't tell me that you went from a girl who didn't want to have premarital sex to one who's going to be happy with making love to a man she barely knows, no matter how much we're attracted to one another. I may be used to sex, but I'm not used to love. I want to take things a little slower and try to do something like going out on a date, taking a trip

92

to the grocery store together, or watching movies with you. I want this to last."

Nodding soberly, Rory said, "Me, too." Brightening, she suggested, "We could do all three today! Let's go to lunch, run by Publix for groceries, and then watch a movie tonight."

"I'd love to, but research needs to come before pleasure. Working on a relationship won't do either of us any good if we let evil reign here at Nostalgia Road."

"Okay, so we'll skip the movie part. We can do research and eat lunch while we work, go to dinner, then pass by the grocery store on the way home. We have to eat, and I do need to buy groceries."

Caden grinned and said, "It's a date. For now, why don't you give me the grand tour of the Roosevelt Library and Museum?"

"I'd be happy to, Sir," she said playfully. "I'll waive the fee this time."

"I'm much obliged."

Extending her arms in a sweeping gesture, Rory said, "Along these two side walls we have many shelves filled with books regarding ghosts and the supernatural. Some of these books are over a hundred years old, while others are fairly recent publications. Beneath the bookshelves are cabinets that hold plastic containers filled with family documents and heirlooms that supposedly relate to the supernatural. On the far wall above the desk, there's a portrait of my great-great-grandfather, Hugh. He and his wife, Annie, were the ones who built this house after the fire claimed the original Cracker House that stood on this spot."

Caden stepped in front of the portrait and studied the subject. Hugh Roosevelt had dark, curly, red hair, blue eyes, and fair skin. Caden realized that Nolan resembled the man and asked Rory if her father and grandfather also looked like Hugh.

"Dad did. The pictures I have of his father show that he did, too."

"I have more questions," he told her. "First, how were all of these things saved from the fire? Or do they all date from after the construction of the new house? You said some books were over a hundred years old, but they could have been bought after this home was built."

"Dad said his mother explained that she was told that what's in here now was in one of the other cottages when the fire happened."

He nodded then asked, "Have you ever wondered why you all look Irish but have a Dutch surname?"

"How do you know it's Dutch?"

"Google," he answered with a shrug, as if there could be no other response. "Why would a family with Celtic lineage possess that surname?"

"I know why. The story is told through a variety of documents and diaries kept in this room."

Looking pointedly at her, he urged, "So, tell me."

"The original members of the Roosevelts who settled this land fled Ireland and came to North America over two hundred fifty years ago to escape persecution. Because of their supernatural abilities, they were thought of as witches. They had money, but there wasn't enough money in Ireland to buy their safety if they remained. A dozen family members escaped and crossed the Atlantic, but two died along the way. By the time they reached their new country, the survivors had agreed that they needed to hide themselves from others who might follow and persecute them. So, they changed their last name to Roosevelt and headed south. They didn't stop until they reached what later became the State of Florida."

"What was the original family surname?"

"Ironically enough, it was Brody."

"According to Elias, Brody is a Hungarian surname. He should know since it's *his* last name."

"It's also an Irish one. It's an odd coincidence but kind of cool, don't you think?"

Caden didn't believe in coincidences. He looked back at the portrait of Hugh Roosevelt and studied the man's face. He pictured the red hair as gray and envisioned the subject with a short gray moustache and beard.

"Holy Mary, Mother of God," he murmured.

"What?" Rory asked, the word suffused with both confusion and concern.

"Elias always told us his parents were from Hungary and that they'd come to the U.S. when he was an infant. He said they were killed when he was seventeen. I think he's a lying SOB. Ever since I was old enough to remember, he's had gray hair. None of us have ever seen pictures of him when he was younger, but I'm betting his original hair color was a deep red. He has the same features as Hugh Roosevelt."

Rory smiled indulgently at him and asked, "Don't you think that's a bit of a stretch? How on Earth could your adoptive father be a relative of mine? It's impossible! He'd have to –"

Her skin seemed to turn a whiter shade of pale, and Caden prompted, "He'd have to what?"

"Oh…my…God."

"What?" When she didn't answer, Caden practically shouted, "Rory! What? Are you all right? You look like you've just seen a ghost."

"A living ghost," Rory muttered. "An evil one."

11 Rory

For a few seconds, Rory felt as if she might pass out. Frightened by what she was thinking, she couldn't ignore her suspicions. Avoiding Caden's worried demands for answers, she turned and went over to one of the cabinets, opened its door, and then withdrew one of the clear plastic containers that rested inside. Carrying it to the desk, she put it down and removed the blue top. It didn't take her long to find the document she wanted to review.

Caden came up behind her and peered over her left shoulder. Tension radiated off him in waves, and Rory stayed still and allowed him to study the Roosevelt Family Tree. She held her breath when she sensed he was nearing the line she'd immediately thought of when they'd begun to make connections regarding Elias Brody and the Brodys turned Roosevelts.

"Damn it all to Hell!" Caden swore. "Charles and Ike. Twin sons born seventy-one years ago to your great-grandparents. According to this, Charles died in infancy, and Ike died when he was twenty. That was the same year your father was born."

"Yes. Dad told me his mother said that his father died in a farming accident before she found out she was pregnant." Feeling queasy, she lowered the paper back into the box and muttered, "It just doesn't make sense. If Elias is really Charles, then why does it say that he died?"

"And if he didn't die, then where did he go and could he be the cause of your grandfather's untimely death?"

"And the cause of my parents' plane crash?" she whispered. "Is Elias the evil my father warned you about?

"We obviously don't have all the facts. Let's start going through the papers and heirlooms under the assumption that Elias and Charles are one and the same and that he's evil."

"Caden, I know he's your father –"

"*Adoptive* father," he corrected.

"– adoptive father. It has to be difficult to think that he might be somehow responsible for harming innocent people."

Wrapping his arms around Rory's shoulders from behind, Caden said, "I've been suspicious of Elias for a while now. A couple of my brothers recently shared with me that they have some issues with him, too. I haven't been able to reach our other brothers, yet. If you and I find out anything definite, it might help all of us to stop him if he is evil."

"What if he's just misguided?"

"I suppose we'd tried to help him. If he refused our aid, we'd probably be forced to break ties with him. In many ways, we've always felt that we owed him our lives. We're not so certain any longer."

The two of them began to search through the containers. They were so engrossed in their efforts that they worked through lunch and well into the afternoon. By 4:00, Rory was exhausted, and Caden appeared weary and disappointed. So far, they'd found no proof of anything about Baby Charles other than the notation of his birth and death.

"Why don't we stop for the time being?" Rory suggested. "Let's go out to dinner like we'd planned and then drop by the store on the way back. I'm really low on a few essentials in the fridge and pantry."

"Okay, but I need to go to Mockingbird Hideaway first to put on a nice pair of pants and a nicer shirt."

"Caden, we're going to dinner at a local restaurant in Sage, Florida. The jeans and t-shirt you're wearing are fine. Speaking of Mockingbird Hideaway, did you leave Astrid there? I haven't seen her all afternoon."

"I asked her to try some new tricks. I figured it'd keep her out of our hair for a while. Did you look up her obituary? If so, when is her funeral?"

"Tomorrow at 2:00. She's going to want to come with us, and I think it's probably a good idea. Maybe the killer will be there, and she'll remember who he was when she sees him."

"Agreed. It would be nice to solve that case although I am getting kind of used to having her around."

Rory shook her head, planted her hands on her hips, and said, "Oh, no, you don't! We are *not* keeping her!"

"You sound like a mother telling her kid he can't keep a kitten he found in a cardboard box by the side of the road." Glancing away, he said, "Well, that's what I *think* a mother would sound like."

Her heart aching for Caden, who had never known the love of a mother, Rory said, "Don't try to make me feel guilty. Astrid needs to move on."

Caden smiled, but the smile didn't reach his green eyes. Rory considered that he needed a pet of some sort. She doubted that Elias Brody had allowed his adopted sons to keep dogs, cats, hamsters, or rabbits. If there had been any animals in the household, they'd probably been attack dogs.

"Why don't you go tell Astrid about our date, and I'll put away everything we've reviewed. I'll leave the rest out for tomorrow."

"Sounds good. I'll be back as soon as I can."

Rory listened as Caden went down the stairs, walked through the house, and then left through the kitchen door. She peered out of the window, studying him as he made his way along the path to Mockingbird Hideaway. His shoulders sagged slightly and his head was bowed as though he were deep in contemplation. She wondered what she could do to help him. Whatever was going on with Elias Brody weighed heavily on Caden. She was certain that his doubts regarding his adoptive father's origins were causing him to question what Elias had told Caden regarding his own origins.

Was that the suspicion he mentioned earlier? Did the Brody sons find out other things that led them to doubt the only parent they've ever known? Massaging her throbbing temples, Rory wondered, *What if Elias is Charles and is evil? He'd be my great-uncle. That would certainly complicate things. But why would his parents give him up and list him as deceased? How would he have found out the truth? And wouldn't he have wanted to know his twin? Why murder Ike, if that was, indeed, what he did? Did he resent the fact that Ike had been kept by their parents, who were already dead when he returned to the Roosevelt home?*

All of the speculation was giving her a terrible headache, so Rory decided to put her worries about Elias/Charles out of her mind for the remainder of the day. She and Caden both needed some downtime. She hadn't been on a date in seven years. For the first time since her date with Dominic, Rory wasn't afraid of what might happen if she let her guard down. She felt certain that Caden wouldn't hurt her. She longed to make love to him, to prove to both of them that she wasn't scared to have sex.

I'm not scared of sex with Caden in particular, she mentally reminded herself. *I'd still be scared of sex with any other man.*

Her youthful dream of finding a lifelong partner and waiting to have sex until marriage had been ripped to shreds when Dominic had forced himself upon her. Rory wanted Caden, and, for some reason, he wanted her. She still didn't understand. He'd probably slept with hot women who looked like Astrid for all of his adult life. Rory felt she was attractive, but she knew she was definitely not supermodel material.

As she closed the door to the room behind her, she had a "light-bulb moment" of her own. Caden had never known love – not the love of his birthparents nor the love of a woman. The only love he'd had was the fraternal kind he seemed to share with his brothers. He'd had sex for release, but there had been no emotional connection between him and his partners. Rory was intelligent, hard-working, and as wholesome as one could be. She'd had a stable home life in a close-knit rural community. Of course, he would be drawn to her. They both had supernatural powers, but Rory was everything Caden hadn't been allowed to be. Compared to him, she was "normal."

I'm a web designer who runs a B&B, she thought. *He kills killers and often witnesses them doing horrible things. I represent everything he's been denied. So, does he just want me because of that? Or does he want me because of who I am inside?* Sighing, she decided, *Two halves make a whole. It's probably both. After all, my background has helped to shape my personality.*

Rory wished that she had the makings of a nice dinner in her kitchen. She wanted to cook a meal for Caden and simply stay at the house and talk. But she'd been telling the truth about being low on many staple items. Besides, it would be good for both of them to leave Nostalgia Road for a while. She could cook dinner for him the next night.

Caden returned to the main house in his Trailblazer. Rory was waiting on the front porch. As he climbed out of the SUV, she walked along the pavers that led to the little gravel parking area. When Caden offered to open the passenger door of his Chevy for her, she suggested that they take her car.

"I don't think I can even *fit* in your car," he volunteered after giving the white Ford Focus a dubious glance. "I'm six foot three. You'd probably have to cut me in half."

"I've been in your SUV, remember? It could use a good cleaning on the inside." Glancing toward her car, she assured him, "You'll fit. You don't know your way around Sage like I do. It would be easier for me to drive, and I'm not comfortable driving anyone else's vehicle."

"I don't have the same qualms, but I refuse to let a woman drive me around. It would be ungentlemanly."

"If I let you drive my car, then we'd be in the same situation as if I rode in yours. I'd still have to be giving you directions."

"So, just ride in my Chevy."

"Caden –"

"I'm not going to budge on this, Rory."

"Fine," she groused. "If it rains and there's a large puddle, then are you going to put your jacket across it so I don't get my feet wet?"

"I'm not wearing a jacket. I'd just pick you up and carry you over the puddle."

"You would not!"

"Try me," he said with a devilish look in his eyes.

She sensed that she didn't have to test him. She knew deep down that he would do it. This man was, indeed, a "real" man. He didn't want a submissive little woman, but he did want to retain his own dominant and protective tendencies.

"Where is Astrid?" she asked once they were on their way toward Sage.

"Still at my cottage. She was having fun and didn't seem inclined to leave, so I told her what we were planning and advised her to stay put until I returned later."

"What do you have her doing?"

"Playing on the Internet. She's been concentrating on depressing the keys on my laptop. She said it took a while to get the hang of it, but she's having a great time now. I think it's making her feel as if she's not dead."

"That could be dangerous."

"Letting her play on the computer?"

"Well, yes. But that's not what I meant. Making her feel more connected to the living may make her less inclined to cross over."

"Is there a rush?"

"You know she doesn't belong on our plane of existence any longer." Staring out of the window at the passing fields, she added, "I am glad she ended up at Nostalgia Road. It's given me an entirely different outlook on what kind of a person she really is. Well, was."

"As long as she's here, I vote for referring to her in the present tense."

Rory grinned, reaching across the seat in order to place her left hand on Caden's right forearm. He tensed, saying, "You're distracting me."

"How?"

"I told you that you make me hard whenever we're together, remember? Having you touch me is making it worse."

"I don't believe you," she said with a small smile.

Caden grinned wolfishly at her and asked, "You don't, huh?"

He gently disengaged his arm from her light grip, took her hand in his, and brought it to the front of his jeans. When she felt the telltale bulge beneath her palm and fingers, Rory blushed and swallowed hard but didn't pull her hand away.

They heard the unmistakable sound of a police siren behind the Trailblazer and noted the flashing lights. Rory hastened to withdraw her hand, and Caden straightened and swore. She threw a look over her shoulder and said, "Relax. It's my friend, Harvey."

"Officer Marsh and I already met twice the day I came to Nostalgia Road. He stopped me for speeding both times, and I promised him I'd try not to do it anymore while in the area. I was so freakin' distracted by how I was feeling that I have no idea how fast I was going."

"It'll be fine. Pull over so that we can talk to Harvey."

"Is he the only cop in town?"

"There aren't many, and he tends to handle this area. They have different quadrants they cover since there aren't a lot of cops. He's a wonderful guy."

Pulling over to the side of the road, Caden said, "Yeah, I was impressed by him both times he stopped me. I don't think he's going to be as pleasant this time."

Caden rolled down his window, and Harvey appeared beside it. He frowned – until he saw Rory.

"Rory Roosevelt! What are you doing out here with Mr. Lead Foot?"

"We're out on a date. We're going to Ren's Creek for dinner then to the Publix in Gladeland."

Harvey's eyebrows shot up, but he recovered himself quickly and said, "My wife and I had a date like that last night." Looking to Caden, he asked, "Do you know how fast you were going this time, Mister Brody?"

"No idea. I was kind of…distracted."

"By what?"

"Rory."

Harvey's face registered some understanding and then surprise, but he merely cleared his throat and said, "Well, maybe you should be 'distracted' more often. You were actually going five miles *below* the speed limit. I was pulling you over to rib you a little but also to commend you." Darting a glance at Rory, he said, "Sorry to interrupt your date. Have a great time tonight."

"Thanks. We plan to. Tell your wife 'Hi' from me."

"Will do." Drilling Caden with his eyes, Harvey said sternly, "You take care of her, you hear?"

Caden smiled and said, "No worries. She's my top priority."

The way he said it made heat burn in Rory's stomach and lower still.

"How far is it to this restaurant where we're supposed to have dinner?" Caden asked once Harvey had returned to his cruiser.

"About five more minutes. Why?"

"Because I don't know how much longer I can hold off when it comes to making love to you."

"If your Trailblazer wasn't such a mess, then I think I'd be fine with you folding down the seats and making love to me in the back right this minute."

"You're serious?"

"Yes. I was just imagining climbing onto your lap and –"

"Rory, stop. I'm trying to hang on to what self-control I have left." Inhaling deeply then slowly exhaling, he said, "Let's get moving. We need to be in a public place as soon as possible."

12 Caden

As they approached the town of Sage, Caden regained complete self-control and asked, "You mind if we take a quick tour before dinner? I'd like to get acquainted with your hometown."

"It will definitely be quick," Rory said with a grin. "Most people out here live in the countryside surrounding the town."

"Like you."

"Yes, but I'm the only one who owns a B&B. Some are farmers, while others have cattle and horses. The actual town of Sage is kind of nothing."

"I'd like to see what 'kind of nothing' looks like."

"Sure. Take the next left, then drive straight down Central Florida Boulevard. There are two stoplights and a couple of stop signs. It's our version of Main Street."

"You're kidding me."

Grinning, she shook her head and said, "Small-town America at its finest."

He laughed, thinking that perhaps she was teasing him. She wasn't. He passed older homes that needed some TLC, an Exxon station, a business called Nash's All-In-One, a few deserted buildings that had FOR LEASE signs in their windows, Ogden Hardware and Feed Store, and Nolan's Bar.

"Your brother couldn't come up with anything more original than that?"

"He said a bar was a bar, and he didn't need any cutesy name for his. I gave him my suggestion, but I knew he'd hate it since he always resented our supernatural abilities."

"What was your suggestion?"

"*Spirits.*"

"That would have been the perfect inside joke."

"Yes. Nolan hated it, but it made me smile."

"Maybe someday he'll change the name."

"Maybe, but I don't think so. He'd have to completely come around, and I don't foresee that happening."

Sensing that this line of conversation was making Rory sad, Caden decided to change the subject by inquiring, "What's *Nash's All-In-One?*"

"A large convenience store."

"Surely this can't be all there is to Sage."

"It's not, but things are pretty spread out. There's a church, an elementary school, a high school, a funeral home, a mechanic shop, the cemetery, a hair salon, and a dog groomer."

"So, where are all these places?"

"Down side streets or country roads. Well, part of Lizbet's house right off The Boulevard is her hair salon, and she has a shed out back that has air-conditioning where she does the dog grooming."

"Okay, wait a minute. This woman, Lizbet, is the local hair stylist *and* pet groomer?"

Rory smiled, shrugged, and then said, "Lizbet saw a need for hair and fur care and decided why not get certified to do both?"

"I can't wait to explore this town more thoroughly."

Rory sobered, asking, "Are you sure? This is a rural area, and you seem to have traveled all around the country and probably outside of it during your lifetime. Sage isn't the most exciting place, but this is my home. I can't leave it, Caden. But could you be happy here if things work out between us? Assuming we survive, that is."

"I *have* traveled all over our country, but not the world. I've seen a lot and have lived in all sorts of places. You know where I tend to live when I'm not on a job?" When she shook her head, he said, "Rural areas. The place I'm leasing right now is outside of Jackson Hole, Wyoming. My previous apartment was in a rural town not too far from Boise, Idaho. I like being near to big cities because I have to be close to airports and other things I might need for work. But I found that once I left New Orleans, I actually prefer the peace that comes with living in more remote places."

"You're not just saying that? I wouldn't want you to settle here and then be miserable."

"I wouldn't. Even if rural life wasn't my thing, then I'd find a way to make it work. I'm falling in love with you."

That she remained uncertain bothered Caden, but he knew there was no way to convince her without actually showing her. He would have to be patient until she accepted that what he'd told her was the truth. A small part of him was concerned that she would always worry about this facet of their lives if everything *did* work out between them. And Caden desperately wanted a future with Rory, although he couldn't quite pinpoint why.

"Turn right at the next road," she directed. "Then, drive until you can't go any further. When that happens, we'll be at Ren's Creek Restaurant."

"Would you give me some background? Is Ren's Creek an important water source in the area?"

"Ren Yeager is the restaurant's owner. The name of the creek is Scorched Creek."

Scorched Creek? he thought, but he didn't want to interrupt Rory in order to ask her about the origins of the creek's unusual name.

"Not only is Ren's business on its banks, but so is her house. The restaurant serves delicious food in a casual but polished setting. Customers can eat outside if it's not too hot, cold, or raining. Otherwise, people eat indoors, but all of the tables have a view of the creek and the area around it. The menu is varied but balanced. You'll see."

Within a few minutes, the restaurant came into view. Caden pulled into the gravel parking lot, which was almost full. True, there was only enough room for perhaps two dozen cars, but that was still impressive, considering the size of the nearby town. The outside of the building had a rustic, yet well-kept feel to it. The exterior was all wood, and a large deck area with tables and chairs was to its right. Indoors, huge windows gave patrons good views of the outdoors, and Caden could easily see the people inside the brightly lit dining room. They looked relaxed and happy. As he pulled open the door for Rory, the sound of music could be heard, but it wasn't loud enough to interfere with the conversations going on at each table and at the small bar area. No one was having to shout to be heard. He listened for a minute and then smiled as he recognized the song that was currently playing: Trace Adkins's "Hold My Beer."

"I like this place already," he told Rory, who gave him a quizzical look. Instead of elaborating, Caden took her in his arms and bent to kiss her. After a few seconds, he noted that all conversation in the restaurant had ceased and felt the eyes of the patrons upon them.

Rory hasn't been out on a date since high school, and everyone in this place probably knows her, he reminded himself, as he deepened the kiss. *Her being out on a date with a local would have caused enough of a stir, but showing up with a stranger and kissing him in public? Hell, this will be the talk of the town for a while.*

He drew back, giving her a broad grin, and then said, "I think we're being watched."

Red crept up Rory's neck, settling in her cheeks, as she confirmed, "We are. I don't care. I like it when you kiss me."

Putting his lips to her ear, he murmured, "I'm glad to hear it because I was just thinking about picking you up, carrying you over to the bar, and then –"

"Rory! Hey, Girl!"

Caden pulled back, trying to mask his annoyance, as he turned to look at who had interrupted them. He was momentarily startled as he caught his first glimpse of the woman he would soon learn was Ren Yeager, the owner of Ren's Creek Restaurant. Were she not five foot ten, he would have assumed she was of only Asian descent. She had almond-shaped, dark brown eyes and long, straight black hair, but she was at least eight inches taller than the average Japanese woman.

There was no trace of a foreign accent when Ren spoke. She wore a red Polo shirt, nice jeans, and a pair of sandals. Her fingernails and toenails were painted red, but she wore no jewelry. The only make-up she'd used that evening was red lipstick.

Rory introduced him to Ren, who smiled politely but appeared to be scrutinizing him while they talked. He didn't mind. She seemed to be making certain he was genuine. He sensed protectiveness for Rory in Ren's gaze and was thankful for it. He wondered how long the two women had known each other.

"Welcome to Ren's Creek," the woman said, as she led them toward a table near a far window. "What do you like to eat, Caden?"

Born and raised around here, he thought. *Rural folks tend to use first names right away if they accept you. I guess I made a good first impression on Ren.*

"I love all types of food. What do you recommend tonight?" he asked, as he pulled out a chair and gestured for Rory to take a seat.

Looking pleased with Caden's manners, Ren waited for him to take the seat beside Rory before answering, "The grouper platter with whipped sweet potatoes and seaweed salad."

"That sounds delicious. Will I have room for dessert?"

She gave him a once-over then said, "A big guy like you? Definitely."

"Great. I have a sweet tooth."

"Check out the desserts on the menu. I'm sure we'll be able to satisfy you on that score."

I have other things in mind when it comes to being satisfied, he thought.

Once Ren had left to put in their orders, Rory asked innocently, "So, what kinds of sweet things do you like to eat?"

"I never met a dessert I didn't like," Caden said truthfully. Leaning toward her, he murmured, "What I'd *really* like for dessert would be to coat your skin with powdered sugar and then lick it all off. I've been fantasizing about it ever since I touched you in your kitchen."

Rory shivered involuntarily but couldn't stop smiling – and blushing. Once their waitress had brought their iced teas, she said, "Speaking of powder, I have to powder my nose. I'll be right back."

Purse in hand, she headed away from their table. He watched her walk to the restroom and thought of Rory's telling him she needed to powder her nose. When was the last time he'd heard someone use that phrase outside of an old movie? She was so sweet and so wholesome.

Rory returned just before their plates arrived. She had opted for grilled shrimp, spicy green beans, and cheesy corn grits.

"Would you like to taste what's on my plate?"

"I will if you'll sample what's on mine."

"I'd love to," she admitted. "I'm drooling over the seaweed salad."

They concentrated on their food, alternating between making satisfied noises after taking bites and sipping their drinks. Caden was happy to note that the silence wasn't an awkward one. He felt as if he and Rory had been together for years, and there was no need for inane conversation.

"Dessert?" Ren asked when she passed by their table after their dinner plates had been cleared.

"I think I'd explode," Rory replied.

"I'll have a piece of the chocolate pecan pie," Caden said. "The strawberry pie is also calling my name, but I'll save that for next time."

"So, you're planning on being a repeat customer?"

"Yes. Hopefully, I'll be eating here a lot from now on."

The woman was obviously startled but merely nodded to Rory and grinned. Rory beamed at her. Caden was glad to see her so happy. Maybe they *could* have a normal relationship in the midst of their abnormal lives.

After Caden had savored every bite of the delectable chocolate pecan pie, he paid for dinner, ignoring Rory's protestations that she should pay for her portion of the meal. Waving goodbye to Ren, they left the restaurant and crunched across the gravel to Caden's Trailblazer. It took thirty minutes for them to reach the Publix in Gladeland where they spent an hour shopping and chatting easily as they wandered. By the time Rory had gotten everything on her list and Caden had picked up a few odds and ends he needed, it was almost 9:00. Because of their proximity to Nostalgia Road, they were back at the Roosevelt home before 9:20.

After he'd helped her unload the cloth bags full of groceries from the truck, Caden did as Rory asked and sat on the couch, listening to her hum contentedly as she put away the groceries. He tried not to think about Astrid's killer, the threat of evil at Nostalgia Road, his brother's death, and the mysteries surrounding Elias. Unfortunately, he wasn't very successful.

Rory came into the living room carrying something in her right hand and asked, "Do you want anything? A beer? Something sweet?" Smiling, she said, "Sweets for my sweet."

"Sweets for my sweet," Caden repeated. "Where have I heard that before?"

"It's an old song by The Drifters. My parents used to play that on the stereo and dance around the living room." Looking wistful, she added, "They were so in love." As she sat beside him on the couch, Rory unwrapped a pink ice pop, asking, "Do you want one? I have other flavors besides strawberry-kiwi."

"I'm good," he assured her, never taking his eyes from her mouth as she inserted the tip of the ice pop into it and wrapped her lips around it. When she noticed his watching her intently, she raised her brows in a silent question without withdrawing the frozen treat from her mouth.

"You have no idea what you're doing to me, do you?" he asked huskily.

Easing the ice pop out, she said with complete innocence, "What?"

"Watching you sucking on something that looks like, uh, a –" After searching his mind for a polite way to phrase what he wanted to say, Caden finally blurted out, "You're going to make me explode without even trying!"

"What?" Then, as realization dawned, she colored and said, "Oh. Do you want me to stop?"

"Hell, no! I want to see you suck on that until it's gone."

"Well, now I feel self-conscious sucking on an ice pop," she mumbled, looking away.

"Don't. You turn me on like nobody else ever has." Nodding toward her popsicle, he said, "It's melting."

Instinctively, she tilted her head to one side and stuck out her tongue in order to lick the rivulets running down the sides. Caden wished that he could take himself in hand, but he wouldn't do that to her, not at this stage in their budding relationship. In the future, he'd want her to touch him and to take *him* in her mouth. But that could – and should – wait until later.

After she'd finished, Rory asked, "Did you really enjoy watching me eat an ice pop?"

"You have no idea."

"Then I think it's time to put that powdered sugar in the kitchen to good use. Let's take it upstairs and indulge your sweet tooth."

"If I do that, then I don't know if I'll be able to stop myself from going further."

"Then don't. I appreciate the chivalry. You can't imagine what it means to me, especially in light of what Dominic did. But tomorrow is Astrid's funeral, and you and I both know that bad things are coming. Astrid was right when she said that we could die anytime. I want to be with you first, and you want the same thing. Why waste any more time?"

Caden replayed Rory's words in his head, as he stood and offered her one hand. She accepted it, got to her feet, and allowed him to enfold her in his arms. He brushed her lips with his before murmuring, "Let's get the powdered sugar and go upstairs."

"Sweets for my sweet," she said with a gentle smile.

He nodded and repeated, "Sweets for my sweet." Leading her into the kitchen, he lifted the bag of powdered sugar from the counter and asked, "Do you have a pair of scissors handy? This is going to be messy. If I cut the corner of the bag, then there might not be as much clean-up afterwards. Even so, we shouldn't do this in your bedroom in case powdered sugar ends up everywhere."

She considered this before saying, "I agree, but I want our first time to be in my bed. We can do the powdered sugar part in a guest room and then shower and, um, finish in my room."

They climbed the stairs, turning left when they reached the landing. She led him past the library and a bathroom. They walked through the next doorway into a simple guest room that was furnished with a full-sized bed, a dresser, and a wooden chair. All of the furniture was oak and looked antique. The bedding was all white, as were the curtains. The wallpaper design involved tiny flowers and vines.

"What should I do now?" Rory asked nervously.

"Are you comfortable with my undressing you, or would you like to do it yourself this first time?" Caden asked, wanting to take extra care with her because of how Dominic Ambrose had forced himself upon her seven years earlier.

"I'd like to undress myself," she replied, sounding nervous.

"Mind if I sit and watch?"

"What?" she asked, bewildered.

"I want to watch you undress. Is that all right?"

"Yes, but I don't know how exciting it will be for you to see me take off my clothes."

"I do."

Caden sat in the chair and watched as Rory slipped off her dress. Underneath, she wore a black bra and pantie set. Caden's breathing quickened, as she unhooked and removed the bra, tossed it on top of her dress, and then pushed down her panties. The sight of her breasts and her short red curls forced Caden to stifle a groan. Her long, red hair was slightly disheveled. She looked nervously at him, as though he might be disappointed.

Rising, he said, "You're even more beautiful like this than I imagined. Before morning, I'm going to know every inch of your body, and I hope you'll know every inch of mine."

"I want that, too. It's only that…well, this is really my first time. You know what I mean? I'm worried I'll do something stupid. I don't have any experience except the bad kind."

"I do, so trust me." Looking directly into her indigo eyes, Caden said with a hint of wonder in his voice, "I think I feel…love for you"

"I think that I feel love for you, too," she admitted. "I can't believe this is really happening."

"That we might be falling in love or that we're having sex?"

"Both. Are you as scared as I am?"

He half-shrugged before admitting, "I'm scared I'll inadvertently wreck things." Stepping forward, Caden slid his arms around Rory's naked shoulders and said, "Let's stop talking and start making love. I feel like that will solidify things between us."

Grinning, Rory said, "Interesting choice of words for people with powers like ours." Wrapping her arms tightly around his waist, she observed, "It feels so odd not to have clothes on while hugging someone who's still dressed. Will you please take your clothes off?"

Caden sat again and removed his boots and socks. Standing, he reached his right hand behind him, grasped the material of his shirt, and pulled it over his head before dropping it onto the floor. His ginger-colored hair was now thoroughly mussed. After unzipping his fly, he pushed his jeans down before pulling them off. Caden added his boxers to the pile and stood, naked, in front of Rory. For the first time in his life, *he* felt exposed in the presence of a woman.

"You think I'll do?" he asked in an attempt to help them both relax.

"*Do*? Caden, you're like an action hero come to life!" Glancing down at herself, Rory looked disappointed and began, "And I'm –"

"Gorgeous," he interrupted, genuine awe in his voice. "I'm ready to satisfy my sweet tooth."

"Do I get to satisfy mine?"

"You want to go first?"

"Oh, no! I wouldn't know what to do."

"Okay, but you have to tell me if I'm doing something you don't like. Are we good?"

"We're good."

When Caden turned to retrieve the bag and scissors, Rory gasped then exclaimed, "What an awesome tattoo on your back! Did it hurt to get it?"

"It hurt like hell. Elias had rites of passage for his sons, but we brothers developed our own, like getting a full-back dragon tattoo when we each turned twenty-one. The individual tattoos are unique. We may not share the same parents, but our tats are another way of showing that we're brothers."

As he returned to the bed, Rory asked, "Why dragons?"

"It was Beck's idea." When she looked blankly at him, he clarified, "My oldest surviving brother. He's half-Japanese and half-Caucasian. Like our African-American brother, David, Beck was a non-white child raised by a white man in a white man's world. Beck's always been fascinated by Japanese culture. Hence, the dragon tattoo idea." Bringing the conversation back to the original topic, Caden explained, "Dragons are perceived in most cultures as being strong, wise, mythical creatures. Often, they're sentinels who protect treasured things."

"Like you and your brothers help protect humanity from killers." After he'd agreed, Rory asked, "May I touch your dragon before we start?"

Caden sat with his back facing Rory, closing his eyes as her fingers crept across where the red dragon's claws gripped the top of his left shoulder. Her fingertips moved over the dragon's foot then traced around one wing before moving down his back. She stroked gently along the tail that hugged Caden's right hip and the outside of his right leg. Rory used her palm to rub his skin as she followed the edge of the right side of the dragon's body, finishing by skimming one of her nails around its head under his neck. Throughout her examination, Caden consciously slowed his breathing and worked diligently not to surrender to climax.

"Caden? Are you all right?"

He nodded and said in a graveled voice, "That was unbelievably erotic."

"It was pretty erotic for me, too," she admitted. "I love the way the dragon looks so alive, especially when you move. It makes me ache to have you inside me."

If she'd had any more experience and hadn't been raped, Caden would have immediately pinned Rory to the mattress or pulled her into his lap and pushed himself inside. But this was Rory – sweet, wholesome, date-rape victim Rory. He *had* to go slowly with her. Like the dragon on his back, he had to be strong, wise, and protect the treasure that was her.

"Lie down," he instructed, as he snipped one corner of the bag then rose to replace the scissors on the dresser. When he turned, she was on her side, facing him. His features softened, and he gently commanded, "Turn onto your back. I want to...to...." Struggling to verbalize how he felt, he said, "I want to *claim* you, to make sure you're mine. Does that scare you?"

Shaking her head, Rory said, "Exactly the opposite. I can see how much you want me but also want to please me. It's what I dreamed of when I was younger. I wanted a man to look at me with the combination of love and lust that I see in your eyes."

Caden was so moved that he couldn't speak. For a millisecond, he wanted to cry. Quickly quashing that impulse, he merely nodded and urged, "On your back, Rory."

She rolled over and looked up expectantly at him. Caden shook some of the powdered sugar into his right palm; then he began to sprinkle it over Rory's torso, continuing down to above her knees. He left her arms and lower legs clean. He didn't believe he could hold off on climaxing if he coated her entire body.

I'll make her come before we both shower and move to her bed for the grand finale, but I need to stay in control. She's counting on me, and I can't slip up. This is too important.

After returning the bag to the dresser, Caden knelt beside Rory on the bed. He bent forward, kissed her, and ran his fingers through her hair then brought his mouth to her neck. She sucked in her breath and clutched at his ginger-colored hair, but Caden didn't pause. Instead, he kissed and licked until all the powdered sugar was gone from her throat. Then, he lazily dragged the tip of his tongue around in patterns across her chest and breasts before drawing one nipple into his mouth. She tensed.

Releasing the nipple, he announced, "I'm not going to enter you here, but I intend to make you come before we shower. Relax."

He sensed that she wanted to argue, but Rory remained silent. His tongue and lips moved between her breasts before exploring her

113

belly. Rory was panting by this time, but Caden stayed focused. She cried out when he flicked his tongue into the depression of her navel.

"Open your legs for me," he directed. When she did, he moved between them, licking the powdered sugar from her thighs in long, full strokes.

"Caden, please," she whimpered, but he could tell it was with pleasure, not pain.

"Sweets for my sweet," he murmured, caressing her sticky, sugar-coated thighs and belly with his hands.

Rory moaned when he slipped two fingers between her legs and returned his mouth to her breasts. After giving the rest of her torso more attention, Caden withdrew his fingers, replacing them with his mouth. She suddenly cried out his name, pulled hard at his hair, and arched her back. Moving his hands to the sides of her hips, Caden kept his mouth where it was and basked in her body's reaction to the orgasm he'd just evoked from it.

"Oh…my…God," Rory said once she could speak again. "That was amazing."

"For me, too. You all right?"

Rory nodded but looked slightly dazed.

"You can cover me in powdered sugar next time," Caden said before suggesting, "For now, let's shower and move to your bed."

"I need to lie here for a minute. My legs feel all rubbery. Will you hold me for a while?"

I'm an idiot! This isn't my typical partner, someone who's only interested in sex. Stretching out beside her, Caden pulled her against him, enjoying the feel of the sticky sugar residue, and thought, *I should talk to her about something personal to show her that I care about all of her and not only her body.*

Having no experience in this area, Caden floundered. Finally, he said, "Tell me about your parents. You said they were really in love. How could you tell?"

When Rory began to cry quietly, Caden mentally kicked himself.

"I'm sorry. I didn't mean to make you think about their absence."

"That's not why I'm crying," she insisted, although the tears didn't stop.

"Why then?"

"Because I had such a happy home life as a child, and you didn't have one at all." Crying harder, she went on, "When my parents would watch TV, Mom and Dad would sit side-by-side with their knees touching. They'd put on old records that used to belong to their parents and dance around the house. Even when they were washing dishes, they'd stand beside each other at the sink and kind of sway back and forth like they were moving to music Nolan and I couldn't hear. They loved each other and us so much and made our house a home." Burying her face against his chest, she went on, "It sounds like you had caregivers, training by Elias in fighting and killing, and no normalcy whatsoever! How old were you the first time you killed?"

"Thirteen," he said quietly.

"Thirteen?" she echoed, her horror evident. "I can't believe Elias did that to you! It's *so* wrong! What about your remaining brothers?"

"David was fifteen, and Sawyer and Thorn were each sixteen." After a brief pause, he said, "Beck was eleven."

Still crying, Rory threw her arms around Caden's neck and kissed him. Despite her distress, he was fully erect and wanted desperately to be inside of her. He realized that this wasn't merely a physiological response. His body was reacting to what his mind craved. He *needed* to be in Rory, to be granted emotional and physical relief as he released in her.

Drawing back, Caden said, "I need you."

Blinking away tears, she said, "We need each other so much for different reasons. I want to make it better for you, just as you want to make things better for me. I can't wait to take you in me. I wish we never had to be apart."

13 Rory

Rory lay under the covers in her bed, listening to the sound of the water flowing through the pipes as Caden showered. What they had already done was mind-blowing, but what they were about to do was monumental. Rory wasn't scared. On the contrary, she had never been more eager for anything in her life. She wanted Caden to enter her but not merely for the sake of physical pleasure. She somehow knew that he needed to bury himself in her and climax in order to soothe the part of himself that had known nothing of real love.

She had no doubt that Caden loved his brothers, but none of them had been allowed to have normal childhoods. They'd had no parents or traditional experiences that would allow them to comprehend what was involved in meaningful connections with partners. Rory couldn't fathom doing the things she and Caden had already done without loving the other person involved. Caden and his brothers had known nothing else. All they'd seemed to learn from Elias was how to fight, kill, and have impersonal sex.

The water stopped, and Rory's heart rate increased. She wondered what would happen if she couldn't reach Caden and he withdrew from her. She couldn't force him to understand. She wasn't certain about what would happen to them if their lovemaking didn't yield the anticipated results. She suspected it would break her heart, not only because she *did* feel love for Caden but also because she'd know that she'd failed to reach him.

"Hey," Caden said from the doorway. Although he was naked and damp from the shower, he declared, "I have to go back to Mockingbird Hideaway."

Hastily sitting up, Rory asked, "Why?"

"I don't have condoms here. I won't take a chance on getting you pregnant."

"Have you ever had sex without a condom?" she asked.

"No. I didn't want to catch some disease or accidentally father any children."

"I'm on birth control. I have, um, trouble with my cycles. My doctor said the hormones would help, and they have. They also make it virtually impossible for me to get pregnant."

"You take it religiously?"

"Every morning when I get up. I've never missed a dose in two years."

He planted one hand on the doorframe and admitted, "I hated the thought of using a condom with you. I want to know what it's like to be totally with someone. You know, with no barriers."

Rory nodded but sensed that Caden was disquieted. Searching for a temporary distraction, she asked the first question that came to mind.

"Do you like my room?"

Dork! she immediately berated herself. *What am I, some starry-eyed teenager? He's going to think I'm an idiot!*

But Caden merely glanced casually around, taking in the sleigh bed with the paisley comforter, the nightstands, the lamp with its fringed shade, the photos of family and friends on the wall, the filled bookshelves, the chest of drawers near the closet, and the miscellany arranged on the surfaces around the room. He smiled at the sight of Paddington Bear sitting in a rocker near the window. Rory wondered if he knew what Paddington Bear was but decided not to ask that particular question just then.

"I *do* like your room. It's comfortable, just like the rest of the house. Well, what I've seen of it anyway. I take it all of your electronics up here are in your office next door?"

"All except my iHome on that bookshelf. I plug my other devices into it if I want to listen to music or part of an audiobook in here before I go to sleep."

"What's your favorite type of music?"

"Blues and jazz. You?"

"Country and blues, but I like jazz, too."

"What about books?" When he looked quizzically at her, she prompted, "What types of books do you like to read?"

"Thrillers."

"I'm shocked," she said with a grin. "I figured you'd say, 'Romance.'"

He chuckled and said, "No, I obviously have a lot to learn about romance."

"I think you're doing an awfully good job."

"Am I?" he asked intently. "I feel like I kind of suck at it."

As a blush deepened in her cheeks, Rory said, "I liked the way you sucked a little while ago."

Caden was instantly hard. His eyes became hooded, and he strode over to the bed and grasped the edge of the comforter before pulling it and the top sheet down to the foot of the mattress. Rory, still naked after her shower, shivered in the coolness of the room but felt heat flare in the pit of her stomach. A slow burn began between her legs.

Caden climbed onto the bed so quickly that Rory almost didn't see the movement. As he proceeded to settle on top of her. Rory felt the definition of his muscles as she stroked his chest, shoulders, and arms with her palms. His hard length teased her as he moved above her.

When Caden pushed his tongue between her lips, Rory explored his mouth while he delved into hers. After a few moments, she felt compelled to suck on his tongue. When she did, he grunted and tightened his hold on her.

Breaking the kiss, she said, "May I touch...*it* before we...before you enter me?"

Rory could sense how difficult it was for Caden to release her and sit back on his heels, but he did it. She scooted back, her legs still spread, until she could sit up and examine his erection. Her neck and cheeks burned with embarrassment, as Caden refused to take his eyes from between her legs.

"Caden?"

"You're so freakin' beautiful," he said, lifting his gaze to her face. "Every part of you. Can I cup your breasts while you touch me?"

Rory intuited that he wasn't used to asking for permission to do things with any woman he bedded. Smiling, she nodded then turned her attention toward his erection with its thick, veined shaft. As Caden cupped both of her breasts, Rory darted a glance at his face, noticing that Caden's eyelids were closed and his jaw was clenched. She suspected that he was struggling not to come. Regardless, he began to knead her breasts and rub at her nipples, making her own need that much greater. She gently ran her fingers up and down his length and heard him draw in a quick breath. She explored the ginger-colored hair that surrounded the base of his shaft before moving her hands lower.

Caden said her name through clenched teeth. Sliding her hands along his hips and then cupping his cheeks with her palms, Rory said softly, "I want you in me. I *need* you in me."

The kiss that followed was so intense that Rory felt as if her lips were being bruised. She didn't care. Raw emotion and physical desire were literally drawing them together. Before she realized what was happening, Caden had her on her back. She spread her legs wider and pushed her breasts up against his chest. Without warning, Caden drove into her.

No pain, she thought with relief. *Oh, God. It feels so good, so right. Yes, yes, yes....*

As Caden began to repeatedly thrust in and pull out, Rory lifted her hips in an attempt to take him deeper inside. She squirmed with pleasure underneath him. Their bodies quickly became slick with sweat. After what seemed like a blissful eternity, Rory knew that she was going to climax soon.

"Caden!"

"I feel it," he panted. "This is...so different...." He dropped his head but didn't stop thrusting as he practically shouted, "God, Rory! I *love* you!"

"I love you, too!" she cried. "Come in me now! Please!"

Rory tightened around him. She could tell that Caden was coming even before she felt it. Her blue eyes locked with his green ones, and neither looked away until both of them had finished. Caden then lowered himself on top of her but didn't pull out. Although he appeared completely relaxed, she knew that he wasn't. If he were, then he would have crushed her with his large body. Neither of them spoke, but she could feel his hot breath on her ear as they held on tightly to one another.

"You okay?" he eventually asked.

"Uh-huh. You?"

Caden withdrew from Rory, wrapped his arms around her, and pulled her against him. He didn't answer her question, and she wondered if she should repeat it. Opting to remain silent, she breathed in the sandalwood and vanilla scent that was now stronger on Caden's body.

"I never understood how sex could be so different when you actually love the person you're having it with," murmured Caden. "I can't ever imagine having it without love again."

"Good, because you're only supposed to have it with me from now on."

"That's all I want. Being in you without wearing a condom and releasing directly in you was…liberating. I imagined…."

"What?"

Caden shook his head and said, "Nothing."

Pushing up and away from him until she could see his face, she prodded, "You imagined what?"

To her surprise, *his* face reddened. She could have teased him about blushing but wasn't about to make him withdraw out of embarrassment. She waited.

"I *did* feel as if I was claiming you." Sighing and shutting his eyes, he confided, "I know it's ridiculous. We still hardly know one another, and it goes against everything I was raised to believe. Up until this week, I never imagined I could actually *have* a life with someone. I figured I'd die young like all the other Brody sons."

"And now?" she asked in a small voice.

"Now I want to have a life with you. I know it's too soon to be discussing that but –"

"I don't think it is," she insisted. "We could both die tomorrow. We're together tonight, and I want much more time with you in the years to come." After a brief pause, she prodded, "What do *you* want?"

"You, of course. Maybe someday we could have a family." After kissing her, he said, "If you even want to have a family with someone like me."

"What's that supposed to mean? You keep telling me how gorgeous I am, and I understand now that you *see* me as gorgeous. It makes me *feel* gorgeous. Yet, you can't see what an amazing man you are? Why wouldn't I want you to make babies with me someday?"

"Because I wouldn't know the first thing about what to do with kids!" he said, his agitation evident. "It's not like I'd be recreating my childhood for them, seeing if they survived my training in order to be 'allowed' to grow up so that I could teach them to fight and kill!"

"Shhh," Rory said, stroking his hair. "You wouldn't do anything of the sort. Let's each dream big. You'll stay here with me. Right?"

"Right," Caden said softly but firmly.

"You said you like rural communities. So, we'll have a normal life here at Nostalgia Road. You'll choose what *you* want to do for a living. No more fighting and killing after we take care of whatever evil is after me or us or the world."

"But I don't know how to be a regular guy. What if I'm a horrible partner and parent." Appearing flustered, he hastily added, "*If* we had kids, that is."

"I had fabulous parents. Personally, I think you'd be a great partner and dad."

Caden turned his head and admitted, "I wonder if Elias did lie about it all. I think perhaps we were taken from our parents. What if mine are still alive and are still looking for me? Or what if Elias killed them so that he could have me?"

"If they're alive and are searching for you, then you'll find out and locate them. If Elias killed them...."

She didn't finish her sentence. They both knew that if Caden's adoptive father had killed his sons' parents in order to take their children, then the brothers would be forced to kill him in order to gain retribution for their dead mothers and fathers. She suspected that the brothers would have to kill Elias anyway since it appeared that he was actually Charles Roosevelt. If that were true, then he'd probably killed his own brother and Rory's parents. Once they were certain, Rory had no doubt that justice would be swift and sure.

"Will you teach me everything you know about sex?" Rory asked, attempting not to allow thoughts of Elias Brody to interfere with the progress they'd made so far that night.

"It'd be my pleasure," Caden said with a wicked grin.

"Good. Plus, I want to see what it looks like when you come."

Caden rolled his eyes and said, "Now you've gone and done it."

"Done what?"

"Got me hard again already. Not that I'm surprised. Remember, I don't even have to be awake for you to make me hard and –"

"Rory! Caden!"

They both sat bolt upright in bed and exclaimed simultaneously and with great exasperation, "Astrid!"

"I know! I know I'm not supposed to bother you in the bedroom, but I had to warn you!" Taking in their appearance, she cried, "Oh, thank God! I was hoping you'd have sex! You two are obviously meant to be together. I am *so* glad I didn't have to interrupt you while you were screwing your brains out!"

"Astrid, what do you need to warn us about?" Caden snapped. "Did you find out something on the Internet?"

"No. Well, yes. But that's not why I'm here. I'm here to tell you that –"

Before she could finish, Nolan stormed into the bedroom. Rory scrambled to pull up the sheet, but she wasn't fast enough. Nolan's face turned almost purple with rage, and he pointed a handgun at Caden before shouting, "You fucked my sister!"

Caden's eyes narrowed, but he seemed unperturbed by the appearance of the weapon. He brought the sheet up a little higher until it was draped over Rory's chest, kissed her, and then slowly got out of bed. He appeared unconcerned that he was still naked and that Nolan was pointing a gun at his belly.

Panicked, Rory called out, "Put down the gun! We're all adults here, Nolan!"

"Shut up, Rory!" he yelled. "I *knew* you were responsible for what happened with Dominic seven years ago, but I never figured you for a whore! How many men have you fucked?"

Within seconds, Caden had knocked the gun out of Nolan's hand and kicked him in the jaw. Several seconds later, he had the younger man pinned to the ground, both arms twisted behind his back. Nolan howled with fury and pain, his speech garbled. Rory, who had managed to hurry out of bed and wrap the sheet around herself, didn't try to approach or comfort him. Instead, she looked sad yet disdainful.

"I did *not* lead Dominic on!" she hissed. "He forced himself on me, Nolan! And all you did about it was make me feel like it was my fault! Not that it's any of your business, but Caden is the first man I've ever been with. Dominic doesn't count since what happened between us wasn't consensual. Real men don't accuse their sisters of inviting rape or of being whores." Scowling down at her brother, she continued, "Speaking of whores, how many women have you slept with over the years? Sage is a very small town with a close-knit community. There aren't many women in our age group who have class and are willing to put out for you, yet I understand from the town gossip that you have an active sex life. So, who's the whore?"

"You go, girl!" Astrid cheered.

"What do you want me to do with your brother?" Caden asked. "Personally, I'd like to beat him black and blue for disrespecting you and for threatening me with a gun, but I doubt if you'll go for that no matter what."

"No. That doesn't mean that I won't do what it takes to make Nolan listen to reason."

"Or leave Sage," Caden muttered.

Her brother insisted that he was not going to leave his bar. At least that was what she assumed he said. It was difficult to understand him with his broken jaw.

"Apologize to me and Caden," Rory demanded. "Let's start over."

He used the middle finger of his left hand to let her know what he thought of her idea. Caden immediately took the finger and wrenched it back, breaking it. Rory winced and felt sick to her stomach, but she told herself that Nolan was getting off easy. After all, he'd just pointed a gun at Caden and would have been dead had Caden not known that Rory would object to that permanent solution.

"I'm sorry, Nolan. You're giving me no choice." Looking to Caden, Rory asked, "Can you hold him for a few minutes while I shower and dress?"

"Easily."

She hurried to the bathroom, carrying jeans, a t-shirt, and underwear. Within five minutes, she was clean and dressed although her hair remained damp. Nolan appeared to have a fresh lump on his forehead. Rory didn't ask how it had gotten there. Instead, she picked up her phone and dialed 911.

"Hey, Dorothea. It's Rory. Who's on duty in my area tonight? Harvey? Great. Could you send him my way? No, there aren't any unruly patrons. My brother just showed up here with a handgun and threatened my boyfriend. Yes, I have a boyfriend. Caden Brody. Yes, the same man I was with at Ren's earlier tonight." Winking at Caden, she said into the phone, "News travels fast through Sage, as usual. Thank you. Yes, he's awesome. I promise to bring him by to meet you. Okay. No, he has Nolan pinned to the floor. I think he broke Nolan's jaw after Nolan waved the gun at him. Thanks. We'll wait for Harvey then. Have a good night, Dorothea."

Nolan managed to shout "How could you?!?" clearly enough so that he could be understood.

"Because you're as much of a bully as Dominic, and I won't stand by while you let your anger drive you to threaten to shoot innocent people. Mom and Dad would be devastated if they could see how you acted tonight." Staring at the gun on the floor, she added, "I'm so sad and disappointed. I hoped someday you and I could be close again. You've made your choices. You'll have to deal with the repercussions."

"What repercussions?" Astrid asked, unable to tear her eyes from Caden's naked body. "They'll probably only give him a little time or just probation."

"Nolan told me once he didn't own any guns. I'm thinking he doesn't have a permit for that one and wonder if it's legal." When Nolan sagged against the floor, she sighed and said, "I'm guessing not. After all is said and done, he'll probably lose his liquor license and, therefore, the bar."

"Fucking A!" Astrid exclaimed. "Well, I think the punishment fits the crime. You turned out to be such a coward and a scumbag, Nolan. If you know what's good for you, then you'll sell the bar to your sister in exchange for her and Caden not pressing assault charges against you."

"Wha–?" he asked, lifting his head in order to look at the ghost.

"She can buy you out, and you can take the money and start over somewhere away from Sage. Maybe you'll actually get your life together if you move away. Perhaps you'll finally grow up."

"Even if I wanted to, I can't afford to buy him out," Rory insisted. "I don't have the money."

"But *I* do," Caden said. "I have more than enough."

14 Caden

"Caden, no!" Rory exclaimed. "I don't *want* you to run Nolan's Bar!"

"I don't plan on running it, but this line of discussion is making me think of all sorts of possibilities."

"Such as?"

"I'll tell you later when we're alone." Leaning forward slightly, he asked, "Well, Nolan? You'll get a fair price. All you have to do is get the Hell out of Sage and stay gone from the town and Nostalgia Road. Deal?"

Looking defeated, Nolan nodded and moaned with the resultant pain.

"We'll work out the details once you've been fixed up and take care of your issues with the authorities. Just don't try to renege on our agreement. If you do, then I'll bust your balls. Literally."

Nolan shuddered involuntarily, and Astrid laughed. Caden was actually glad that this incident had happened. It would resolve Rory's dilemma with her brother, although he knew it wasn't the resolution she'd hoped for. It would also allow Caden to initiate a plan that he'd begun to formulate in his mind the moment Astrid had suggested that Nolan sell his bar. If his plan worked, then Caden and his brothers might have the opportunity to be a happy family for the first time in their lives.

If they go for it. They may all turn me down. What if only a couple of them agree? I want us to stay together.

Harvey Marsh arrived. Although taken aback by Caden's nudity and the disarray of the bedclothes, Harvey didn't comment on what he'd certainly surmised had happened between Rory and Caden. He handcuffed Nolan and then asked Rory to tell him about her brother and the gun. She blushed – that beautiful, sweet blush Caden loved to see – but lifted her chin before beginning.

"Caden and I, um, were in bed when Nolan burst in waving a gun. He said some terrible things about Caden and about me while pointing the gun at Caden. When I yelled at Nolan because of what he was doing and saying, it momentarily distracted him. Caden knocked the gun out of his hand, kicked him in the jaw, and pinned him to the floor. I, um, showered and dressed while he held him there, and then I called 911. I'm sure I should have called right away, but I was embarrassed by the thought of you coming in and seeing me wrapped in a sheet."

"It's okay," the policeman assured her. "I understand. The situation was under control. Wanting to be modest in front of others isn't a bad thing." Throwing a glance at Caden, who was now standing but still naked, he added, "Although not everyone is concerned about modesty."

Grinning, Caden said, "You saw everything when you walked in. My clothes are in another room, and I wasn't about to leave Nolan unrestrained until you cuffed him. Now that you're here, I'll get dressed if you'll stay with Rory."

"I'm not going anywhere except to haul Nolan's butt to the hospital in Gladeland. We'll keep him under guard. The fact that he had a gun ramps things up regarding how much of a threat he is." Glancing toward Nolan, he asked, "Do you have a permit?" When Nolan shook his head and moaned, Harvey added, "Damn it, Nolan! It's an illegal piece? You could have purchased a gun through legal channels. What is *wrong* with you?"

Nolan didn't reply, but the middle finger on his right hand twitched. Caden said, "Don't even think about it, or I'll break that middle one, too."

"He's got a broken finger on his other hand?" Harvey asked.

"He couldn't talk, so he told Rory to fuck off with his finger. I didn't think that was very nice of him and showed my disapproval."

Harvey nodded, smiled, and asked in a leading tone of voice, "So, this happened during your scuffle with him?"

"Of course," Caden answered innocently, but he was grinning.

"Ex-*cuse* me! Hel-*lo*, Rory and Caden!" Astrid called out in a singsong voice. "My funeral is tomorrow. You need to let Harvey take Nolan away so that you can be rested and alert when we attend the service!"

"Do you want our formal statements now?" Caden asked. "I may be escorting Rory to a funeral tomorrow at 2:00."

Glancing at Rory, Harvey asked, "You're going to Astrid Hass's service? Wasn't she always kind of a bitch to you and your friends?"

"She was kind of a bitch to everyone," Rory admitted. "But I knew her almost all my life, Harvey. I suspect there may have been more to Astrid than she let on. Even if I'm wrong, I don't believe in holding grudges."

"Holding onto anger is like drinking poison and expecting the other person to die," Caden muttered. When Harvey and Rory looked admiringly at him, he said, "Don't give me the credit. Buddha said that a long time ago. I read it somewhere, and it stuck with me. I tried to remember it when I want to kick the crap out of someone just because. But if he or she deserves it –"

"I think now would be a good time for me to take Nolan out of here," Harvey interrupted. "I don't want to hear anything that might land *you* in jail, Caden."

"Me neither. Thanks. You're a good guy who does a great job."

"I do my best, considering how understaffed our local police force is at the moment." Hauling Nolan to his feet, Harvey added, "I'll take your statements before I leave so that will be out of the way. You'll probably have to give more details, depending on what the Chief says. That can be done later. Let me get Nolan locked up in the back of my patrol car; then I'll return to bag the gun. Don't touch it."

Caden watched Rory take a step toward her brother. He figured that she wanted to hug him despite what he'd done and what he'd tried to do. Nolan turned his back to her, and she sighed, staying where she was.

"I'm going to shower and put my clothes back on," Caden told her once Harvey was heading down the stairs with his prisoner. "I won't be long."

Rory's lower lip trembled, but she didn't cry. Caden took her in his arms and told her he was sorry about her brother. That was when she burst into tears, surprising him with the intensity of her sobs. When Harvey returned for the gun, Caden was still standing naked, holding Rory as she wept. Harvey averted his eyes and slipped on a pair of gloves before lifting the handgun, locking the safety, and slipping the weapon into an evidence bag.

"I'm real sorry about Nolan, Rory," Harvey remarked. "I'm glad your folks didn't have to see him like this."

"Me, too," she said through her tears. "Thank you for everything."

"You're welcome. We've been friends a long time." Looking at Caden, he said, "You take care of her, you hear?"

"I plan to."

"Good, because if you don't, I'll come out here and kick your butt, Hollywood action hero lookalike or no."

Caden simply smiled. Harvey smiled back. They both knew Harvey wouldn't stand a chance against Caden, but he would do whatever it took to protect his friend no matter what the odds. Caden respected that. They nodded to one another in mutual understanding; then Harvey took their official statements before leaving to transport Nolan to the hospital for treatment.

"I'm going to shower, dress, return to Mockingbird Hideaway to get a few things, and then come back here and spend the night with you," Caden said once Harvey had driven away.

"I don't think I'm up to making love anymore tonight."

"You think that's all I want? I meant that I'd like to lie next to you and comfort you. I want to wake up beside you in the morning. You know, just spend the night."

Rubbing a hand over her face, Rory said, "I am *so* sorry. It's been an emotional couple of days. I'm upset and tired. Tonight was magical until Nolan barged in saying those awful things and waving that gun. I hate that he ruined the rest of our night."

"We did have a fantastic evening together before he showed up."

"Yes, we did." Turning toward Astrid, Rory said, "Thank you for trying to warn us."

"It's too bad I didn't get here sooner. I guess you were right when you told me that ghosts don't keep track of time as living people do. I was having so much fun on the Internet that I have no idea how long I was using it. You wouldn't *believe* the things I found out!"

"Like what?"

"Well, the biggest news was about Dominic Ambrose. He and his family moved to New Jersey after we graduated. I knew he'd moved somewhere, but I didn't know where. Anyway, you'll never guess what happened to him!"

"If we'll never guess, then why not just tell us?" Caden asked irritably.

"You're sexy when you're cranky," she said with mock sweetness.

"Astrid, will you please just share what you learned?" Rory asked. "I have a major headache, and I suspect it's only going to get worse after you tell us all of your 'exciting' news."

"I suspect you're right," she remarked. "Okay. So, Dominic and his family moved to New Jersey. A few months later, he was drinking and driving and smashed his car into a pole. No one else was hurt, but Dominic was killed."

"That's an awful thing to have happen to anyone," Rory said. "Although I can't say I'm sad that he's dead after what he did to me."

"I'd call it karma," Astrid said. "The rapist pig!"

"Tell us what else you unearthed during your playtime on the computer," Caden urged.

"I found a bunch of pictures of me partying!"

"Yes, I came across a lot of those pictures when I did my initial search after you showed up here," Rory said. "None of them had captions under them that read, 'The person in this picture really wants to murder Astrid Hass.'"

"No, but I realized that I was right when I looked at some of the shots!"

"What did you realize?" Caden asked impatiently.

"That I was in love with a stunning-looking man although I still can't remember his name. It's so annoying."

"Do you think you angered him, and he killed you?" Rory asked, perplexed.

"I don't think so. When I saw him in the photos, all I remembered was us being in love. There's no *way* I would have committed suicide either! I *knew* it!"

"Rory, why don't you pull up the pictures on your computer so that we can see this guy," Caden suggested. "Maybe he did kill Astrid and will be at the funeral."

"He didn't kill me!" Astrid insisted. "He loved me!"

"Maybe, but you obviously don't recall everything. Perhaps you argued, and then he murdered you in anger."

"Caden's right. Until you recall the whole truth, we need to know everything we possibly can about your mystery lover. If he didn't kill you, then where is he? Why didn't he come forward? None of the papers have mentioned a lover being singled out for questioning."

"I can see my family working to keep that news out of the papers. They might not be able to cover up my supposed suicide, but they could shut down some other scandals. I wonder if I'd told them about the man I loved or not. I wasn't close to my parents or sisters, so I doubt it."

"Caden, why don't you shower and dress?" Rory said, as she walked toward the door on the far side of her bedroom. "Astrid and I will be in my home office pulling up the pictures she found."

"Good idea. I'll be only a few minutes. I'm eager to see the photos in preparation for the funeral tomorrow. Maybe we can identify the man in the crowd of mourners and get an explanation from him."

Quickly retrieving his clothes and boots, Caden hurried into the bathroom, hastily showered, and dressed. He hoped that Astrid's discovery would lead to a break in her murder investigation. If they could solve it, then he and Rory could concentrate on the warning her father had delivered to him the previous week. He felt his pulse rate increase as he made his way toward Rory's home office. He walked through its doorway – and froze.

"There are three good views of the man," Rory said without turning toward him. "However, we're not finding a match to a name or personal information anywhere on the Web." When he didn't comment, she twisted around in her chair and asked, "Did you hear me?"

Caden found that all he could do was stare at the computer screen. He saw Astrid in a skimpy cocktail dress similar to the one she currently wore, other partygoers, and his youngest brother, Anderson. The man was looking adoringly at Astrid, and she was beaming at him. Caden felt physically ill as he realized what must have happened to his brother and Astrid.

Rory rose slowly from her chair, and Astrid frowned. Looking worriedly at him, Rory said his name. The only thing he seemed able to do was stare at his little brother, whose funeral was also supposed to be the following day.

"Caden? Caden, you're scaring me. What is it? What's wrong?"

"I know the man," he said in a low voice. "His name was Anderson."

Rory stiffened, and Astrid screeched, "Anderson! Oh, my God! That's *it*! Anderson! That was his name. He was a few years younger than me and was so smart, sexy, and sweet. We fell in love, and I – I got pregnant! Oh, my God! I remember now. We were going to run off, get married, and raise our baby, but then...something happened."

"Who killed you, Astrid?" Caden asked grimly, suspecting he now knew the answer.

"I told you, I don't know! I still can't remember that!"

"Show her a picture of Elias," Rory suggested, evidently thinking the same thing he was.

"I can't. Elias never allows anyone to take his picture."

Astrid put her hands on her hips and asked, "How did you know that man in the photos was Anderson?"

"Because he was my youngest brother. Our father told us he'd been hurt on the job and was in a coma. He died. His funeral is tomorrow, just like yours."

"He died?" Astrid repeated in disbelief. "What are the odds of that happening to us around the same time?"

"The odds of its being coincidental are extremely low," Caden said. "I suspect our father killed him and you. Anderson was working in California when he ended up in the coma. Shit!" Picking up a book that rested on a nearby table, he hurled it across the room and shouted, "Shit! Shit! Shit! How could Elias do something like this? How could he kill Anderson and a pregnant innocent?"

"You don't know if he did," Rory pointed out.

"I'm afraid I do. Something he said to me the other night made me think he'd kill anyone who interfered in his grand plans, and that included his sons and innocents. I can see him killing me and you if he found out I loved you and planned to leave the fold in order to marry you and raise a family. So, I can also see him doing that to Anderson and Astrid. Goddamn it, Rory! We trusted him! We loved him!"

"So, your adoptive father is probably my murderer," Astrid said with shock. "He killed his own son, the man I loved. He killed me and the baby." Looking at Caden, she asked, "What are you going to do about it?"

"Call my brothers and tell them we have to meet. I'll explain that it's an emergency and that it's on the down-low because it involves Elias. I'll get them to meet me here, and we'll work something out. Maybe having them at Nostalgia Road will help in our efforts to stop this evil that's after Rory and this place." Walking over to where the book he'd thrown lay on the floor, Caden bent to lift it and said, "I'm sorry I lost my temper like that. I hope this isn't a rare book."

"No. It's just my diary. My father said his mother told him every caretaker of this land kept diaries, but we never could find any. Dad told me he'd tried to keep a journal but couldn't get into it himself. I started keeping my own when I inherited this place and became the caretaker. I felt as if it was an act of respect, kind of like going to the family cemetery. I wanted to keep the Roosevelt tradition alive."

Caden stiffened and demanded, "Why didn't you tell me about the diaries? The answers to all of our questions probably lie in them!"

"Because I forgot!" Rory snapped. "I've been a little overwhelmed recently!"

After putting the book down, Caden took Rory in his arms, apologizing before saying, "I know you would've told me if things hadn't been so crazy, lately. I'm just so stressed, pissed, and frustrated that I don't know what to do with myself."

He kissed her and was thankful when she melted against him, eagerly responding. After a few minutes, he broke their contact and said, "I need to go back to my cottage and get a few important things. I won't be long."

"I'm coming with you," Rory insisted.

"No. It's after midnight now. Why don't you get ready for bed? As soon as I return, I'll come up here and join you. Tomorrow, I'm going to move all of my stuff to the main house."

"I'm glad." After chewing on her lower lip for a moment, Rory asked, "Will you be calling your brothers while you're at the cottage?"

"My phone battery's almost dead. Let me plug it in so that it can charge while I'm gone. When I get back, then it should have enough battery life for me to make the four calls."

"You can use my phone."

"My brothers won't answer a call that comes from a number they don't recognize. Plus, if Elias is somehow tracing our calls, I don't want him to see any originating from your number."

"If he's actually my great-uncle and maybe killed my grandfather and parents, then surely he knows about me and this place. After all, he would have been here years ago."

"But he wouldn't suspect that you might be on to him. I want to keep you safe. I'll use my phone to make the calls."

Looking uncertainly at him, Rory nodded and said, "Just don't be too long."

"By the time you remake the bed, put on your nightclothes, and lie down, I'll be on my way back here." Glancing around, he asked, "You want me to plug my iPhone in to your computer, your iHome, or somewhere else?"

"The iHome is fine."

Caden looked at Astrid and ordered, "Stay with Rory. If anything out of the ordinary happens, come get me right away."

The ghost nodded and then asked hopefully, "Will Anderson be waiting for me when I cross over?"

Caden shrugged and admitted, "I have no way of knowing. If you two really were in love, then I hope so."

"Elias Brody may be evil, but somehow he managed to raise at least two good sons."

"All of us Brody brothers are good, although we each have our faults. We made a pledge to one another when we were children to never stray from the path of goodness nor stop fighting evil, regardless of where it lay."

"What if your brothers resent being called here?" Rory asked.

"They won't. They'll want to work together to straighten out this mess. When Astrid made the comment about your buying Nolan's Bar, it gave me an idea about how I could bring my brothers together. I think we're all kind of done with being the ones who are responsible for stopping the depravity we have to deal with in our jobs. We need to let others continue that fight and find new callings before we get killed. We're pretty burned out, but we never considered any other options before now."

"And?" Rory prompted.

"Sawyer would be the perfect brother to buy and run the bar. He's cocky and has no interest in having any meaningful relationships. However, he's also got a good heart, is a great fighter, and has wonderful business sense. He'd probably enjoy bartending, breaking up brawls, and making the place more successful."

"And the others?"

"Thorn is a computer whiz who, like you, can work from anywhere. I'm not certain what Beck and David would do, but perhaps they'd like to settle out here, too. If all five of us were here at Nostalgia Road, then we could be a *real* family. If each of us lived in one of the houses, then we'd be virtual and literal protection for the elements your dad mentioned. Maybe we could start over and live happily ever after here. Would you mind?"

"I've never met your brothers, so I'm not sure. I'd love for both of us to have them close by, but what if we don't all get along? I'd want to meet them first. Plus, how would I pay for upkeep, taxes, and insurance on the cottages if I didn't rent them out?"

"My brothers would have to buy you out. They have the money. They wouldn't own the cottages if you didn't want to sell, but they could pay you for lifetime use without having a deed."

"Would they go for that?"

"We'll have to wait and see. I'm trying to tackle one life-changing thing at a time."

15 Rory

Rory jerked awake and then looked at the clock on the nightstand. It was 5:04 a.m. Although she hadn't planned on falling asleep, her exhaustion had evidently overtaken her after she'd crawled into bed shortly after 1:00. Caden was not lying next to her.

She considered that he was in another room, calling his brothers. After all, he wouldn't want to wake her. However, when she glanced at his phone, it remained plugged into her iHome. She doubted it had been unplugged while she'd slept. Once she'd risen and checked the charge, Rory was certain of it. The display read 100%.

"Astrid!" she called out, her heart pounding in response to the dread building within her.

"Here," Astrid said, as she appeared through the door.

"Did Caden come back from Mockingbird Hideaway, yet?"

"No. Why?"

"Because it's been four hours. Would you go see if he's there?"

Astrid didn't answer. She merely left the same way she'd entered. Rory wanted more than anything to head to the cottage. Yet, she knew that if something had happened to Caden, then she needed to remain in the house and stay as secure as possible. She wondered if any place was actually secure in instances where Elias Brody was involved.

I could try to go back to sleep and see if my astral form manifests itself. No one can hurt my astral body. Of course, someone could simply kill my physical body while I slept. That's definitely not an appealing prospect and won't help me or Caden. I'm too tense to sleep anyway.

Hurriedly slipping on jeans and a blue t-shirt, Rory brushed her red hair while pacing the room. She hoped Astrid wouldn't get distracted and would return quickly to the Roosevelt House. Thankfully, she was back within fifteen minutes.

"He's not there! I checked all of the other cottages, and he's not in any of them either. I even looked in the barn and that little storage building. It's so dark in there!"

"What about his SUV?" Rory asked nervously.

"It's in the parking area near the cottage."

"Were there any signs of a struggle?"

"No. Everything was in its place, so to speak. No overturned chairs, things strewn about, blood spatter –"

Her heart constricting at the thought of Caden's being injured, Rory interrupted by saying, "Okay, Astrid! Thanks. At least we know it can't be Nolan since he's been arrested." Cocking her head, she asked, "By the way, how did Nolan get in? How'd you find out about it?"

"I was finally getting bored with the computer and wanted to come back here. I saw him using a key to enter through the rear door of your house. He knocked last time. Then, I saw the gun in his hand and knew I had to warn you."

"Thanks again. You may have saved Caden's life."

"Last night. But what about today? Where is he?"

"I have a feeling his father took him."

"What? Where?"

"I don't know."

"What are you going to do? His adoptive father sounds like a really big prick and evil to boot! You can't just go after him, Rory! You're not the superhero type. No offense."

"None taken. You're absolutely right. Brains can't trump brawn in a fight to the death, not that I think Elias is stupid. Plus, I don't know exactly what sort of supernatural powers he has. I'd be woefully unprepared."

"So, what will you do?"

Sighing heavily, Rory admitted, "I have no choice but to reach out to Caden's brothers and hope they don't contact their father."

"Wait a minute. If Anderson's funeral is today, then odds are his adoptive father will be there. Doesn't he live in Louisiana? How could Caden's father kidnap him during the night and get back to New Orleans in time for the funeral?"

"It would only take a couple hours by plane to get from here to there. I wonder if he tucked Caden away somewhere near Sage or took him someplace else."

"Or killed him."

Rory rubbed at her temples and said, "I was trying not to think about that. Thanks for reminding me of the possibility."

"Oh. My bad. I was only considering possible scenarios."

"I'm not going to consider that particular scenario. I believe Elias is holding Caden prisoner nearby. I just don't know where."

"What if he's torturing him?"

"Astrid, please! Keep those kinds of questions to yourself."

"Call his brothers! Use his phone, and leave them messages!"

"In a minute. I have to think about what I want to say. I need to phrase it properly."

"Well, think fast! I'm sure every moment counts!"

"I'm trying, but it's difficult when you're pressuring me! I know you want Caden to kill Elias if he killed Anderson, you, and your baby."

"I do, but that's not the only reason I want Caden to be all right. You two are good people and seem to love one another. I want you to be happy, Rory. I want him to be happy. *Someone* should come out of this alive and happy! If the two of you survive this, then promise me that you'll make love to that man every chance you get and have a family with him. Anderson and I will never get to be married or have our baby. At least you can live the life I longed for without regret. Please, promise."

Rory stared at Astrid for several moments then said, "I promise that I won't waste a minute of my time with Caden when I get him back."

"Good. I'm going to leave you alone so that you can figure out how you want to approach his brothers. I'll be downstairs if you need me."

"Thanks, Astrid."

The woman gave her a melancholy smile then vanished through the door that led to the landing.

Rory unplugged Caden's phone and pulled up the contacts screen. Sure enough, there were only six listings: Anderson, Beck, David, Elias, Sawyer, and Thorn. Deciding to begin at the top and work her way down, Rory skipped Anderson and touched Beck.

As she listened to the rings, she wondered what the eldest Brody brother was like. She knew he was half-Asian and had been the one to suggest using the dragon symbol for the brothers' tattoos. He was also supposed to be on a mission of some sort, but it didn't sound as though Caden knew where the man was or what the mission entailed.

What are his supernatural abilities? she wondered. *Obviously, all of the brothers can see ghosts, but what are their individual talents?*

The call went to voicemail, and a man's voice said, "You know what to do." Then, there was a *beep!*

"My name is Rory. Caden's in trouble. Come to Nostalgia Road Bed and Breakfast near Sage, Florida as soon as you can, and *don't* tell Elias. Please, hurry."

Her next call was to Caden's African-American brother, David. Again, the call went to voicemail. Rory left him the same message she'd left Beck.

She then phoned Sawyer, the brother Caden had said would be best suited to buy and run her brother's bar. After leaving him an identical message to the ones she'd recorded on Beck's and David's phones, she sighed. Thorn was the only brother left. Expecting to have to leave another voicemail, she hit his name on the screen and listened to the ringing of the phone. It continued for so long that she wondered if the number was no longer in service. Suddenly, she heard a sleepy male voice ask, "Caden, what's up?"

"Is this Thorn?" Rory asked, her pulse rate skyrocketing.

"Who is this? How'd you get this phone?"

Noting that all traces of sleep were gone from the man's voice, she answered, "Caden's in trouble. My name's Rory. Get your brothers and come to Nostalgia Road Bed and Breakfast near Sage, Florida as quickly as you can. *Don't* tell Elias. Please, hurry."

"Wait a minute. Who are you?"

"I'm Caden's girlfriend. I think Elias has him. We think Elias killed your brother Anderson and his pregnant girlfriend because he wanted to marry her and settle down. Caden said Elias had threatened to hurt Caden and any, um, 'innocent' who might interfere with his plans. Now, Caden's disappeared. I didn't know what else to do, so I just called each brother using Caden's phone."

"Why didn't Caden have his phone with him?"

"He left it charging in my bedroom while he went to get a few things. He never came back, and he's nowhere on the property. His SUV and his things are still on site. The only powers I possess are being able to see and interact with ghosts and taking on an astral form while I sleep. I have no idea what sort of powers Elias has. I don't even know what he looks like. Well, I kind of do because we think he's my great-uncle and there's this portrait in the family library...."

Rory knew she was babbling, but she couldn't seem to stop herself. She was on the verge of panic and was aware that if she couldn't get Caden's brothers to help then she and he were probably doomed.

"Wait a minute," Thorn said, interrupting her ramblings. "Your great-uncle? But Elias was the only child of Hungarian immigrants."

"We believe that he lied about all of that, as well as the true origins of his adopted sons. It appears he's my great-uncle but that his parents faked his death when he was a baby and sent him away. Caden and I have no idea why they did that, unless they recognized that he was evil early on. It's safe to say that we believe he murdered his twin brother, who was my grandfather, and is responsible for my parents' deaths in a small plane crash three years ago. Some terrible evil is supposed to be after me and my brother, and Caden and I think the terrible evil might be Elias. Do you know where Elias might have taken Caden?"

"There could be hundreds of places." After blowing out a breath, Thorn directed, "Stay in your house, and keep Caden's phone with you at all times. Anderson's service is at 8:00 a.m. That's still a few hours away. As soon as it's over, then David, Sawyer, and I will make our excuses and head your way. I have no idea where Beck is, but I'll try to reach him myself to verify your situation."

"But won't Elias be suspicious if you all leave right after the funeral?"

"No. We each have assignments waiting for us. We'll simply use those as excuses and take our leave. However, we will probably travel separately. Then we can all sit down and talk this out in order to formulate a plan."

"Caden already has a plan, but it's for afterward."

"Afterward?"

"I'll explain once you're here. Please, hurry."

"We'll be there as quickly as we can." Emphasizing each word, he said, "Stay in your house, and don't let anyone in. I mean no one. Understand?"

"I understand."

"Rory, I want you to take a selfie and text it to each of us."

"So, if I go missing as well then you'll know what I look like?" When he didn't answer, she said, "As soon as we hang up, I'll do it."

"Good. Odds are that none of us will be in contact with you until we arrive. Sit tight. Do not leave the house for any reason."

Feeling tears prick the backs of her eyelids, Rory asked, "Will you tell me what I'm up against in case Elias makes it here before you do?" When the man hesitated, she practically shouted, "Thorn! He may have already killed Caden! What am I dealing with?"

"He can see ghosts, of course," Thorn answered. "He also knows magic and has psychokinetic powers."

"You mean he can move things with his mind?"

"Yes. Psychokinesis, or PK, means one can influence physical systems without physical interaction."

"So, he can hurt or kill without getting his hands dirty."

"Yes," he said soberly. "Listen, do you have Internet access where you are?"

"I'm a web designer who runs a B&B. It's all good."

"Excellent. I'll get to work on my end. Sawyer, David, and I should be there before midnight. Is anyone else aware of the situation?"

"Astrid."

"Who's that?"

"Anderson's dead, pregnant lover. She and I grew up together. She's hoping to be reunited with Anderson once she crosses over."

Thorn was silent for a long time before saying, "I suspect we've each been questioning Elias's motives and judgment for quite a while, but none of us shared our doubts until after Anderson was hurt. I wish we'd talked about it sooner. It might have saved him, his lover, and their child."

"It may be too late for them, but I don't want it to be too late for those of us who are still living."

"I couldn't agree with you more. I look forward to meeting you, Rory."

"Same here. And Thorn?"

"Yes?"

"Be careful."

"You, too."

Once they'd ended the call, Rory took a few selfies and texted the clearest one to Caden's four remaining brothers. Then, she left her bedroom, went downstairs, and forced herself to eat two eggs and a piece of toast and to drink some milk. Her stomach was in knots, but she knew she needed to keep up her strength and remain hydrated. She prayed that Thorn would be able to convince his brothers to join him in his efforts to help her.

What about Beck? she mused. *When is the last time anyone spoke to him? Has Elias already killed him? Perhaps his "assignment" was actually a trap Elias set in order to lure him to his death.*

Telling herself that this line of thinking was not going to help reassure her of a positive outcome, Rory called out to Astrid and updated the ghost once she appeared. After putting the woman on sentry duty, Rory informed her that she was going upstairs to sift through more Roosevelt family papers in hopes of finding something they'd missed or hadn't gotten to the previous day.

"Okay. Too bad you'll miss my funeral. I was kind of wondering how it'd turn out, but I guess I can just read about it online."

"I'm sorry, Astrid. I really was planning to attend. But I think Thorn's right. I need to stay locked in the house until the brothers arrive."

"I think so, too. I don't want you to get killed just so we can see how my funeral goes."

Rory grinned and said, "You are *dying* of curiosity, aren't you?"

"Now you sound like me, Little Miss Snarky!"

"Maybe I've been around you too long."

Astrid tossed her blonde hair over her shoulder, inadvertently revealing the telltale bullet hole on the side of her head. She seemed to be deep in contemplation. Finally, she asked, "Does Caden have a dragon tattoo on his back? When I saw him nude, I was kind of fixated on his front, you know? I remember Anderson having a full back dragon tattoo."

"According to Caden, each of the Brody brothers has a dragon tattoo on his back." Intrigued, she prompted, "You're remembering more about Anderson? Did he talk about his father and brothers?"

Frowning, Astrid said, "He didn't like his father. He said he knew how ruthless the man could be. He loved his brothers. He wanted a life with me and them away from his father's reach. I think he was trying to figure out how to achieve that when he…we…died." Looking questioningly at Rory, she asked, "Is there a way to tell if I was pregnant with a son or daughter? I'd have wanted a son. I'd have worried about raising a daughter the way my mother raised me."

"I'm afraid I don't know of any way to tell if you were having a boy or a girl. I didn't even know that you were pregnant when you appeared to me, remember? Even if you were further along, I wouldn't be able to sense that or tell your baby's sex. I don't have those kinds of powers."

"Have you ever had a pregnant ghost appear to you before?"

Fighting a sudden wave of nausea, Rory nodded and battled to keep her breakfast from coming up. When Astrid asked her what was the matter, Rory answered, "I don't want to talk about it."

"But now I have to know!"

"No, you don't."

"But I do! I can already see that you have from your reaction, so tell me what happened."

"No," Rory said firmly, beginning to climb the stairs.

"Tell me!" Astrid insisted. Moving through Rory and causing her to shiver, she stood at the top of the stairs, crossed her arms over her chest, and said, "How many other pregnant ghosts have come to you for help?"

Gripping the handrail, Rory stared at the floor and said wearily, "One."

"What happened to her? Rory, come on!"

Whipping her head up, Rory snapped, "You want to know? Fine! The woman who appeared to me was almost full-term! Her boyfriend didn't want the baby but told her he'd changed his mind the week before her due date. He asked if they could talk about patching things up. He suggested they take a walk along the creek behind her house. That was where he strangled her and dumped her body in the water after he weighted it down by tying a rope to a log and wrapping the rope around her neck. She and her son didn't stand a chance."

Astrid looked horrified, which gave Rory some satisfaction. After all, the woman had pushed her to talk about the pregnant ghost Rory tried not to think about whenever she saw or read news reports about the murders of pregnant women.

"What was the woman's name?" Astrid asked in an unusually subdued tone of voice.

"Naomi. She said her baby's name was Wayne. She'd had an ultrasound and knew she was carrying a boy."

"Did you help get her justice?"

"I didn't have to, but I did help her cross over."

"How?"

"I found out that her boyfriend had hanged himself from the tree above where he'd dumped her body. I guess his conscience got the better of him, but it was too late for Naomi and Wayne. Once she knew the man who'd betrayed and killed her was dead, Naomi crossed over."

"That's so sad."

Rory didn't give a verbal reply, but she nodded and slowly continued up the stairs. When she reached the door to the library, she heard Astrid say, "You do good work. I know it takes its toll on you, but you help so many of us through what you do."

Without turning, Rory said, "I wish there weren't a need for me to help anyone, but that's the way it is. I'm glad I make a difference in people's lives, even if it is after their lives are technically over."

Once she was inside the library, Rory stood, staring vacantly at the portrait of her ancestor. She wished more than anything that she could identify Caden's location before his brothers' arrival, but she knew the odds were slim. She thought of his admission to her the previous night regarding his desire to spend the rest of his life with her and to have children together. The prospect obviously scared him, but Caden Brody was not one to be easily deterred. She *would* find him; they *would* get married; and they *would* have babies.

Lots of little Cadens running around the property having normal childhoods, she thought with a slight smile. *Well, with the addition of a few supernatural powers, I'm sure.* Shaking her head, Rory mused, *I can't believe I've gone from being afraid of being with any man to imagining marriage and children with Caden in such a short time. That has to mean that we were meant to be together. It will happen. All I have to do is find Caden, and everything will be all right.*

16 Caden

Caden stirred in the darkness and groaned. He hurt all over and couldn't seem to clear his head. In spite of his clouded mind, he recognized that he'd been beaten and had suffered a blow to the skull. Deducing that he must have a concussed brain, he slowly extended his right hand in an effort to determine his location without causing further injury. The effort proved too great, and he paused, listening intently. He heard no noises outside of the harsh sounds of his own quick, ragged breaths.

Slow your breathing, Brody, he silently commanded himself. *Nice and even. In and out.*

Once he was satisfied with his rate of respiration, Caden attempted to move his left hand. Again, he couldn't manage self-directed movement of his body. Everything hurt and felt heavy. So, he stopped trying, not wishing to waste valuable energy. He needed time to regain enough strength to do…whatever it was he had intended to do. Just then, he couldn't recall what that was.

As he lay in the dark, Caden turned his attention toward his last clear memories. It took effort. He caught snatches of recollections that involved eating with Rory, shopping with her, dusting her body with powdered sugar, and then making love with her. Her brother had stormed in with a gun, but Caden knew he hadn't been beaten by the man. He'd quickly and efficiently overpowered Nolan. The policeman had arrived….

Why can't I remember the cop's name? Nice guy. Good guy. Henry? No. That doesn't sound right. Whatever.

The cop had taken Nolan away, and Caden had done something in anger that had necessitated his offering an apology to Rory. They'd kissed, and he'd then connected his phone to her iHome so that it could charge before he'd left her house in order to return to his cottage.

The cottage….

Caden strained to recall whether or not he had actually made it to Mockingbird Hideaway. The only thing he could call to mind was walking toward the place. He'd wanted to hurry, to get back to Rory so that he could be with her and protect her.

Something grabbed me, he thought. *But how? I was on alert.*

Caden coughed and then choked back a cry. Several ribs on his left side felt broken. His mind muddled from what he hoped was only a mild concussion, he decided to perform a head-to-toe inventory of known injuries. Unfortunately, this would involve movement, which would involve an increase in pain. Plus, he would need to move at least one hand in order to feel as much of his wounded body as he was able. With concentration, he found he could make a fist with the fingers of his right hand. However, when he attempted to raise it, his right shoulder and elbow screamed in protest.

Okay, let me try the left hand, he told himself. *That's it. I made a fist. Now, all I have to do is release it before bringing my hand up. If I do it gradually, then it might not hurt my ribs as much. That's it. Come on. I can do this. I –*

A wave of pain brought with it a wave of nausea. Caden knew if he didn't roll onto one of his sides, he could choke to death if he vomited. Because of the broken ribs, he opted to divert all of his attention and energy toward rolling to his right. It took every bit of effort he could muster, and he howled with the resultant pain he experienced in various locations on his body before succumbing to dry heaves.

Dry heaves? How long have I been out? I should have had something in my stomach, even if it was only water. Have I been unconscious for days, or have I already thrown up while I was out of it?

Caden lay as still as he could and battled a bout of the chills. His right arm throbbed, and he was thankful he'd managed to turn onto that side without pinning it underneath him. Exhausted, hurting, and dizzy, Caden worked at slowing his breathing and heart rate. After a while, he decided that assessing his condition without trying to move more was presently in his best interest.

Concussion? Check. Eyes? Able to open them but can't see in the blackness of wherever I'm being kept. Nose? Likely fractured. Lips? Swollen but not split. Cheekbones? Not broken but abraded skin. Teeth? All there. Chin? Sore. Neck? Stiff. Chest? Sore. Left ribs? Several broken. Right ribs: Okay. Right arm? Sprained.

Left arm? Probably okay. Wrists? Not fractured. Hands? Bruised. Belly, hips, and back? Sore but okay. Dick and balls? Tender. Right leg? Gashes on upper thigh and across knee. Left leg? Bruised shinbone. Ankles? Not broken. Feet and toes? Sore but not fractured. In short, my injuries aren't life-threatening. Things could be a lot worse.

Caden wanted to sit up but knew that wouldn't be advisable in his condition. He still tried, failing but giving himself kudos for his efforts. He would try again soon.

Gradually lifting his left arm, Caden reached forward. Nothing. He then lifted his arm. Nothing. He extended it behind him as far as it would go. Nothing. Grunting with pain, he lifted it above his head. Nothing.

Well, I'm not in a coffin or a box, he thought encouragingly. *Everything is dark, but I can feel the passage of air. So, I shouldn't die of carbon monoxide poisoning. I'm cold, but I can tell I'm not lying on a dirt floor. Am I underground? If so, then there has to be a ventilation system in place. It might be natural or man-made. If I'm above ground, then this place is air-conditioned. I don't hear any machinery. This location is either very high-tech or very low-tech.*

Caden dealt with another round of the chills although perspiration coated his skin. He had to concede that his physical reaction might be due to his injuries rather than the coolness of his cell, whatever and wherever it was. He also noted for the first time that he was naked.

I guess that head injury might be worse than I first imagined, he thought, unable to stop his swollen lips from twitching. *Damn, I'm cold.*

Wondering whether his attacker had been human or supernatural, Caden shook and struggled not to worry about Rory. She was as smart as she was beautiful. Once she realized that he wasn't coming back to the house, she'd send Astrid out to see if she could locate him. When she couldn't, Rory would then use his iPhone to call his brothers and plead for their help. Perhaps she'd be able to reach Thorn directly since he still hadn't set up his voicemail. If not, he prayed that he or one of the others would quickly respond to her without notifying Elias.

146

Elias. Caden knew that his adoptive father was somehow responsible for all of it – Anderson's coma and death, Astrid's murder, Rory's grandfather's fatal farming accident, and her parents' plane crash. He firmly believed that Elias and Charles were one and the same, but he couldn't figure out how Rory's great-grandparents had come to know that their baby was evil and had given him away. Had the adoptive couple been aware of the presence of evil in the baby and accepted the responsibility anyway, or had they thought they were receiving a perfectly normal child? Had Elias actually been the one to murder his own adoptive parents? Had he fabricated the story of their deaths at the hands of another as the motivation for his adopted sons to train in order to fight and kill evil men and women?

That's what I don't understand. If Elias is evil, whether he's Charles or not, then why did he raise us boys to fight evil? Why not raise us to do evil instead? And how do Rory and Nolan fit into all of this? Does Elias want to use them or kill them? If it's the former, then what purpose does he have in mind?

Shivering again, Caden clenched his jaw in order to stop his teeth from beginning to chatter. He prayed that his brothers would come to Nostalgia Road, find him, and help him and Rory stop the threat of evil – and Elias. It was evident that he was a serious menace to all of them and to humanity. Someone had to stop him if he wouldn't listen to reason, and Caden doubted that he would listen.

Caden lost consciousness for a time, but Rory was there with him in her astral body. She touched him, and he could feel vibrating heat each time she placed her palms on him or kissed unmarred areas of flesh. He wanted her to strip and lie naked beside him in order to provide him with some much-needed warmth and comfort. She seemed to innately sense this and removed her clothing before stretching out next to him. Caden automatically laid his head on her shoulder while she gently rubbed his flesh with her hands and body so that she could help to ease his chills. He inhaled the fragrance of her skin and relaxed slightly.

When Caden regained consciousness, Rory was gone. He moaned with longing for her, but the longing had little to do with desire. He wanted her with him. He needed her innocence and her strength. If Elias harmed her before he was able to escape, Caden vowed to kill him.

A groan suddenly emanated from the darkness beyond his feet. Caden asked in a graveled voice, "Who's there?"

"Nolan. Help me."

The man's speech was almost unintelligible, but Caden understood it. Nolan moaned again and coughed several times before asking Caden in garbled words to come closer.

"How did you get here? Do you know where we are?"

The answer to the first question sounded like, "I don't know." The answer to the second was definitely, "No."

"Where is...the cop?" Caden asked, still unable to remember the policeman's name.

"Hurt."

"Is he here?"

"No. Left in car."

So that Rory will be notified about the details of Nolan's disappearance, Caden thought. *A trap. Will she fall for it? Nolan may be a self-centered ass, but he's her brother. Would she risk her life for his? Of course she would, just as I would despite Nolan's bad behavior. The guy's a jerk, but he's not evil. That makes him an innocent.*

"We're going to get out of this," Caden told him. "After we do, you'll get fixed up, maybe do a little jail time, then take the money from the sale of the bar and leave the area forever. Right now, I need you to help me. Got it?"

Nolan didn't answer.

Coward, Caden observed. *Total coward. All he cares about is himself. Never mind that his little sister is in danger.*

"You were unconscious when you were brought here?" Caden pressed.

"Yeah."

"Did you see who attacked you?"

"No." A moan then, "Stop talking. Hurts."

"It's your own Goddamned fault for bursting into Rory's bedroom waving a gun and then aiming it at me. What were you thinking?"

"Should have protected her years ago. Trying to do it now."

"Very admirable if you're sincere. You're seven years too late. You should have helped her when Dominic Ambrose raped her. *That* was when she needed you."

Nolan was silent, and Caden wondered whether or not he'd lost consciousness. However, after several minutes, he said, "My fault. Was wrong."

"You're damned right you were wrong. Do you have any idea how much you messed up Rory's life since that day? You had her believing the rape was her fault. She cut herself off from the world because of what Dominic did and the way you handled her admission afterwards. You wronged your sister. You're just as guilty as Dominic Ambrose."

"I know. I –"

Caden waited, but Nolan didn't continue. Eventually, he hissed, "Nolan! Are you awake?"

"Yeah. Remembered."

"Remembered what?"

"Dominic and some other attacked. Took me."

"Dominic Ambrose was killed in a car accident seven years ago."

"Was a ghost. Helped other man."

"What did the other man look like?"

"Jaw hurts. Finger hurts."

"Screw that! This could help us to survive! It could save your sister's life!" He repeated, "What did the other man look like?"

"Older. Slim but muscled like you. Not tall. Gray hair, beard, and moustache. Gray eyes. Intense."

Elias, thought Caden. *Well, at least that confirms our suspicions about his involvement.*

"Nolan, did you sustain any more injuries during your attack?"

The man moaned and then confirmed that he had.

"What? Damn it! Don't make me drag everything out like this!"

"Stabbed me in the belly."

"You've got a gut wound?"

"Yeah."

"Are you bleeding heavily?"

"Was but not anymore. Bleeding out."

Because of what Nolan had just shared, Caden was inclined to agree but said, "You don't know that. Maybe whatever was used to stab you didn't penetrate deeply."

Nolan mumbled, "It did."

"What was it?"

"Pointed piece of metal."

"A knife?"

"Not sure. Went down at an angle. Deep. Doubt if I have long."

"Why didn't you say anything about it before now?"

"No point. Save Rory and kill the bastards."

"I will, and you'll help me."

"Too busy dying."

The man sounded as if he was about to lose consciousness. Caden barked an order for Nolan to stay awake. When Nolan didn't respond, Caden gritted his teeth, rolled onto his back, and turned onto his left side. Suppressing a scream as his broken ribs protested, Caden paused in order to catch his breath for a moment and then pushed up into a sitting position. Without light and nothing upon which to fix his gaze, dizziness threatened to return him to the floor. Refusing to allow this, Caden clenched his jaw and commanded his limbs to move until he was on his hands and knees. He stayed still as the world spun and the injured parts of his body sang with pain. Finally, the vertigo subsided, but Caden knew he'd have to move slowly and carefully if he didn't want it to return.

He crawled in the direction from which Nolan's voice had come. With every few inches he gained, his head, right arm, ribs, and left shinbone reminded him that he shouldn't be moving at all. Everything else hurt, but the pain from those areas kept threatening to halt his progress. He pushed past it and continued to crawl until he touched what he assumed was Nolan's leg. Caden rested his right hand on the man's ankle and squeezed – hard. Nolan moaned softly.

"Stay awake!" Caden snapped. "Where is the entry wound on your belly?"

"Center under ribs," he mumbled. "Need to lie down."

"You're sitting up?"

"In a corner."

His voice was growing fainter with every word, and Caden knew the man had no hope of survival. Regardless, he crawled forward until he touched the wall where Nolan's back rested. Sitting heavily beside the dying man, he reached out and placed his left palm on Nolan's chest then moved his hand downward. He felt what was unmistakably dried blood on Nolan's belly and found the entry wound. It was perhaps the size of the tip of his index finger. He wondered how long the piece of metal had been and why Elias hadn't simply killed his great-nephew outright.

If he's been watching Nolan and Rory, then he knows what a wuss Nolan is, Caden thought. *He likely wanted him to suffer. Elias doesn't tolerate cowards. He'd want to teach Nolan one final lesson that would end with his elimination. As usual, Elias got his way.*

"Won't have to sell bar now," Nolan muttered. "Rory's after I die. Call it 'Spirits' like she wanted. She was right about everything." As the man's body suddenly jerked then settled back against the wall, he whispered, "Mom. Dad." Tears slid down his cheeks and fell onto his body and Caden's arm before he gave a final shudder and then slumped sideways in death.

Caden shivered as the man's soul left his body. Unfortunately, he continued to shiver long after Nolan's heart ceased to beat. He wanted more than anything to lie down once more but didn't want to have to struggle in order to sit up again.

At least I reached a wall, he reminded himself. *Once I'm a little stronger, I can crawl around the perimeter to gauge the size of this room and try to stand to see how much clearance there is. Maybe I'll find some breach and be able to escape. If I can orientate myself, then I can head toward home.* He smiled, even though it pained him and thought, *Home. I guess that's what the Roosevelt place is for me now. Hell, I'd put on a pair of ruby slippers and click my heels together if that would get me back to Rory right away.*

Closing his eyes, he muttered, "There's no place like home. There's no place like home. There's no place like –"

And then Caden lost consciousness again.

17 Rory

Rory frowned when she heard the knock on her front door at 4:34 p.m. She doubted that any of the Brody brothers could have made it to Nostalgia Road that quickly after Anderson's funeral. She considered that someone had come to attack her and wondered what she would do if they had.

Maybe it's Beck, she reasoned. *After all, he wasn't going to the funeral. Perhaps he got my message or was reached by Thorn. He might have been close by. He could be the first arrival.*

She went cautiously down the stairs. Astrid stood near the front door and said, "It's that Japanese girl who went to school with us. She was a few years older. Jen or something like that?"

"Ren," Rory corrected. "Why would Ren be here?"

"No clue. Does she drop by often?"

"No. We just see each other around town or if I eat at her restaurant."

"Why don't you open the door and find out what she wants?" Astrid asked impatiently.

"What if it's a trick?"

"What if it's not?"

Ren knocked again. Rory squared her shoulders, forced a smile, opened the door, and exclaimed, "Hey, Ren! It's great to see you. What brings you to Nostalgia Road?"

Ren hurried in and said, "Harvey's been attacked."

"What?" Rory asked, butterflies fluttering around in her belly. "When?"

"Dorothea called me from the station. She told me last night Harvey arrested your brother because Nolan had threatened your boyfriend with a gun and had gotten a broken jaw and finger as a result. Harvey was driving him to Gladeland, but the two of them never made it to the hospital. Dorothea said someone passing on the highway spotted Harvey's cruiser on the shoulder. It was all smashed up, so the guy pulled over to check out the scene."

"Harvey and Nolan?" Rory asked in a small voice.

"Harvey's hurt, but he'll live. Nolan's missing. They don't know if he was responsible for all the damage or if someone else caused it and took him. Harvey has a head wound, wasn't making sense, and told the doctors he'd been attacked by some invisible force that had beaten him and trashed his car before it hauled Nolan away. The few other officers we have are working the case and didn't want to take precious time away from the investigation by coming over to update you. Dorothea didn't want you to just get a call from her with the news. She asked if I'd drive over here and tell you and Caden in person about the situation." Glancing around, Ren asked, "Is he here?"

"Not at the moment. He'd planned to escort me to Astrid's funeral, but we didn't make it."

"Astrid Hass? I didn't know her well at all but knew of her reputation. I'm kind of surprised you'd attend her funeral. Wasn't she nasty to everyone outside her social circle?"

"Yes, but people change. I thought someone should be there who understood that maybe she wasn't as bitchy as everyone believed."

"That's very sweet of you. I think most people who are going are doing it out of sheer curiosity. It's morbid. I doubt if anyone from around here will truly miss Astrid. I guess she brought it on herself. It's still sad."

"Very." Swallowing hard, she added, "I hope they find Nolan soon."

Ren startled Rory by hugging her. She hugged back, fighting the impulse to surrender to tears. She would have liked nothing more than to share everything with Ren and to be told that all would be fine, whether it was true or not. She knew that Elias, with his psychokinetic powers, must be the "invisible force" behind Harvey's attack and Nolan's kidnapping. She was certain he was responsible for Caden's disappearance. Rory wondered whether or not Nolan and Caden remained alive.

Both women jumped visibly when someone knocked on the door. Rory laughed nervously, as Ren remarked, "God, we're skittish today."

Astrid announced, "It's a guy. Whoever he is, he looks Asian but has blue eyes. He's *tall,* too!"

Heart racing, Rory opened the front door and caught her first glimpse of Beck Brody. If it hadn't been for his light blue irises and the fact that he was six feet tall, Rory would never have suspected that Caden's older brother was anything except pure-blooded Japanese. Beck's straight, black hair fell past his shoulders, and he possessed Asian facial features. Wearing a black shirt, black jeans, and black boots, he was slender but muscular, reminding her of fighters in the martial arts movies she'd watched with Nolan when they'd been teenagers and he'd dreamed of becoming the Caucasian version of Jet Li, Sonny Chiba, or Bruce Lee.

Beck looks lethal, Rory thought. *Neat, clean, and deadly. Holy crap!*

"Rory," Beck said in greeting, as if they'd already met.

He didn't smile, but Rory, who was relieved to see him, did. She would have hugged him had he not been so...aloof.

"Hello. Come on in." Turning to her friend, she continued, "Ren, this is Caden's older brother, Beck Brody."

Ren's expression was inscrutable, and Rory wondered if the woman was suspicious of Beck. Neither of them reached out to shake hands, nor did they smile at one another. Rory sensed wariness on both their parts. Well, she was wary of Beck Brody, too.

The man stepped into the foyer and glanced around before stating gruffly, "We need to talk."

"Yes, we do." Looking to Ren, Rory said, "I'm so thankful you came out here to tell me about Harvey and Nolan. Please let me know if you hear any updates, and I'll do the same."

"Of course." Ren hugged her again and whispered, "Are you sure you want me to leave you alone with him? He looks kind of scary."

"I heard that," Beck remarked idly without looking away from the picture he was studying on the wall in front of him. "I am scary, but I would never hurt Rory, you, or any innocent. I kill only those who are evil."

Rory broke away from Ren, planted her hands on her hips, and snapped, "Well, aren't you the master of tact and discretion?"

"I never claimed to be either. I am what I am."

"What is going on?" Ren asked, a worried look shadowing her face. "What do you mean you kill evil people?"

"It's why we Brody boys were adopted. It's what our father raised us to do," he answered matter-of-factly. "We stop murderers wherever and however we can."

"Rory, he's insane!" Ren exclaimed. "Is Caden delusional, too?"

Trying to ignore the persistent throbbing in her head, Rory insisted, "Neither of them is crazy or delusional." Rounding on Beck, she asked, "Why are you involving her?"

"I'm not. She involved herself when she came to your house. If Elias is watching, she's now on his hit list. She needs to be informed and protected." Staring at Ren, he said, "You can't leave."

"The hell I can't!" she shot back.

"Fine," he hissed. "Leave and see what happens. You'll probably be dead before tomorrow."

"Is that a threat?"

"No. It's a fact. It turns out that our adoptive father is evil and is after us, Rory, and her brother. He wants something else, too. I'm not quite certain what. I've been digging around on this for months, but I haven't been able to narrow things down enough to uncover Elias's real goal."

"You mean the assignment you've been working has been trying to uncover the truth about Elias?" Rory asked, as realization dawned.

"Yes. I couldn't very well tell my brothers about it. I wasn't certain how they'd react, although I suspected they were having doubts about Elias themselves. I've been surreptitiously investigating our father and his background."

"Then you probably know what Caden and I already figured out."

"Maybe. Maybe not. The others will be here soon. We'll wait for them so that we don't have to repeat ourselves over and over."

"And how long will that be?" demanded Ren. "I have a restaurant to run!"

"Looks like you'll be calling in sick," Beck said coolly. "My brothers won't be here for a while, and then we need to get our shit together to save Caden and stop Elias."

"Save Caden?" Ren rounded on Rory and asked, "Caden's in trouble? Why didn't you tell me?"

"Because I wasn't supposed to tell anyone!"

"Let me guess," Beck said, as he braced himself against the doorframe beside him. "Thorn told you to stay inside, stay quiet, and stay safe."

"Yes. Considering I don't have any kick-ass training like you do, I thought that was my best bet."

"It is," he agreed. "From what I know about you, you can see ghosts and walk in astral form while you sleep. Kicking ass seems to be out of your realm of expertise."

"You can see ghosts?" Ren asked incredulously. "And walk in astral form? How? Why?"

"Tell her," Astrid urged. "You might as well give her an explanation of the basics before the others arrive. It may be hours."

"Astrid, *please* be quiet."

Ren glanced around and said, "Astrid? Astrid Hass? You mean her ghost is *here*?"

"Yes," Rory admitted with a sigh. Glaring at Beck, she said, "You might as well hear this, too. If I have to repeat it, then I do. I can't keep Ren in the dark when there's so much at stake, and your brothers won't be here for a while."

"It's okay by me," he said. "Got a beer handy? I think I could use one."

"I do. I think *I'll* have one, too. Ren?"

"At this point, I think I could use some alcohol. Let me step into the living room to call the restaurant. I'll join you both in a minute."

Once the three of them were seated at the kitchen table, Ren stared unabashedly at Beck and asked, "You're a half-breed like me."

His expression clouded, but he merely nodded.

"Do you know who your parents are?"

"I thought I did. But not anymore. My brother, Thorn, will review the situation when he arrives." Cocking his head, he asked, "Do you know who *your* parents are?"

Shaking her head, Ren said, "My parents settled here in Sage. They'd been missionaries in Japan when they adopted me. They hadn't planned on going overseas and returning with a kid. I was four and living in an orphanage when they came across me. They were told my mother was Japanese and my father was an American, but that was it. Being a mongrel in my native country, I was treated like an outcast. I wasn't…pure, and I was verbally and physically abused as a result. Mom and Dad said they felt they couldn't leave me there. So, they petitioned to adopt me. Their request was granted quickly. I think the local authorities were glad to get rid of me."

Rory's mouth hung open. She'd never known the story of Ren's early life and adoption. Now she knew why her friend had kept silent. What small girl would want to tell such a tale? Although she hadn't been verbally or physically abused in their close-knit community, Ren was definitely different from the average Sage resident. She was the only person of Asian descent in the area.

Beck rubbed thoughtfully at his chin and asked, "You still speak Japanese?"

"Yes. My adoptive parents spoke it. That's how they'd ended up as missionaries in Japan. They didn't want me to lose the language, although they didn't entrench me in Asian culture. They told me I should consider myself 100% American once I was their daughter but that everyone should know other languages in order to spread God's word."

"You're a Christian then?"

Rory couldn't miss the derisive tone in his question. She was certain Ren caught it, too.

"I am, but I'm no Holy Roller." Hesitating, she asked curiously, "Are you a Christian?"

"We Brodys were raised to believe in good and evil, but Elias only took us to church at Christmas and Easter each year. I believe in God, but He isn't only found in churches."

"I couldn't agree more," Ren said with a slight smile. "That's why I haven't set foot in one since my parents died. There's no need."

"But you believe in Good and Evil?"

"Of course. I'm a proverbial cheerleader for Team Good."

Beck's expression softened a little, and he murmured, "I'm glad to hear it. We need all the cheerleaders we can get."

"I'm not *just* a cheerleader," Ren insisted hotly. "I work to promote Good every day!"

"I'm certain you do." He paused then added under his breath, "Good with a dose of Asian spice."

Rory could almost feel the heat flowing between the man and woman seated next to her at the table and thought, *Oh, brother. Do we really need another complication?*

She cleared her throat and explained about the Brodys turned Roosevelts, the family's supernatural "gifts," the unusual events of the past few days, and Caden's disappearance. By the time she'd wrapped up her summary, Ren had finished her bottle of beer, and Beck was on his third. Rory had drained half of hers before she'd started speaking.

"You probably think we're crazy," Rory told Ren once she'd sat back in her chair and picked up her beer bottle again.

"No," Ren said slowly. "I'm just amazed that you and your family managed to keep your supernatural side hidden from the community for so many years. After all, it can be tough enough for one person to hide her supernatural powers, but generations of one family? I'm impressed."

Beck straightened in his chair and said plainly, "You're speaking from experience."

"I – I don't know what you're talking about," Ren insisted, but Rory could tell that she was withholding something.

"We're not going to tell anyone," he declared. "We need to know. It could make the difference between life and death."

"I told you –"

"Don't fucking lie to me!" Beck shouted, pounding his fist on the table and causing the women to startle. "My baby brother is dead, and another brother is missing. I need to be aware of every advantage we might have available to us! I don't give a damn if you've hidden it all your life. Rory's just shared her family secrets with you. Drop those goddamned defenses and tell us what powers you possess! You think *we're* going to out you?"

Ren's eyes glistened with tears, but she didn't look away from Beck's fierce gaze. Instead, she said resolutely, "I'm a surveyor."

"I thought you said you owned a restaurant," he countered.

"I do. I'm not talking about surveying property. I'm talking about a special…talent I possess. I've never told anyone about it, though."

"Sounds like it's time to talk."

Rory leaned forward and said, "I think I know what she means. I remember a character in an *anime* I watched as a teen where the girl was a 'surveyor' in her world. Basically, she'd put her hand in water, and she could sense or see or whatever you want to call it everything that was happening anywhere in the water."

"You mean around her hand?" Beck asked.

"No, it's not only that," Ren corrected. "For instance, if I put my hand into the creek, then I could…explore every aspect of the creek and the river it fed into and the bay it connected to, etcetera. I can't see or sense *everything*, but I can see a lot. I don't really know if it's a useful talent, but it is extremely relaxing and makes me feel connected to the world in a way a person can't be connected in daily life." Sighing, she admitted, "There's no way I can explain it properly using words. You'd have to experience it."

"Which we obviously can't."

Looking quizzically at Beck, Ren asked, "What do *you* do?"

"Yes, I've been wondering the same thing," Rory said. "I know all you Brody boys can see and interact with ghosts. I also know that Caden can sense when others have supernatural powers but –" She stopped, blinked, and said, "Wait a minute. If that's true, then why didn't Caden tell me Ren had special abilities?"

"It's not our place to out anyone who has supernatural gifts," Beck reminded her. "If we went around doing that, then we could ruin a lot of lives. Many people don't even realize they have powers and would flip out if we told them. Caden explained once that it wasn't his right to tell anyone about people's gifts unless he had no choice. He just tucks away the information for future reference wherever he happens to be."

Rory nodded. She understood, but a part of her was hurt that Caden hadn't confided in her regarding Ren's power. However, she put herself in his place and released her anger. His approach was best, and she didn't want her personal feelings to cloud her judgment, especially not in such dangerous times.

"Right," she said. "So, Caden can sense others who possess supernatural gifts. What do the rest of you do?"

"When my brothers get here," Beck said, his words clipped with annoyance.

Her own annoyance flaring, Rory was about to demand that he immediately explain everything when they heard a knock on the front door. Beck was swiftly on his feet, commanding her to answer the knock but move out of the way if he indicated there was trouble.

Rory rolled her eyes at Ren in a way that conveyed her exasperation with his bossiness, and Ren rolled her eyes in a similar fashion. The two women grinned at each other, and then the three of them rose and headed for the foyer.

The large African-American man with buzzed hair, a short beard, and a thin moustache waiting on the porch was bulkier than Caden and Beck. Rory silently wondered how many hours he spent at the gym daily in order to maintain the bulging muscles all over his body that seemed to strain the fabric of his clothing. Unlike most bodybuilders she'd seen in magazines or on television, the muscles on the new arrival didn't make him appear disproportionate or grotesque. They seemed to suit him.

"You must be Rory," he said with genuine friendliness. "I'm David." His eyes lifting, he said, "Hey, Beck."

"Hey yourself," Beck said with more warmth than Rory would have thought possible from the man. "How close are Sawyer and Thorn?"

David shrugged and said, "They should be here within the hour. We each took different flights so that we wouldn't be driving for twelve hours and agreed to regroup here. Any updates?"

"A few," Beck replied in his typical taciturn manner.

"Come in, and get out of that heat," Rory urged David, reminding her of the first day Caden had arrived and asked her if he could come inside in order to escape the blistering summer temperatures. When Ren said her name with obvious concern, Rory shook her head and admitted, "Just thinking about Caden."

No one spoke, as David stepped into the foyer and gave his older brother a tight, quick hug. Then, he noticed Astrid and exclaimed, "Damn, Woman! Look at that dress you're *not* wearing. You think men want to see everything right away?"

Sounding unusually contrite, Astrid said, "I didn't know it would be the last dress I ever wore. It should have been...I should have been...." Shaking her head so that the bullet hole flashed in and out of view, she admitted, "I don't think Anderson minded."

"What is she wearing?" Ren asked quietly, reminding Rory that Ren was the only person who couldn't see or hear the ghost.

"A red cocktail dress that leaves little to the imagination." Turning toward David and Beck, she said, "I suppose I might as well make the formal introductions. Astrid Hass, meet David and Beck

Brody. David and Beck, this was your little brother's fiancé." Directing her gaze at David, she added, "Astrid was pregnant when Elias staged her suicide and injured Anderson, leaving him comatose."

David's face grew somber, and he closed his eyes then turned away from the others. Beck placed a hand on his brother's shoulder and squeezed before swearing, "We *will* stop Elias. We'll find Caden, determine Elias's goal, and then kill him."

Without turning, David nodded and said tightly, "We have no choice."

"We do have a choice," Beck insisted. "We simply have to choose wisely."

Half an hour later, Sawyer Brody arrived riding a black Harley Davidson motorcycle. The man had shaggy, blonde hair and brown eyes and looked as though he'd just stepped off the cover of a magazine entitled *50 of the World's Handsomest Badass Men*. Tall, lean, and muscular, Sawyer Brody's body type was more like that of Caden and Beck's than David's. Rory could see the cockiness Caden had mentioned reflected both in the man's eyes and his swagger. She expected him to be a handful, and Sawyer did not disappoint.

"What's the deal?" were his first words when she opened the door. "Let's talk so we can kick some ass and get Caden back!"

"In time," Beck said firmly. "Remember your manners."

"Manners?" Rory echoed. "I'm still waiting for evidence of yours, so don't lecture your brother about his lack of manners."

David and Sawyer guffawed at her remark. Beck remained stoic, but Rory thought she detected the faintest of twitches at one corner of his mouth. Ren smiled, and Astrid snorted. Sawyer was just stepping into the house when they all heard the sound of an approaching vehicle.

"Thorn," Sawyer said. "What's up with him and those damned vans?!?"

"He says they're the best way for him to haul all of his electronic crap," David commented. "He's probably right, but, man, do they always have to be so butt-ugly?"

After the nondescript white van had parked in the little lot, a brown-haired, brown-eyed man climbed out and approached the porch. His straight hair hung down his back, and tattoos were visible on his arms. His musculature resembled that of Beck, Caden, and Sawyer, but he didn't appear to possess his brothers' self-confidence. He looked younger than the others, although Rory suspected he wasn't the youngest by many years.

Thorn smiled shyly at her when he reached the front door and said, "Hello, Rory. I spoke with you on the phone. I'm sorry I couldn't get here sooner. I had to gather some gear after renting the van once I landed in Orlando."

"You're here now, and I'm so glad," Rory said, ushering him inside. Then, "Oh, my God! You have the Companion Cube from *Portal* tattooed on your right forearm!"

Thorn looked momentarily taken aback before grinning and saying, "You know *Portal*?"

"I know just about every video game that's ever existed," she answered.

"I think I'm in love," Thorn said with a wide smile. "Caden has all the luck!"

A chorus of indignant protests sounded from the other brothers, but Thorn merely shook his head and said, "I don't see any of *you* with girlfriends, so don't look so pissed. Right now, we need to find Caden and take care of business." Glancing back to Rory, he went on, "But you and I have some serious gaming time in our future."

She smiled at his attempt to lighten the mood and played along by saying, "I bet you a hundred-dollar GameStop gift card that I can beat you at any multi-player game of your choosing."

"You're on!"

After Thorn had hugged his brothers and had been introduced to Ren and Astrid, Rory led them all to the living room, preparing to provide her explanation to the three new arrivals and receive the updates and information from the four brothers now present. It needed to happen, but she wasn't looking forward to it. At least it would distract her from her worry about Caden and what he might be enduring – if he was even still alive.

18 Caden

Caden shivered once more in the chill of his dark prison. Rory's astral body appeared beside him. Thankfully, Nolan's body was nowhere around. Caden wondered where it had gone but didn't dwell on the question for long. He was too busy fighting the chills.

Once again, he felt Rory's naked astral form touch him, heating his cool skin. While she was with him, he didn't focus on the hurts and the blackness of the room. He simply *was*. He was more than ready to be away from his dark prison cell.

Rory caressed the skin above his broken ribs, and he felt as though someone had placed a heating pad on the injured area. As her fingers and palms moved over his body, Caden relaxed and sighed with temporary relief. This time, her hands found their way between his legs, and he was instantly hard.

"Don't stop," he murmured. "I need you now more than ever."

He sucked in his breath when he felt her mouth close over the tip of his erection. His ribs complained, but he ignored them. Instead, he directed his attention to the vibrating heat of Rory's mouth as she swirled her tongue over the head of his dick. He wished he wasn't hurt. He ached to push his hips upwards so that he could show her how much he loved what she was doing and how much he wanted to pleasure her in return.

God, that feels phenomenal, he thought. *I should tell her how I love it.*

As if she could hear him, astral Rory intensified her efforts. Caden came fast and hard, shouting her name as he did so. He fully expected the apparition of Rory to be gone once the spasms in his body subsided, but she remained.

Caden reached for her, pushing aside the pounding in his head, his aching right arm and lower left leg, and his aggravated broken ribs. Astral Rory curled into his embrace and nuzzled against him. He felt so…contented. After a while, he also felt aroused again.

Rory looked up at him. Her glittering astral body illuminated the two of them and nothing else. She pulled away, and he cried out in despair. Then, she reappeared, straddling his hips. He wanted to participate in whatever she had planned, but his body felt weighted down. All he could do was watch. As she moved while astride him, Caden felt her channel quivering around him. He groaned when she leaned her head back, her long, red curls tickling his thighs. When she rocked her hips back and forth, he murmured, "God, yes." Rory's hips rocked faster, and he felt her inner muscles tighten around his dick. Powerless to hold off, Caden exploded within her. She came a moment later, and they shuddered together.

"Love you," he whispered, as she sagged against his chest. "Stay with me."

Astral Rory began to shudder again. This time, ecstasy wasn't responsible for her movements. She was crying in his arms. He wished he could tell her everything would be fine, but he had doubts about that. So, he simply continued to hold her and repeated that he loved her until he was hoarse.

19 Rory

Rory had just finished explaining recent events to David, Sawyer, and Thorn when she experienced a wave of erotic pleasure followed by a sudden bout of vertigo. She shivered as if she were cold but instantly broke out into a sweat as heat coursed through her. Before she realized what was happening, her knees gave out. The next thing she knew, she was lying in Beck's arms as he knelt on the floor.

He actually looks concerned, she reflected. *I wonder if he really cares what happens to me or if he's just worried he'll lose his only solid link to Caden.*

"What's wrong?" Ren said urgently. "Should we call 911?" When Beck offered her a terse "No," she pursed her lips before asking her friend, "Do you want some water?"

Rory shook her head and instantly regretted it. Her world spun again, and she dealt with another round of alternating chills and sweats.

"Love you," she mumbled. "Miss you."

"She must be sick," Sawyer observed. "No woman loves Beck. He wouldn't allow it."

Rory felt Beck's body tense at his brother's remark, but he didn't dignify it with a response. However, Ren voiced her disapproval at Sawyer's comments, and he grudgingly apologized.

"What happened?" Beck asked pointedly, never taking his eyes from Rory's face. "Are you ill?"

"Caden," Rory murmured. "It was Caden."

That got everyone's attention. The others stared at Rory for a few moments before the questioning began. They were all talking at the same time, but the only thing Rory could hear was Caden's voice repeatedly uttering the words, "I love you."

Beck lifted Rory and then carried her to the couch. Ren got her a root beer, and Rory allowed her upper body to be propped up against a square pillow before beginning to sip the soda as directed by Beck. When she began to feel queasy but had stopped shivering, she looked around at the four brothers, Ren, and Astrid and said, "I was…with Caden."

"What do you mean?" asked David, the coffee table groaning under his weight as he sat on the edge.

"Caden and I were…together."

Rory blushed, not wanting to tell them that she'd felt as though she'd had an orgasm but remembering the sensation all the same. She also recalled pressing her body against Caden's and hearing him tell her over and over in a hoarse voice that he loved her.

A solid link, she silently repeated, recalling her earlier thought about Beck and his need to use her in order to find his brother. *But how could I develop a link to Caden that would connect us across space?*

"I felt as if I was with Caden," she explained. "He was naked, hurt, and shivering. It's cold wherever he is. I was in my astral body. Caden told me shortly after we met that I feel hot when I'm in astral form and that it's like I vibrate and glitter."

"Okay, this is *way* weird!" Astrid exclaimed.

"Says the ghost with the hole in her head," remarked Beck. Never taking his eyes from Rory, he ordered, "Tell us everything you remember."

"I, um, don't think I can."

"Why not?"

"Because I, um, was…that is…we were…."

"The two of you were screwing," Sawyer said with a shrug. Frowning, he asked, "You can have sex while in your astral body?"

"I never have before."

"So, you didn't realize what was going on until you climaxed?" Thorn asked, his tone mercifully clinical. "Usually, you're in control when you're in astral form and are completely aware?"

"My physical self is asleep, but my astral self's mind is aware," she clarified. Feeling less embarrassed, Rory said, "This time, I was talking one minute, felt like I, um, you know, and then got dizzy. I felt cold and hot simultaneously. Then, I heard Caden saying he loved me as he held me in his arms. He kept saying it again and again, and it sounded like he hadn't had any water in a long time. His voice was all raspy. Then, I was back here and collapsed."

"How often have you and Caden had sex?" Beck asked.

Her cheeks flaming, Rory snapped, "You can add lack of subtlety to your list of things you need to work on!"

"I have a point," Beck said calmly.

"We Brody brothers each have a point," Sawyer said with a gleam in his eyes. "But Caden's point is only for Rory."

David's black fist made contact with Sawyer's upper arm hard enough for the younger man to yell, "Knock it off!"

"When you show some respect, I'll be happy to," David said firmly.

"You didn't answer my question," Beck reminded Rory. "How often did you and Caden have sex?"

"Um, like only touching or like full-on sex?"

Thorn coughed and put a hand over his mouth in an effort to hide a smile. Sawyer snickered, and David pressed his lips together in an obvious effort to contain a grin. Only Beck remained seemingly unaffected by her question.

"Rory," David said gently. "I'm going to ask you a very personal question. I'm not being nosy. We just need to know. Okay?" When she nodded, he asked, "Was Caden your first partner?"

Her lower lip quivered, as she answered, "Yes. Well, no. I don't know what to say!"

"Tell them the truth," Astrid prompted. "They won't share anything about what Dominic did to you with anyone else."

"But I don't want to tell them!"

Astrid sat on the edge of the couch and said, "I think you have to. Any little detail might be important, and what happened with Dominic wasn't simply some little detail."

After releasing a sigh filled with resignation, Rory turned her head toward the back of the couch, shut her eyes, and told the story of how Dominic Ambrose had date raped her seven years earlier. When she got to the part where Dominic had used her panties to wipe her blood off of his penis, she thought she heard David growl. He sounded more like an animal than a man, but she didn't look at him. She couldn't look at any of them. She felt ashamed by having to share her assault with this room full of virtual strangers. Ren took one of her hands and gently squeezed it.

"If I know my brother – and I damn well do – then he was…careful with you," Beck said. "He wouldn't have pressured you to have sex with him. Am I right?"

Rory nodded.

"Back to the original question," Thorn said in that clinical tone of voice he'd used moments earlier. "How many times did you and Caden have sex. Uh, 'full-on' sex."

"We did it for the first time last night."

"Did he use a condom?"

"No. I'm on birth control. My cycles aren't regular."

"La-la-la-la," Sawyer chanted, pretending to put his fingers in his ears.

"Well, you told me you needed to know everything," Rory muttered. Slowly sitting up, she said, "And then there was this time just a little while ago. I mean, we *couldn't* have been having sex. I'm here, and he's somewhere else. But it felt so real."

Beck appeared thoughtful for a minute before saying, "I have a theory."

"Let's hear it," David said.

"Yeah, what's your theory?" Sawyer asked.

"Tell them, Thorn," Beck ordered. "I'm sure you're thinking the same thing I am."

"What's he thinking?" inquired Ren.

"That Caden has never had sex without a condom before last night," Thorn replied. "None of us has ever had sex without protection. Hell, that's a Brody Brother mindset. None of us ever planned on falling in love and settling down." Looking at Astrid, he asked, "Did Anderson have sex without condoms, or did you get pregnant because one busted?"

"I don't remember," she admitted. "There's still a lot I can't recall."

Nodding, he continued, "Well, Caden wanted sex but didn't want to get any girl pregnant or catch a disease. He evidently fell in love with Rory and made love to her without using a condom. Now, she's had this 'experience' with him. That means one of two things. Either just having sex with her triggered some sort of physiological and telepathic link with her, or she somehow got pregnant despite being on birth control medication and the baby is providing this link." Looking to Beck for reassurance, Thorn asked, "How was that?"

"Perfect. You're damned good at combining deductive reasoning with thinking outside the box."

"That's why he's the genius," Sawyer muttered.

"Except that Beck thought of it first," David reminded him.

"I'm the eldest and have more experience," Beck pointed out. Fixing his gaze on Rory, he asked, "Do you take your birth control pills regularly?"

"Every day."

"And you're not on antibiotics or anything else that could reduce its efficacy?"

"No. I can't be pregnant!"

"The odds are against it," Thorn noted.

"I know. That means we'll assume that Caden somehow became integrally linked with Rory when he came in her."

"If that holds true for him, then perhaps it holds true for each of us," David said.

"It obviously doesn't hold true in relation to oral sex," Sawyer said. "Otherwise, we'd have developed links to other sexual partners over the years. But if not using a condom while having 'full-on sex' as Rory put it leads to the formation of a supernatural link with a partner, then maybe that's why Elias was so adamant about our not having sex without protection."

"Anything's possible when it comes to Elias," Thorn said. "Until another one of us tries it, then we won't know for certain."

"We'd better be damned sure if we decide to have unprotected sex with any woman," David declared. "I don't want to be linked to any woman for life if I don't love her."

"Maybe it only provides a temporary link…."

Rory excused herself to wash her face. She was mortified that they were all discussing her body and what she and Caden had done. She knew it was unavoidable, but it was embarrassing all the same. By the time she reached the downstairs bathroom, she was in tears, stress combining with embarrassment to make her more emotional than usual. She locked the door behind her and wept. She felt dirty again, just as she had after Dominic had raped her.

There was a tentative knock on the bathroom door. She expected it was Ren and asked her to go away for a while.

"I can't," Sawyer said. "I told the others I had to take a leak."

"You're not going to do it in front of me," she informed him. "Just go away."

"Rory, I don't need to pee. Actually, I need to talk to you. It's really urgent."

Mistrustful but intrigued, Rory unlocked the door and allowed Sawyer to enter. Once he'd lowered the lid of the toilet and taken a seat, he said, "I'm sorry we had to push you like that for information. We're doing everything we can to find Caden before Elias kills him." As she nodded, wiping at her wet cheeks with fresh tissues, he murmured, "You can't forget what happened to you seven years ago, but you can tuck it away so that it doesn't drag you down so much."

"How would you know?" Rory asked, confused but not angry.

"I, uh, want to tell you something I've never shared with anyone before." Lowering his head, Sawyer said, "I've always been pretty wild. Early on, I started occasionally sneaking out of Elias's compound and roaming the streets. The other guys knew I did it and tried to discourage me, but I can be really stubborn."

"You? I can't imagine," Rory said with no small amount of sarcasm in her voice.

"Yeah, well, when I was fifteen, I ended up at this party where everyone was drinking and doing drugs. Elias would have had a shit fit if he'd known where I was. Anyway, this girl was coming onto me, but we Brody boys had all been told by Elias that we were *not* to have sex until we turned eighteen. Then, he'd take us to a high-class brothel so that we could learn what good sex without emotional involvement was like. So, even though I wanted this girl, I wasn't going to follow through. I knew Elias would literally kill me if I did. As it turned out, I didn't have a choice."

"You were date raped?" Rory asked in disbelief. "How? How does a girl rape a guy?"

"With help. When I kept refusing, the girl got angry. She had…friends at the party. Before I knew it, I was being held down. The girl unzipped my pants. I couldn't help being hard, but I kept telling her no, that I wasn't going to have sex until I was eighteen. She laughed and said that I was pinned to the floor, and what was I going to do about it? At least she put a condom on me before she got on top. I was fifteen. My body reacted instinctively, but I don't even remember what it felt like to come in her. I was being held down, and all these other kids my age and older were watching me being forced to have sex."

"That's horrible!"

"Yeah, it was. When it was over, I slunk home and never went to a party by myself again until I knew I was old enough and strong enough to handle any situation. I've never forgotten what happened, but I've learned to compartmentalize my brain so that the incident stays where it should. You can't imagine how much I admire you for telling all of us your story."

Rory smiled weakly at Sawyer. He'd never shared his own humiliation with anyone besides her in the decade or so since it had happened. She hoped someday he'd tell his brothers or find a woman who could handle him and would make him feel comfortable sharing his experience with her.

"Thank you, Sawyer. I really appreciate what you just did. It took guts."

Sawyer stood, gave her a rakish smile, and said, "You've got guts, Rory. You may be an innocent – and I do mean that in an almost literal sense – but you're tenacious and good-hearted. I'm happy Caden found you and fell in love with you. He deserves it. He's the spirit that binds us Brody brothers. Beck's the eldest, the most controlled, and the head of the family; David's the nice guy who's loyal but deadly when he has to be; I'm the smart-mouth, cocky fighter who knows how to make a buck and keep it; and Thorn is the geek who's probably stronger than all of us put together but isn't comfortable with himself, yet." Running his fingers through his hair, Sawyer said, "I always sensed Caden wanted a normal life for all of us, not only himself. If we find him, then I think we should make that happen."

"*When* we find him," she corrected.

He nodded and said, "Why don't you wash your face like you wanted, and then I'll go ahead and pee before returning to the living room? I wouldn't want to be a liar."

"You're not quite what I expected."

"I'm certain I'm exactly what you expected," Sawyer replied. "I'm just even more awesome."

Shaking her head but smiling, Rory did as he'd suggested. Once she was seated on the couch again, she said, "I've told you everything I intended to say and more. Your turn. We need to know everything we can about each of you, your backgrounds, and Elias. That way, we can maybe exploit this link between Caden and me in order to find him. Perhaps if I know all, then we can figure out a way to make it happen."

"The problem is that now we don't know if anything regarding our origins is true," Thorn explained. "We were each told stories of how we came to live with Elias. Recently, I discovered encrypted files that even *I* can't hack. They're lumped in a folder that says it contains information about our 'actual' origins. This would lead one to believe that the stories we were told were filled with lies. Until I can break the encryption codes, we won't know."

"What *can* you tell us?" Rory persisted. "What were your lives like?"

"We were brought into Elias's household as babies," Beck explained. "Other boys, too. Elias began training each boy to fight and kill when he deemed him ready. Some of the boys didn't make it through training, but Elias dismissed their deaths, stating that they'd proven to be too weak. We didn't question him. We felt we owed him our lives and our loyalty. After all, if we survived training, he'd adopt us. We'd have a father."

David added, "Everything we did revolved around honing our skills so that we could become the best fighters of evil."

"What were your daily lives like?" Ren asked.

Sawyer answered, "Up at 5:00 a.m. Breakfast then homeschooling with tutors until 11:00 a.m. Lunch. Training until we were too exhausted to do more than shower and go to our rooms. Dinner at 6:00 p.m. then homework. Bedtime at 9:00. Start over the next day."

"No playtime?"

"We horsed around when Elias was out or at night when we were supposed to be sleeping," David confided. "We boys all slept in one, big room. Elias believed he could keep a tighter rein on us that way. I guess he could, but that also enabled us to develop an even closer bond. Those of us who survived became blood brothers. We developed our own rituals that were kept secret from him and apart from his rites of passage."

"What kind of rituals?" Astrid asked.

"Whenever a boy was adopted, the others who'd already been adopted would get up at midnight, stand in a circle, make a cut on the tip of one finger, and then squeeze drops of blood into a glass," Sawyer said. "The blood would be swirled around in the glass before it was set in the center of our bedroom. Then, everyone would return to bed. It made us feel like we were of the same bloodline. We were blood brothers."

"When each brother turned twenty-one, he got a full-back dragon tattoo," Thorn volunteered. "Beck suggested the tattoo ritual and the idea that it always be of a dragon, but each of us selected our own design. There were other minor things we did, but the blood ceremony and the dragon tattoo held major significance. They were only for us, not Elias."

"If your adoptive father is evil, then why didn't he train you to do evil instead of fight evil?" Rory asked.

"We're not sure," Sawyer answered. "Just like we're not sure of his end game."

"What are your other supernatural abilities?" Rory inquired. "You know mine and Ren's. You definitely know Caden's. Other than the being able to see ghosts part, what about you?"

Beck sighed and said resignedly, "We have to tell you, but it means we're breaking our vow to Elias. But I think all vows made to him are null and void at this point. It still feels wrong somehow."

"I agree, but it's time to move forward, Beck," David said.

The man nodded and confided, "I have the ability of pyrokinesis. I can create and control fire by using my mind."

David continued by saying, "I'm a shapeshifter. When I choose to, I can become a German shepherd. I don't have to wait for a full moon or anything like werewolves do."

"Werewolves are real?" Astrid asked.

"We're talking about pyrokinesis and shapeshifting, and you can still doubt that there are werewolves?" Rory asked tiredly. "Have you forgotten that you're a ghost?"

"That would be difficult for me to forget, wouldn't it?"

"Look, I'm sorry," Rory said apologetically. "I'm really stressed and tired right now." Turning to Sawyer, she asked, "What about you?"

"I can scout anything in my vicinity without moving. I clear my mind, and I'm soaring like an eagle. Well, my conscious mind is. My body doesn't go anywhere."

"O-kay." Finally looking at Thorn, she asked, "And you?"

"I can teleport anywhere I imagine I need to go."

"That's awesome!" exclaimed Astrid. "Can you take people with you?"

"No. I've tried. Each time I attempt to teleport someone with me, he gets left behind."

"It may still happen," Beck told him. "You're only twenty-four. We'll all be perfecting our ability to control our powers until we die."

"No more talk of dying," Rory insisted. Standing, she asked, "Who's hungry? I know I need some energy, and cooking would be a wonderful distraction for a little while."

Everyone agreed that they were ravenous. Ren excused herself to call her manager at the restaurant to make certain there were no problems. Rory explained about the cottages and suggested that each brother take one for the duration. They all declined, stating that they needed to stay together in the house until the danger had passed.

"But it's what Caden wanted," she stated before she realized what she'd said.

"What do you mean?" Beck asked.

"Caden hoped that each of you would settle out here with us. Even if you travelled for work, he wanted to live with me in the main house and have one of you in each of my guest houses. Nostalgia Road wouldn't be a B&B anymore; it would be the Brody homestead."

The men were silent for half a minute until Sawyer said, "I'm in. Caden's always known what's best when it comes to our family's heart. I trust his judgment on this."

"Good because he also wants *you* to buy my brother's bar and run it."

Looking devilishly at her, Sawyer said, "Hell, why not? I'll try anything once."

"I can think of several times where that didn't work out so well for you," David muttered. "But I'm all for using this place as a home base and trying to have a normal family life once all of this is over. Thorn? Beck?"

"I'm in," Thorn said hastily as Beck nodded but remained silent.

That must be his version of enthusiasm, Rory thought. *They each want in. Now, we just need Caden to complete things. After that, we can make all things right with the world.*

20 Caden

Caden was shivering, but it wasn't a result of the cold. He had forced himself onto his hands and knees again, and the effort and pain had proven to be too much for him. After suffering another bout of dry heaves, he was now shaking from exertion and the intensity of the resultant pain. His sprained arm, bruised shinbone, concussed brain, and broken ribs didn't appreciate his movements, whether they were directed or reflexive.

Have to get out, he thought, as a moan escaped his lips. *My injuries may not be life-threatening, but lack of food and water will kill me.*

Standing was an agony, but he managed it with only one resultant bout of dry heaves. He was weak, and his balance was tenuous at best. Between his compromised physical condition and the total darkness, it was difficult for him to remain vertical. So, Caden leaned against the wall and focused on his breathing and heart rate. Once he felt as if he wasn't going to pass out, he straightened as much as his body would permit and began to feel his way along the wall. Limping, he nonetheless tried to count off paces in order to determine the size of his cell. He stopped, realizing he had no frame of reference that would allow him to know where he'd started. Moving forward, he waited until he reached a corner then began softly counting off again. His throat felt as though it were lined with sandpaper, but the sound of his own voice gave him some reassurance. Therefore, he continued to count aloud.

He had no idea how long it took, but Caden finally ended up back where he'd started. The room was approximately two hundred square feet and seemed to be completely empty save for him. He'd felt no seams for doors or windows and wondered how that was possible. The floor and walls appeared to be made of concrete, and he continued to sense ventilation of some kind.

Where am I, and how did I get here? I can't reach the ceiling, and there's no ladder. Where did Nolan go? Perhaps there's a ladder in the center of the room. Nolan's body could be there, too. Do I chance trying to make it across? Oh, what the hell!

He wandered around blindly with his hands extended in front of him. Occasionally, Caden would bump into a wall, but he never came into contact with anything or anyone else. Eventually, he stumbled and collapsed to the ground, crying out with pain as he landed hard on his right side. He lay trembling, feeling as if he were going to pass out again. He didn't fight it. Instead, he welcomed it. Being unconscious seemed to provide him with some link to Rory. Perhaps he could use that to his advantage. If not, then at least he could take comfort in her presence.

Allowing himself to be sucked into unconsciousness, Caden waited. Sure enough, astral Rory appeared and began to soothe him with her touch. She kissed him on one temple, and he opened his mouth to speak but found that he couldn't. His mouth was too dry, and he was too drained.

No, damn it! I have to tell her what I know. Someone has to find me soon. Otherwise, I'll die here alone. Rory will be alone and unprotected. I can't let that happen.

"I'm in the dark," he said, barely able to recognize his own voice. "The room is about two hundred square feet and is lined with concrete. No doors or windows. I can't touch a ceiling or find a ladder. I don't think I have long, Rory. Are my brothers with you?"

Her glittering face was somber, but she nodded.

"You like them?"

She nodded again but gave him a little smile and a half-shrug.

"I know Beck can come off as cold, but there's a lot more going on under that façade of his. David's just a flat-out good guy. Sawyer's a mess, but he's a wonderful mess. And Thorn…Thorn is different. He's an efficient killer like the rest of us, but he's not…he's insecure. I don't know why. Maybe it's just his personality. I wish I understood and could help him see how capable he is. We're all damned good at what we do, but Thorn won't allow himself to…shine." Clearing his throat, he continued, "You two should get along great. He's a computer geek like you. If I don't make it, then maybe you and he can get together. You probably have more in common. Maybe he'd be better for you. He's only a year younger than you are and –"

Caden felt Rory's warm, vibrating hand across his mouth. He hadn't realized he'd closed his eyes until he opened them to see her shaking her head. She pointed to his chest then back to hers. Then, she leaned forward and lightly kissed his swollen lips before returning to her soothing caresses.

Caden sighed and let his muscles loosen under Rory's warm touch. He missed her, wanted her, and loved her. His dream of having a long life by her side seemed improbable due to his current circumstances, but he wouldn't give up hope until he took his last breath. He prayed for rescue, as he drifted off into the darkness.

21 Rory

Nausea and vertigo hit Rory fast and hard, and she dropped the clean casserole dish she was about to replace in one cabinet. This time, it was David who caught her. She flinched when she heard the dish shatter. It had been in the Roosevelt family for decades.

Feeling sick to her stomach, Rory closed her eyes and said, "I guess the link will get stronger each time Caden and I connect."

"David, put her on the couch!" Beck ordered. Once she'd been deposited there, he commanded, "Tell us everything you can, Rory. Any detail, no matter how seemingly insignificant, might be of enormous help."

"It was dark and cold again. There was no, um, sex this time. Caden's…declining. He told me the room is about two hundred square feet and that the walls and floor are made of concrete. There are no doors or windows, and he couldn't find a ladder."

"Can you tell where he's hurt when you two link?" Sawyer asked.

"No, but I get the feeling his injuries aren't what's killing him. It's the lack of care."

"The lack of care?" Ren repeated.

"No medical attention and no food and water. I get the impression he's been alone at all times while he's been conscious. I suspect that Caden expects he'll die soon if we don't find him. He seems sort of dazed."

"He could have a concussion," Thorn noted. "That would affect his reasoning as well as his physical state. Also, if he's completely in the dark and is having no interaction with others, he may believe he's been held for longer than he actually has. He may not be in danger of dying at this point."

"When we find him, then we can take him to the hospital in Gladeland," Ren announced. "He can be examined and treated there or moved to another facility if need be."

"No way," Sawyer declared. "We all have medic training. As long as his injuries aren't life-threatening, then we'll treat him here. We can't risk exposure when it comes to the authorities or Elias."

"Then what?" Rory asked.

"We continue to figure this out and plan our offense or defense, depending on the circumstances," Beck replied.

Rory stared at the ceiling in contemplation for several moments before saying, "I have an idea, but I don't know if it will work."

"We won't know if any plan will work until we try it," David pointed out. "What's your idea?"

"I'll try to reach Caden through this link, but I'll hold Thorn's hand while I do it. Maybe I can be a sort of connection between them. Then, Thorn can teleport to Caden and teleport him back here."

"But I already told you I've never been able to transport anyone when I teleport," Thorn reminded her.

"I know, but this might be the impetus that will push you to do it. Unless we can figure out where Caden's being held, then you're his only avenue for escape."

"But I *can't*," Thorn insisted. "I've *tried*."

"You've tried in training," Beck pointed out. "You've never tried it when one of our lives is on the line. Rory's right; you're Caden's only hope, providing she can somehow psychically link you to him."

Thorn surprised Rory by giving the closed door behind him a roundhouse kick. His long, brown hair flew out behind him, as he angrily struck the wood with his foot. The doorframe splintered, as the door itself was torn away from it. The others seemed as startled as she, so Rory deduced that Thorn wasn't typically given to fits of temper. David said his name and began to approach his younger brother, but Thorn waved him off.

"If I fail, then Caden could die!" he shouted.

"At least you'll know you tried," Beck said calmly. "We have no other viable options at this point. If we don't do anything, then Caden may not survive, period. Right now, we have no idea where Caden is or how to identify his position."

"You're right," Thorn said resignedly. Not meeting Rory's eyes, he mumbled, "I'm sorry I broke your door. I'll pay to have it fixed."

"Don't worry about that now," she told him. "It's okay. I don't care about the door; I care about getting Caden back."

She sat up slowly in order to ensure that she didn't succumb to the queasiness and dizziness that tended to accompany her supernatural meetings with Caden. She wondered how she was going to reach him and voiced her concern aloud.

"Just shut your eyes and concentrate," Sawyer suggested. "Hold Thorn's hands or something."

"We have no idea what we're doing!" Thorn snapped. "Even if I reach Caden and can somehow teleport him out, what if I teleport us both into a wall or a tree?"

"Your abilities have never led you astray in the past," Beck said. "Trust in yourself, Thorn. If Rory can get you to Caden, then you *will* be able to get him out."

Thorn sighed then looked to Rory and said, "How do you want to do this?"

"I suppose we could try what Sawyer suggested. If that doesn't work, then we may have to wait until Caden…summons me, however he does it."

"But we don't get any warning with that," David noted. "Thorn would have to hold your hand continually until the link was established if you can't make contact yourself."

"Whatever we have to do," Rory said resolutely. "Ren, would you sweep up the debris from the broken dish in the kitchen?"

"David, gather the medic supplies we have," Beck directed. "Sawyer, go find blankets."

"The extras are in the guest room next to the library upstairs," Rory said when he started to walk away. "Bring a few pillows, too!"

As Sawyer jogged up the stairs, Thorn sat on the couch and took Rory's hands in his. She smiled encouragingly at him before announcing, "Here we go!" Then she closed her eyes and thought of Caden. She imagined she was with him in the cold, dark room. She did this for a while before sighing and opening her eyes.

"It's not working," she told the others.

"Try again," Beck urged. "Don't only think about Caden. Think about Caden's being alone, hurt, and cold. *Feel* yourself in that room with him. Feel his need for you. Will yourself to join him."

Rory did as he suggested. At first, nothing seemed to be different. Then, something changed, and she was in the dark with Caden – and Thorn. Still holding Thorn's left hand with her right, she cupped Caden's cheek with her free hand. He whispered her name but didn't move. She glanced at Thorn and found him staring wide-eyed at her. That was when she remembered that no one except Caden had ever seen her in her astral body. She nodded to Thorn and then jerked her head toward Caden before kissing the injured man tenderly on the lips. Thorn placed his right palm on his brother's chest, and Caden stiffened, looking wildly around. Rory stroked his disheveled hair and kissed his jaw before letting him go. The link was broken, and she tumbled back into her body in the living room. David was cradling her against his chest, and she knotted his shirt in her hands and fought not to throw up as she asked, "Did it work?"

"Thorn teleported but hasn't come back, yet," he replied. "Now, we wait and see if he returns alone or with Caden."

"I feel sort of woozy," she admitted. "David, will you sit beside me on the couch so that I don't fall over?"

"I think I can handle that," he answered with a grin. "Ren, would you get her another root beer? I'm thinking these episodes are messing with her blood sugar."

Ren hurried to comply, and Astrid asked what she could do to help. Rory looked at her and saw only sincerity in her expression and question. Although there wasn't much the ghost could do, she wanted to reinforce the woman's desire to assist, so she suggested she patrol the house in case Thorn reappeared with Caden somewhere other than the living room. Astrid immediately began to wander throughout the home, and Rory smiled tiredly with satisfaction.

Time seemed to move more slowly while they waited. Ten minutes passed. Fifteen. Twenty. With each passing minute, the tension in the living room grew.

"What if Thorn's trapped now, too?" Sawyer asked. "Maybe whatever material lines the walls and floor prevents anyone from leaving."

"Thorn's teleported from rooms lined with sheetrock, concrete, steel, other metals, glass, and wood as well as teleporting outdoors," Beck reminded his brother. "The only thing that might stop him would be a supernatural barrier."

"You mean like someone cast a spell?" Ren asked. "Does anyone do magic?"

Beck, David, and Sawyer exchanged glances before Beck admitted, "Elias knows how to use magic, but none of us do. Elias never –"

They heard a loud clattering noise, and then Astrid yelled, "In the kitchen! They're back!"

Everyone dashed toward the room. Rory was relieved she'd asked Ren to clean up the pieces of the broken dish. As they rushed forward, they spotted Thorn sprawled on the floor near the sink. His arms were firmly locked around Caden's chest.

For an instant, they all stood frozen, dumbstruck by what they saw. Caden remained naked, but he appeared to be perfectly fine. Thorn had bruises and cuts on his face and on the exposed part of his right arm where they could see the skin that wasn't tattooed. He groaned but didn't release Caden, who showed no signs of regaining consciousness.

"David, tend to Thorn while I check Caden!" Beck barked. "Sawyer, start an I.V. on Thorn. I think when he teleported with Caden he somehow…I don't know…assumed Caden's injuries. That doesn't mean Caden's not in bad shape from something that's not visible to us."

"I think you're right," Thorn said in a graveled voice. "I feel dehydrated and am starving. My head and face hurt. I think the ribs on my left side are broken. My right arm feels sprained, and my left shin hurts like a son-of-a-bitch." Moaning as David gently lifted Thorn's right arm away from Caden's chest, he asked, "Is Caden okay? I don't care if I hurt like hell. Tell me I got him out without killing him!"

"His pulse rate and respiration are good," Beck said with an uncharacteristic sigh of relief. "It looks like he's simply unconscious." Leaning across Caden's body, he touched Thorn on one shoulder and said, "You did it, Brother. You saved him."

Thorn smiled then winced at the pain before saying, "Then it was all worth it. I'll mend. Better that I'm laid up than him right now. This is his fight."

"True," Sawyer agreed. "It may involve all of us, but Caden's the one who set things in motion to stop Elias. He needs to be in top form in order to fight."

Rory looked at Beck, knowing that the man had actually been conducting his own investigation of Elias before Caden. Beck merely gave his brothers a brief smile and returned his attention to the man she loved. There was obviously more to Beck than she'd first imagined.

Caden told me that while he was hurt, she remembered. *He said Beck might seem distant on the outside but was anything but on the inside. I'm thinking he's spot on about all of his brothers. If that's the case, then maybe what Thorn did will help to boost his self-confidence.*

"Rory, get over here and rouse Caden," Beck directed. "Thorn, once you've had something to drink, then maybe you can tell us what happened."

After gratefully sipping some water offered to him by Sawyer, Thorn shifted, gritted his teeth, and said, "I hate this damned I.V."

"You need it right now," Sawyer insisted. "I'll remove it once I know you're hydrated."

"Are you able to tell us what happened between the time Rory left you and your teleportation back here?" David asked Thorn, as Rory knelt beside Caden and bent to kiss him. Ren also covered him with a blanket and tucked a pillow under his head, but he stayed motionless on the kitchen floor.

"Rory linked us. She looked...spectacular. I've never seen anyone in astral form before. She...glittered. She touched Caden then gestured for me to reach out to him. Once I did and he reacted, Rory vanished. I wanted to get Caden out of his prison, but I wanted to see if I could tell where he was being held or locate a physical means of escape. It was pitch black after Rory left, and there was no evidence of lights, furniture, or a way out. I did find a man's body on the floor across from where Caden was propped up. I couldn't see him, but I checked him before returning to Caden. He was dead."

Caden stirred and murmured Rory's name. She kissed him enthusiastically, and he responded in kind. Opening his eyes, he smiled and then put his arms around her shoulders before pulling her against him.

"You kept me going," he said. "Off and on throughout my ordeal, you were there for me." Fingering a few loose red curls, he said, "I love you."

"I love you, too," she said, her vision blurring with tears. "Thank God, you're okay."

"Time is of the essence," Beck said. "Do you know the identity of the dead man who was imprisoned with you?"

"Nolan," Caden answered soberly. "Nolan Roosevelt is dead."

Rory squeezed her eyes tightly shut and asked in a small voice, "Are you sure it was him? You had a concussion, and it was dark."

"We talked. He had a belly wound. He said he wanted you to rename the bar *Spirits* like you'd suggested when he opened it since you'd inherit it after he died. I thought he'd been taken out of the room while I was unconscious, though."

Rory swiped at the corners of her eyes. As much as she'd come to dislike Nolan, she still loved him. However, now was not the time to grieve for her older brother. Now was the time for action. She could mourn his passing later.

"He told me Dominic Ambrose was a ghost and was helping Elias. I never saw either of them the entire time I was imprisoned." Taking Rory's face in his hands, Caden said, "I'm sorry you've lost your brother."

"Thank you," she said softly. "I know he was a jerk when you met him, but he wasn't always like that." Forcing herself not to dwell on Nolan's death for the time being, she asked, "How do you feel?"

"Great, actually." Turning his head toward Thorn, he added, "Sorry you ended up taking on all my injuries, but I can't thank you enough, Thorn. You rescued me. I'm so proud of you."

Everyone echoed his comments, and Thorn grinned in spite of his discomfort.

"How did you teleport him back?" Beck asked the youngest Brody.

"Once I'd explored the cell, I wrapped my arms around him and tried to teleport. Nothing happened. After three tries, I got the idea to concentrate on reuniting him with Rory while teleporting. That did the trick, and we were…here."

"Take Thorn to an empty bedroom and fix him up as best as you can," Beck told David and Sawyer. "Caden, try to sit up. Then you can have something to eat and drink, and we'll review everything we know at this point."

Caden sat up slowly with Beck's help. He swayed slightly but didn't fall back to the floor. Beck lifted him then deposited him into a chair at the kitchen table. Once the blanket covered his bottom half, he requested coffee and something to eat. Rory hurriedly made a fresh pot of coffee and placed two banana nut muffins onto a plate. She, Beck, Ren, and Astrid waited until Caden had eaten and drained one cup of coffee before Beck explained about his own investigation into Elias, the brothers' mission, and their determination to stop their adoptive father, hopefully *after* getting the answers they wanted from him.

"This news about Elias utilizing the ghost of Rory's rapist does put an interesting twist on things," Beck noted.

"I was thinking about that," Rory said. "If Dominic became a ghost after his death, then it can't be coincidence that he'd end up with Elias, especially if Elias is my great-uncle."

"Elias had to seek him out," Caden said thoughtfully. "But how? We can't seek out ghosts; they find us."

"We can't, but how do we know exactly what Elias is capable of? We all doubt him and his motives. I'm thinking he controls forces we never imagined could be harnessed."

"Forces greater than psychokinesis and magic?" Caden asked.

"Supernatural energy?" Rory speculated. "You recall I told you that my father instructed me to keep the paths to the elements clear. Maybe Elias plans to come back to claim some supernatural power or object that he feels is his birthright."

"A birthright that was denied him when his parents faked his death and gave him up as a baby," Beck put in. "They must have somehow known he was tainted and sent him far away."

"But Charles Roosevelt has a grave in the family cemetery," Rory told them.

"Your great-grandparents would have to mislead people into thinking one of their twins had died," Caden said. "Thus, they'd have put in a headstone with false information on it."

"Yes, I —"

When she suddenly stopped, Caden raised one ginger-colored brow and looked questioningly at Rory. Feeling as though her brain was running on overdrive, she asked, "What if they didn't merely make a pretend grave?"

"What do you mean?" Beck asked.

"My father told me the caretakers of our family land kept diaries, but we could never find them. Perhaps they buried the diaries in the fake grave."

"What better way to preserve them than to hide them in a safe place no one would think to look?" Caden mused. "I don't care that it's dark. We need to go dig up that grave."

"After you get dressed and we check on Thorn," Beck said. "If he's up to it, then he can work on breaking that encryption from his bed as he recuperates. We'll look for the diaries and hopefully find Elias and rid the world of him and this Dominic guy. Dominic sounds as if he was a real prick when he was alive, so I'm sure it didn't take much for Elias to persuade him to do what he wanted. I wonder what he promised Dominic in return."

Rory shuddered involuntarily. Whatever had kept Dominic Ambrose tethered to Elias Brody, it couldn't be good. She wondered if she'd have to come into contact with Dominic again. She'd thought that part of her life was behind her after she'd met Caden and shared her secret with him. Now, she wasn't so certain, and that thought scared her almost as much as confronting Elias Brody himself.

22 Caden

"Here you go," Sawyer said, as he entered the guest bedroom and handed Caden clothing and a pair of cowboy boots. "I also brought back more clothes, your laptop, and your iPad from that cottage where you were staying. The rest of your clothes are in Rory's room. The electronics are downstairs on the kitchen table."

"Thanks, Man." Turning to Thorn, Caden said, "And thank *you*, Brother, for saving my life and assuming my injuries. I know you didn't anticipate that second part, but I also know you would have done it even if you'd been aware of the outcome. If it's any consolation, the ribs are probably the worst of the injuries. You should be up and about soon, but I know you're really hurting right now."

"S'okay. Having you here and knowing I was responsible for getting you out makes all this worthwhile."

Caden grinned down at Thorn and thought, *Maybe this was what had to happen in order for him to be more comfortable with his teleportation abilities. Hopefully, he won't second-guess himself so much in the future.*

"Caden, you need to shower –" Beck began, but Caden cut him off.

"I will, but not yet."

Looking aggravated, Beck asked, "What do you mean, not yet?"

"I need to spend some time with Rory first."

"The danger's still very real, and all you can think about is your dick?" Sawyer asked petulantly.

"No. All I can think about is the woman I love and how I thought I'd never see her again. I'm not talking hours here. I just need a while to be alone with her. When you fall in love with a woman, then you'll earn the right to give me relationship advice, whether I agree with it or not. Until then, shut up and give me a little while to be with Rory."

"Thirty minutes," Beck proclaimed.

"We'll be showered and ready to go in an hour."

Caden left the guest room before Beck could argue, shutting the door behind him. He went to Rory's bedroom and knocked on the door. When she didn't answer, he slowly cracked it and spotted her seated on the edge of her bed. He cleared his throat and waited where he stood.

"I feel conflicted about Nolan," Rory admitted without looking in his direction. "And I've been so worried about you. I was scared I'd lost you forever."

Closing the door behind him after he'd entered the bedroom, Caden said, "I was pretty scared myself. I was afraid I'd never get to return to you. I worried you'd be unprotected and attacked. If you hadn't appeared to me in your astral body, then I don't know if I would have had the strength to stay hopeful." Sitting beside her on the bed, he put his arms around her and added, "You gave me such comfort."

"I'm so glad," she murmured, as she snuggled against him. "I hated to see you hurt and cold, but at least I knew you were alive. How do you think that link between us worked? One of your brothers – I don't remember which one – suggested that it was because you and I had sex without a condom and that perhaps it somehow linked us."

"That was probably Beck's interpretation."

"With everything that's happened, I honestly can't remember. There was speculation that maybe that was the real reason Elias told you all never to get emotionally involved with a woman or have unprotected sex. Perhaps there's something about you Brody brothers that psychically links you to a woman if you do that."

"Hm. Either that or I got you pregnant last night, and the baby linked us."

"I told you that I take my birth control pill without fail every day."

"Then the first explanation seems to be the best, unless it's merely love that bound us and not the actual act of sex." After a minute of contemplation, he mused, "I wonder if it will be the same with the others or if it's something unique between me and you. I guess we'll find out if any of them follow suit."

Caden thought of David and the man's confession that he'd loved a woman but had lost her due to his inability to commit. Perhaps once all of this was over, David could return to his lover and make that commitment. He hoped so. He wanted each of his brothers to know the joy of what he'd come to quickly understand was true love.

"I do want babies," Rory announced, interrupting his thoughts.

Caden chuckled and asked, "How many babies?"

"I don't know. How many babies would you want?"

He waggled his eyebrows at her and said mischievously, "A dozen or so."

Laughing, Rory exclaimed, "A dozen! I don't know if I want *that* many!"

"Then when we're ready for kids, we'll start with one and go from there."

"That sounds like a workable plan."

Caden stared down into her bright, blue eyes and expectant face and was instantly hard. He was glad the only thing he wore was the blanket wrapped around his waist. However, to his dismay, Rory was not wearing one of her sweet yet alluring dresses. Of all days, she'd put on jeans and a blue t-shirt. Well, he would overcome those obstacles as quickly as he could.

"Oh, God," Rory panted once they were done. "I'm sorry I bit your shoulder, but I didn't want the others to hear me screaming when I came. Did I hurt you? I didn't mean to bite you. Really, I didn't."

Resting his damp forehead against hers, Caden smiled and admitted, "I think that's what pushed me over the edge. I could feel the intensity of your orgasm. Literally. I'm happy you came so hard that you couldn't stop screaming. I doubt if you drew blood. Even if you did, I wouldn't care. You can bite me anytime."

She blushed and giggled, turning him on even though he wouldn't be able to get hard for another quarter hour or so. He kissed her before lying beside her and drawing her close. They both sighed contentedly, but Caden knew neither of them had forgotten that their time together in the bed was as limited as it was precious.

"We'll shower, dress, and then head out to Charles Brody's grave," Caden told her. "I want this mess over and done with, and I want some answers. That way, we can put it all behind us and start our new lives."

"I think your brothers are going to move out here the way you wanted and try to be a family at Nostalgia Road."

"So, you told them. I'm glad. I hope they stay. Even if they don't, at least they know they can always return here whenever they want. We'll remain a family, regardless." When she didn't comment, he asked, "Or have you changed your mind about having them live in the cottages?"

"No. I was just thinking again about *my* brother."

"Damn it, Rory. I'm sorry. Here I am talking about my brothers and being a family when I know Nolan's gone and –"

"And your brothers will be my brothers," she interrupted. "Having them here will make things easier for me to deal with when it comes to losing my parents and Nolan." Shifting in his arms, she asked, "Did Nolan say anything right before he died? I know you told me what he said about the bar. Was there anything else?"

"Verbatim?"

"Verbatim."

"He said, 'Mom. Dad.' then started to cry like he was happy before he stopped breathing."

"They were waiting for him," she said softly. "I'm glad they're together. He'll be at peace now. He hasn't been happy since he and I had our falling out after Dominic attacked me and then the plane crash that killed our parents. I wasn't happy either, not until I met you. But I didn't hate myself like he did."

Caden held Rory tightly for several minutes. Then, she kissed him on the jaw before sitting up and suggesting they shower and dress.

"Ladies first," he told her. "I'll jump in once you're done."

Wrapping the blanket around his waist once more, Caden went to check on Thorn while he waited. When he entered the guest room, all four of his brothers turned to look at him. Beck seemed displeased, but David, Sawyer, and Thorn were grinning. His brow furrowed in confusion, and he asked them what was going on.

"*You* tell *us*," Sawyer said. "Those are some impressive teeth marks on your shoulder. No wonder her screams weren't as loud as they could've been. Still, they were enough to get me hard."

"Don't go there!" Caden growled. "Rory's not just some woman I'm having sex with for kicks. I want to marry her and have kids with her. If you ever disrespect her, then I'll kick your ass!"

"Whoa!" Sawyer exclaimed, lifting his hands with the palms facing his older brother. "I didn't mean any disrespect. I don't know how to talk about sex and women any other way."

"Thanks to Elias," David muttered.

"I like Rory a lot," Sawyer continued. "She's sweet, cute, smart, and stronger than she looks. I want the two of you to be happy. But I am only a man, Caden. When I hear a woman screaming like that when she comes, I can't help but get turned on." Glancing at his other brothers, he asked, "Are you honestly telling me you didn't get hard-ons while listening to that?"

"I'd be lying if I said I didn't," David answered. "It did sound pretty hot, Caden. No offense to Rory. I'm jealous."

David wasn't smiling, and Caden knew his brother wasn't teasing. David *was* jealous and Caden hated that the man didn't have what he wanted, the relationship that Caden and Rory had. He relaxed and nodded to first David, then Sawyer.

"I *am* going to marry Rory," Caden announced, as thunder rumbled in the distance. "She says you've all agreed to move out here with us. No matter what goes down with Elias, I don't want to lose my brothers. Even if you decide to go to other places, I want you to think of Nostalgia Road as home. We're family."

"We are," David agreed. "A fucked-up family but a close-knit one nonetheless."

There was a light rap on the partially opened door. Dressed in her jeans and t-shirt, Rory stood barefoot with her long, damp, red hair tumbling around her shoulders. Her eyes noted the teeth marks on Caden, and she frowned. He merely grinned, kissed her, and then headed for the bathroom.

A tremendous thunderstorm hit while Caden was in the shower. It continued to rage on throughout the night and well into the next day. Everyone used their time of confinement in order to rest, but they were frustrated by the delay nature was imposing upon them. The longer they waited, the more agitated each of them became.

Finally, the storms passed. By the time Caden, Rory, Beck, Ren, David, and Sawyer reached the Roosevelt family cemetery, it was 5:15 p.m. If there hadn't been four Brody brothers with shovels present, Caden would have wondered whether or not they'd have time to dig up Charles's grave before sunset at 8:30. None of them wanted to work in the dark unless there was no other option now that the ground was saturated and water dripped from the branches of the trees. The sky was cloudy, and he prayed it wouldn't rain again. While Rory, Ren, and Astrid watched, the men began to dig up ground that hadn't been disturbed in seven decades. By 6:40, they'd unearthed a coffin. It was not infant-sized.

Caden looked between Rory, Ren, and Astrid and said, "I hope the diaries are in here, but there's a chance that Charles Roosevelt is really inside. I know it's an adult-sized coffin, but the family could've buried the baby in it because they had nothing else available. If you don't want to look –"

"I don't, but I think I have to," Rory interrupted.

"Me, too," added Ren. "My heart's racing a mile a minute."

Astrid surprised Caden by turning her back. Perhaps it was because she'd been pregnant at the time of her death. Perhaps she was simply squeamish. It didn't matter to him. At least he'd given all of them fair warning.

David dropped down into the grave, holding the crowbar he'd lifted from their pile of tools. His large muscles bunched with his efforts, but it didn't take him long to pry up the lid to the coffin. Moving around, he pushed the piece of wood away from the box.

"Holy shit!" Sawyer cried. "How many do you think there are?"

Astrid whirled around and peered down into the open grave along with the rest of them. She gasped, as did Rory and Ren. Inside the coffin were at least a dozen metal boxes. Caden assumed that these held the missing Roosevelt diaries.

There was a loud rumble of thunder, and Beck directed, "Let's haul the boxes out and put them in Caden's SUV before it starts pouring again. We'll open them when we get back to the house."

"We should fill in the hole before the storm hits if we can," David remarked, adding, "At least as much of it as possible."

"I agree," Caden said, as they began to remove the boxes from the grave.

"Once the SUV is loaded, then I'll drive it back to the house," Rory said. "We women can carry in the diaries while you fill in the hole."

Caden paused, wanting to argue. The boxes were heavy, possibly too heavy for Rory and Ren to carry. However, they were grown women and could decide what they were physically capable of once they arrived back at the main house.

"One of us will come back for you," Ren declared once all the boxes had been stowed in the back of the SUV.

"Don't open those until we're all together!" Beck ordered. "We don't know what to expect."

"Aye, aye, Sir!" Ren said sarcastically. Then, "You really need to get a grip."

Beck tensed visibly but didn't respond. Instead, he focused all of his attention on shoveling wet earth back into the gaping hole in the ground. Once the three women had left in the SUV, Sawyer said, "You want Ren, don't you?"

"It doesn't matter what I want," Beck replied without raising his head. "It's never mattered."

"Well, it should," David volunteered. "We have to stick together, but we also need to be our own men, Beck."

"We are our own men," he countered. "We're independent and formidable."

"And alone," Caden said, dumping another shovelful of dirt into the hole. "We've always been so isolated. I'm ending my self-imposed exile. You should try to do the same."

When Beck said nothing, his younger brothers remained silent. By the time raindrops began to fall, Ren was back and the hole was as filled as it could be. They would have to get more dirt in order for the ground to be level once more.

"We got all of the boxes inside," Ren told them, as she drove back through what was now a downpour toward the main house. "Rory had a dolly, and we loaded them onto it and made several trips. Getting them up the porch steps was tricky, but we managed."

"Not counting Thorn, there are six of us who can start going through the diaries," Caden said. "We can each take one box to start. I counted fourteen. As we go through the diaries, we can put them in order by year along Rory's dining room table. It'll be easier to refer back to them if we do that."

Beck agreed and then said, "We need to discuss what we're specifically looking for before we start reading. I know we might come across something we never expected that will answer all our questions, but we should approach our search with some sort of plan in mind."

The men left their muddy footwear on the porch, followed Ren into the house, and automatically headed toward the formal dining room. Rory stepped out in front of them and said "Oh, no you don't!"

"What?!?" Beck snapped. "We need to get started!"

"You're muddy, sweaty, and soaked because of the rain," she pointed out. "We're getting ready to review diaries that are old and may be in fragile condition. We all need to be clean at the start so that we don't mess them up. They might already be in bad shape if they've deteriorated or been damaged by time and the conditions of the ground."

Beck nodded, appearing irritated that he hadn't thought of those things himself. Caden forced himself not to smile. His older brother liked to be in charge and in control of himself, and he knew it irked Beck to lose either of those advantages. The man was an anchor for his family, but he also hid his emotions far too well for Caden's liking. He worried about what was really going on in Beck's head.

"We'll get cleaned up and check on Thorn," Caden told Rory, as the men headed for the stairs. "Then, we'll get to work."

"When I checked on Thorn before you got back, he asked me to help him sit up. I think he's working on breaking that code for the folder about your actual origins. He said there wasn't any time to waste, and I suppose he's right. But he should be resting."

Caden nodded and said, "I'll get him to rest for a while."

"While you guys clean up, I'll make dinner," Rory told them. "We should eat before we start. I have a feeling we won't want to stop once we get going with the diaries, if that's actually what's in the boxes."

"Me, too. I think it's going to be a very long night."

23 Rory

"This is an awesome find," Sawyer muttered before taking another sip of coffee. "Fucking amazing."

"Freakin' amazing and totally overwhelming," said David. "There's so much here."

Rory scanned the table then looked down at the list she'd compiled on her iPad before saying, "All the metal boxes are empty, and we've got everything sorted beginning with the diary we found from 1900 up through fifty years ago."

"Now, all we have to do is read through each one," Caden noted. "That should only take us a few days, right?"

Rory nodded tiredly. She wished that she liked coffee; she could have used the caffeine. The stress of the past few days was catching up to her, as was her grief for her brother. She was exhausted, and they hadn't even begun the "real" work, yet. However, when Caden suggested that she sleep for a while, Rory declined, stating that there was no way she could rest again until they knew what was in the diaries.

"I wonder why there was none before 1900," Ren mused. "The Roosevelts have been on this property a lot longer than that, and I thought you said your father told you all of the caretakers in your family kept diaries."

"The house that used to stand on this spot burned down in 1900. That's when this place was constructed. Odds are that the other diaries were destroyed in the fire although it sounded like Dad thought they still existed somewhere."

"If we don't find our answers in these, then we'll attempt to figure out where the other diaries might be," Beck offered. "I don't relish the thought of digging up more graves or going on the hunt for the proverbial needle in the haystack."

"Don't put the cart before the horse," Caden said. "Practically, how should we tackle this?"

"We should start from the beginning," Rory suggested. "Each of us takes one diary and reads through it before moving on to the next available one. Take note of anything out of the ordinary."

"Why not simply find the ones that include the year Charles and Ike were born?" Sawyer asked. "Someone could be reading those while the others are reading the earlier diaries."

"There may be some clues in the earlier journals about an evil to come and what exactly it is," Rory pointed out. "If we jump ahead, then we might miss something vital."

"Rory's suggestion is the most logical," Beck said with what sounded like approval. "We have to be methodical. If all of these involve mundane notations, then it shouldn't take us long. If the authors wrote about serious issues, then it may take us quite a while but will be worth the time spent."

Sawyer grumbled but agreed. Each of them reached for a diary and prepared to begin.

"What do *I* do?" Astrid asked with irritation. "I can't just hang around while all of you read and take notes. I have to be *doing* something!"

"You can do something very important," Rory said. "You can patrol the grounds."

"Busywork!" the ghost huffed.

"Not at all," Rory contradicted. "If Elias and Dominic are planning some sort of attack, they could be anywhere on the property. There's a lot of it. I don't expect you to move around the entire area that belongs to me. It's huge, and you wouldn't know where the property lines are. But if you roam the grounds surrounding the five houses, barn, and outbuilding as well as the lake, then you could alert us to the presence of anything out of the ordinary. It might save our lives."

As Rory had expected, Astrid immediately warmed to the idea. She proudly lifted her chin and said, "I'll make certain everything is secure around the main area and within the buildings. I'll let you know right away if I see anything suspicious."

"Thank you," Caden said with sincerity. "That will be a big help."

Once the ghost had left the house, Sawyer asked, "I'm not saying what you suggested is a bad idea, but why are you worrying about the woman's sense of importance?"

"Because she may be dead, but she's still here and came to me for help," Rory answered. "At first, I was annoyed with her because she acted like the snotty bully she'd always been since childhood. Then, I started to see another side of her."

"That must have been the side Anderson saw," David remarked. "Our youngest brother didn't go for shallow, bitchy partners. He liked smart people who had a good sense of humor, although, to my knowledge, he'd never actually been seriously involved with anyone."

"None of us had been seriously involved with anyone until Anderson and now Caden," Beck said. "Elias forbade it."

Rory saw Caden and David exchange glances but pretended not to notice. Instead, she suggested they get started in earnest on their reading. The four men and two women each took a diary and settled into various locations on the first floor with their tablets in order to take notes if need be. Rory and Caden sat side-by-side on the couch, their knees touching.

Rory had barely begun to read when she sat up straight and called out, "Everyone, come in here! Hurry!"

Caden asked her what was wrong, as the others rushed into the room.

"You know I have the first diary, and…oh, my God. I think everyone should hear this before we continue. Thorn should probably listen in, too."

"I'll carry him downstairs," David offered. "If you two will clear off the couch, I'll put him there."

Rory sat in one of the stuffed chairs next to the couch where Thorn was soon deposited. Everyone in the room was tense and expectant. Rory cleared her throat and then began to read from the first page of the diary.

"My name is Hugh Roosevelt. My family came to America from Ireland, changing their surname from Brody to Roosevelt in order to escape persecution. Our bloodline had once been honored by all who knew of us because of our unusual abilities, but many eventually became jealous of both our wealth and our talents. We have treasured the items we brought with us from our ancestral home and have kept records of our family's lineage and lore. It is with a heavy heart that I inform the reader that the home which housed most of those things has recently burned to the ground after a fire accidentally started in the kitchen. We were able to save some items and will work to recreate the family tree and other lost records, but much was irreplaceable. All of the journals kept by me and my predecessors were destroyed.

"More troubling than the loss of said items and papers pertaining to our history is my knowledge that a great evil is coming, and it will stem from our own line. The Brodys – or, as we have been called for over a century, the Roosevelts – have ever been the protectors of good and destroyers of evil. My own young son, Edmund, is but a babe. I, who have the gift of foretelling, can see that he will not marry until he is well into his fortieth year. His bride will be a young woman of good standing, and she will bear him twin sons. However, one will be a reflection of all that has been in our bloodline for as long as anyone can recall, while the other will be as if spawned from the loins of Satan himself.

"How I will despise having to someday tell Edmund of this, but he must know. If both twins are kept within the family, then the evil son will destroy not only his parents and brother but also many others. He will strive to open the gateway to Hell in order to attempt to gain great power instead of utilizing the abilities he has for the sake of goodness.

"How my son will be able to tell which of his children is virtuous and which is consumed by evil, I do not know. Perhaps if the one twin is sent away, then the destructive course of events will be altered. I pray for this, but I do not know if it is possible. If the evil twin is not stopped, he could upset the elemental balance in this part of the world.

"Every area of Earth has portals, gateways that remain sealed as a result of protection of the elements that must be kept in balance. The portals may be circular or in the shape of a pentacle, a five-pointed star. The portal protected by the Brodys in Ireland was circular, but the one here in the United States of America is in the shape of a pentacle. The elements comprising the pentacle are, clockwise and beginning at the top point, spirit, water, fire, earth, and air. Here on the property our family procured so long ago, we built dwellings on each point of the pentacle in order to safeguard the five elements. The pathways between the elements must be kept clear in order to maintain the strength of the barrier that keeps the ultimate evil out of this realm.

"I pray for my son and both of the sons he will father. I pray for their children, for I sense that six descendants, some of our blood and some not but all Brody, shall be forced to defeat the evil twin if his path does not alter. Beyond this conflict, I cannot see. The six will be charged with ending the life of this evil seed that will manage to corrupt the goodness of our lineage. May God bless them and protect them."

Rory lowered the diary into her lap and said, "Six descendants, some of our blood and some not but all Brody. The five remaining adopted Brody brothers and me."

"Destined to stop the ultimate evil from entering our realm," Caden added grimly.

"Maybe it was a blessing that all of the previous diaries were destroyed in that fire," Thorn said. "Otherwise, we wouldn't have gotten such a succinct summary from Hugh Roosevelt regarding the past, what was going to happen, and what our roles will be when it does."

"We still don't know how we're supposed to stop Elias," Sawyer said. "Let's skim through the other diaries we pulled and see if we can get to the births of Charles and Ike."

"In light of what we just heard Rory read, I think that's wise," Beck remarked. "Thorn, do you want to go back upstairs?"

"I'd rather be here, helping you guys," Thorn answered. "I'm pretty much in the same position as when I was in bed, so I'm as comfortable as I'll get for the time being."

"Sounds good," Caden said. "Rory?" When she didn't respond right away, he repeated, "Rory?"

She looked up at him and said, "Light bulb moment."

"What?"

"I just had a light bulb moment. There are five points on a pentacle. Each point corresponds to an element: spirit, water, fire, earth, and air. The pentacle is protecting the gateway in the center."

"Yes. That's what your great-great-grandfather wrote."

"There are five of you who can all see ghosts and who are sworn to fight evil." Pointing to Caden, she said, "You're the spirit of the family and can sense others with supernatural abilities. Therefore, you are Spirit and belong here in the house at the top of the pentacle." Turning toward Sawyer, she said, "I think you're Water, because you have the gift of sight or soaring...however you put it...which actually goes along with qualities associated with that element, believe it or not. Your point would be Mockingbird

Hideaway, the cottage where Caden's been staying." Facing Beck, she continued, "You have pyrokinetic abilities, so you're obviously Fire. Your point would be Orange Blossom Retreat."

She heard Caden snicker and gave a small smile herself, thinking of the no-nonsense Beck in the midst of the most feminine décor of all the cottages. When Caden explained this to the others, David and Sawyer laughed, and Thorn grinned madly, evidently trying not to laugh because of his broken ribs. Beck did not look amused at all.

Once the laughter had subsided, Rory went on, "David, because of your ability to shapeshift at will into a German shepherd, you're probably more closely linked to the world and are Earth. You'd be in Hurricane House." Sitting on the edge of the couch beside Thorn, she finished by saying, "Because you're able to teleport, you're Air. Your position would be at Palmetto House."

"And you?" Caden asked. "You're the only one of the six of us who is a Brody by blood. Where do you fit in?"

"I'm the caretaker, remember? It's my responsibility to make sure the elements remain in balance so that the portal can stay closed. I suppose that puts me in the center. Physically, that's the location of the barn."

"So, the gate that's holding back this awful evil is under a barn," Ren observed. "What do you think Elias will do to get this portal to open?"

"We have no idea, which is why we need to continue reading these diaries," Beck answered. "Maybe one of them will tell us what he's planning and how to stop him."

"I still want to know what happened regarding baby Charles and then adult Ike's death," Rory admitted. "I hope the diaries don't leave us hanging."

They returned to their reading. It was 3:00 a.m. by the time Caden picked up the diary that he soon discovered held the story of the twins' birth. The others gathered around him, much as they'd gathered around Rory earlier that night.

"My darling wife has given birth to two healthy sons, whom I've named Charles and Ike," Caden read from one of Edmund's diaries. "I know of my father's warning to me about my sons, but I can't imagine either of our handsome and innocent newborns containing such evil. My wife and I still have concerns but hope and pray that my father's vision has somehow been deflected and that both of our boys will grow here fine and strong." Pausing, Caden read to himself for a moment then said with a heavy sigh, "Here it is. Damn."

"What?" the others asked in unison.

"This part is dated when the babies were eleven months old. Edmund hadn't recorded anything for a month before this entry revealing Charles's evil nature."

"How can an eleven-month-old have an evil nature?" Rory asked.

Caden read, "My heart is heavy. My wife and I have noticed in the last month the preternatural look in Charles's eyes and the way he tries to harm others. Even at such a young age, he appears to intentionally try to hurt me, his mother, and Ike by hitting and biting with malice. Things have also begun to levitate and to be flung about when he's in a foul mood, which is most of the time. His mother was severely injured last night when a scissors flew across the room at her after she didn't immediately go to Charles as he began to fuss because she was feeding Ike. The scissors barely missed Ike's head and lodged in my wife's shoulder. We know now that my father was right. When the trouble started, I began to investigate options for placement of Charles with a couple who had no children and were trained in containing those born with such evil in them. Through my efforts, I've located such a man and woman in New Orleans. They've made it their mission to handle raising such children until they become adults in the hope that they can teach them to purge the evil from their souls. My wife and I can't keep Charles any longer. If we do, then we risk our lives and Ike's. I cry for the loss of one son but am grateful for the well-being of the other and their mother."

"Man," David muttered. "Can you imagine an infant actively attacking his family and knowing your choices would be to locate a suitable home for him, find some unsuspecting family and leave him with them, or kill him?"

Rory tried not to think about this as she asked Caden, "Does Edmund talk about the couple? What about after Charles's departure?"

Caden scanned a few pages before going on, "My wife and I are inconsolable, but we know we had no choice but to surrender

Charles to the couple from New Orleans. They instructed us to tell our friends and neighbors that Charles died suddenly and is buried in the family cemetery. They suggested we put up a marker and think of him as deceased. We'll follow their advice, for we love him despite his innate evil. He's our son, and he didn't ask to be born with this curse. We pray that his new parents will be able to purge him of whatever's corrupting his soul. Perhaps if they do, then they'll tell him of us and he can one day come home. Until that day comes – *if* it comes – all we'll know of our lost son is that his new name is to be Elias."

No one spoke for a long time. Finally, Caden said, "Well, at least now we know."

"We know this part, but there's still so much more we *don't* know," Rory said. "Is there anything else noteworthy in that diary?"

Caden skimmed the remainder of the journal but eventually said, "No. All Edmund talks about is his wonderful son, Ike. Ike was athletic and intelligent, according to his father. He wanted to farm the Roosevelt land and make it more prosperous. He seemed to like being outdoors a lot. He married his childhood sweetheart when they were both eighteen. The diary ends shortly after their marriage."

"When Edmund died," Rory commented. "I remember the family tree. His wife died when my grandfather was sixteen, and Edmund died when Ike was eighteen."

"So, the next diary should be Ike's," Ren said excitedly. "I wonder if he knew anything about what really happened to his brother."

"Who wants to tackle that one?" Sawyer asked.

"Rory should," Beck replied. "It's the last journal. It's her grandfather. It's her right."

Rory smiled at Beck and said, "Thank you."

The man didn't answer, merely wordlessly handing her the final diary. She opened the cover and began to read. No one moved or spoke. After a few minutes, Rory said, "Life was good. Ike loved his young bride, and he dreamed of having a hugely successful strawberry farm. The only problem seemed to be that they wanted children but weren't having any luck getting pregnant, no matter how hard they tried." Blushing, she added, "And they seemed to be trying every spare moment they got."

Caden grinned, leaning forward to kiss her before whispering, "You know what it does to me when you blush like that."

She giggled, nudging his shoulder with hers before saying, "You're going to make me blush even more. Just let me finish the last few pages so that we can all get some sleep."

"Caden, stop distracting her!" Beck snapped.

"I'm thirty years old, Beck. You're my older brother, not my boss. I know this is serious, but we're all tired and need some sort of break after the last couple days."

"He's right, Beck," David put in. "We've got to lighten the mood here and there or else we'll be too tightly wound to do anything at optimal levels."

Beck looked away but didn't argue. Rory returned to reading. Her eyes widened after several minutes, and Caden stiffened, asking what was the matter.

"Ike's wife wrote in his diary after he died. Supposedly, she, um, got pregnant by sleeping with Ike's ghost in the week *following* his death."

24 Caden

Rory held out the diary to Caden, saying, "Everyone should hear what my grandmother wrote word for word, but I don't think I can read it aloud."

Nodding, Caden took the journal from her and read, "My Ike is gone. He was killed two days ago in an accident here on the property. I don't know what I'll do now. I've been crying nonstop since it happened. He's dead and buried. I'm so alone, and I have no idea how I'm going to protect the elements that Ike was destined to safeguard. We never had a baby, so what happens to the portal now?" Reading forward a few pages, Caden frowned and continued, "My Ike appeared to me tonight. I know he said ghosts looked like regular people but had evidence of injury if they died in an accident. Perhaps it's because I wasn't born with the ability to see ghosts that I saw and felt Ike as if he were a real man with physical form. I don't know how he managed to come to me. He had no signs of injury, not even the scar on his left arm from where he cut it last year while he was fixing the fence. He didn't speak, but he came to me after I'd gone to bed. Oh, the night we had together! He was wild with passion for me and did all sorts of things he'd never done when he was alive. It felt almost sinful, and he was so powerful. I lost track of how many times we made love. After the last time but before he disappeared, he placed a hand on my belly. I *knew* he meant there'd be a baby now. I cried after he was gone, but I'm so grateful that he returned to me one last time and left me with this precious gift, our child."

"Holy shit," Sawyer whispered. "Elias."

Rory nodded slowly and said, "He must have come back here, killed his twin, and then pretended to be his ghost in order to get my grandmother pregnant. That would have been the ultimate revenge for having been disowned. Everyone would have assumed Ike got his wife pregnant right before he was killed." Looking frightened, Rory murmured, "Elias is my grandfather. Oh, God."

"You don't know that," Caden responded. "Ike *could* have gotten his wife pregnant right before his death, and she just didn't know it, yet. They were obviously having sex often while they were trying for a baby. Maybe she conceived just before Elias killed her husband."

"But what about the night she spent with Elias and his touching her belly?"

"He could have somehow sensed she was already pregnant," Beck said. "Who knows what he's capable of when it comes to his supernatural abilities? He might simply have enjoyed knowing he was sleeping with his murdered brother's pregnant wife."

"But wouldn't he kill her afterwards?" Ren asked. "Why not just end it there?"

"Maybe he needed the baby she was carrying in order to someday move his plans forward," Thorn speculated. "He'd let it live then watch and wait."

"Biding his time until your father procreated," Caden bit out. "I think Elias was waiting for you and Nolan, Rory."

"But what if he really *is* my grandfather?" Rory persisted. "He's evil." Looking to Caden, she said, "What if I'm carrying some evil in me and have evil babies?"

Caden took her face in his hands and said, "Charles – Elias – is the only evil person noted in your family's history. For whatever reason, he was cursed. That doesn't mean that his curse will carry on to his descendants, if he actually had any."

She didn't appear convinced, and Caden worried that she would now and in the future wonder if their children would be destined to endure the same fate as Charles. If she suspected that, then he doubted they would ever have a family. She wouldn't take the risk. He honestly wondered whether he would be willing to risk such a thing.

"Once we have this final showdown with Elias, then we'll find a way to get him to admit whether or not he knows if your grandmother was already pregnant when he slept with her. If she was, then it might put our minds at ease." When Rory continued to look skeptical, he added, "Your father wasn't evil; Nolan wasn't evil; and you're not evil. Try not to dwell on this, okay?"

"We all need sleep," Beck observed. "Most of us haven't gotten much real rest for a couple days. Unless Astrid sounds the alarm, let's crash for a few hours. Then, we can figure out what our next step will be."

"I need to call the hospital first and check on Harvey again," Rory said. "Then, I'll call Dorothea and ask if they've found Nolan."

While Rory made her calls, Thorn was carried back up to the guest room bed. Ren, who'd been assigned to sleep in Rory's parents' former bedroom, returned to it, while David opted to sleep in Nolan's room. Beck stretched out on the couch, and Sawyer chose to push back in a faded recliner in one corner of the living room. Caden climbed the stairs and then removed his clothing, lying down in Rory's bed to wait for her to finish making her calls in her home office.

The muffled sound of her voice as she spoke on the phone soothed Caden, and he soon drifted off to sleep. He dreamed of himself, his brothers, Ren, and women he didn't know sitting at a long picnic table near the lake behind the Roosevelt home. Children played and laughed in the yard and lake, and Rory sat beside him. She was blushing as she nursed a baby despite the fact that a lightweight blanket covered her exposed breast. He leaned forward, kissed her, and then lifted the blanket just enough for him to see the red-haired infant, who sucked contentedly on his mother's nipple.

Caden woke slowly. He felt both relaxed and aroused. He turned toward Rory's side of the bed to see if she was awake. Longing to tell her about his dream, Caden was disappointed to find that she wasn't there. He glanced at the clock: 10:03 p.m.

The house sounds quiet. We were all so exhausted, but I'm surprised we slept the rest of the day away.

Returning to his back, Caden stared at the ceiling, recalling the dream. There was a fair amount of children in it, some redheads, some brunettes, some blondes, and at least two with black hair and Asian features. The adults and children alike had been relaxed, happy, and...home.

My version of Heaven, I guess.

He stretched then rose and dressed. After checking Rory's home office and finding it empty, he left the bedroom and checked the library. It was also deserted, so Caden moved on to the guest room. When he opened the door, Thorn's eyelids fluttered open and he asked for the time. Caden began to tell him but stopped short when his youngest brother sat up, effortlessly swinging his legs over the side of the mattress. Thorn looked as surprised as Caden felt.

"There's no pain," the younger man explained with a look of incredulity on his face. "I feel fine."

With a half-shrug, Caden suggested, "Maybe if you teleport someone who's hurt, you take on their injuries but only for a limited time. That's the only plausible thing I can think of."

"Seems like a good explanation to me. Where's Rory? And what time is it anyway?"

"A little after 10:00, and I'm not sure. She was on the phone when I fell asleep, and she wasn't in bed when I woke up. Maybe she's downstairs cooking or baking. She likes to do those things."

"Yeah, she made us some fantastic baked spaghetti while you were gone."

"I guess I'll have to request that she make it again so that I can have a taste."

"She saved you some. She said you could have it when you got back." Standing and stretching, Thorn said, "She's amazing, Caden. She's stronger than she looks."

"Damn straight. Come on. Let's get the others up, find Rory, eat, and work on that plan to stop Elias."

Caden and Thorn next woke David, who was thrilled by Thorn's recovery but, like his brothers, was uneasy regarding the length of time they'd all slept. After waking Ren, who excused herself to make a quick trip to the bathroom, the three men went downstairs and woke Beck and Sawyer. Caden was becoming more and more alarmed. They still hadn't located Rory.

"Rory?" he called out. "Rory, are you in the house?"

He was answered by silence. Everyone present fanned out through the first floor to see if they could locate Rory. Sawyer went to the parking area but returned with the news that her car was in its usual spot. They all went out through the back door, and Caden cupped his hands around his mouth and cried, "Rory!" as loudly as he could. His voice echoed in the night air.

"Astrid!" Beck called out. "Astrid, are you there?"

The ghost didn't reply nor did she appear.

"Maybe she's patrolling further out," Ren offered.

"Maybe, but what about Rory?" Thorn asked. "She wouldn't leave the house without telling someone where she was going."

"She wouldn't leave the house alone right now, period," Caden said grimly. Looking to Beck, he proposed, "It has to be Elias. He must have used magic."

"That's what I'm thinking. I can't believe we all slept without stirring for so many hours. It's highly improbable. Plus, if Astrid's disappeared as well as Rory, then Elias must have figured out a way to restrain her somehow. Otherwise, Astrid would have come to rouse us and explain what was going on."

"How would one restrain a ghost?" Sawyer asked curiously. "I've never heard of that."

"Me neither," Beck admitted. "That doesn't mean Elias can't do it. We have to stop him."

"Goddamn him!" Caden growled. "How are we going to locate Rory and Astrid?"

"I say we check the barn first and then hit all of the other buildings," David suggested. "If they're not in any of those places, then we can determine our next step." Once they'd all agreed to his proposal, David said, "Ren, I need to shift into canine form. No one outside the family has ever seen me do it before. It might freak you out. If you want to turn away, then I won't be offended."

"Are you kidding me?" Ren asked. "It was unbelievable watching Thorn just plain disappear when he teleported to Caden. I'd love to see *all* of the Brody brothers in action. I've spent my entire life thinking I was the only person in the area with any supernatural talents, and now I find out there are so many others around me who have their own gifts. It makes me want to cry!"

Ren's voice quavered with her last few words, and Caden wondered if she would, indeed, cry. However, she quickly regained her composure and thanked David for allowing her to watch his transformation.

Grinning, David said, "Just remember that you asked for it. You're about to get quite a show."

"What do you mean?"

"If I have advanced warning, then I strip before I shift. That way, I have clothing waiting for me to come back to and don't have to spend as much on my wardrobe. I also don't have to fight to untangle my canine self from clothes or shoes." Raising an eyebrow at her, David asked, "You *have* seen a naked man before, right?"

Caden's temper flared. He almost launched himself at his brother. Rory and Astrid were missing, and David was wasting time coddling Ren. The man must have sensed Caden's anger, because he said, "Chill, Caden. She's the adopted daughter of missionaries. I don't want to offend her. She's been a trouper during our time with her."

"Thank you," Ren said. Then, she added, "You won't offend me. I have actually seen a naked man once or twice. I'm twenty-eight, after all. I *will* tell you that I've never seen a naked *black* man before...."

"Enough talk!" Beck snapped. "David, strip and shift. We're wasting precious time."

Caden was in total agreement but sensed a hint of jealousy and anger in Beck's tone. He wondered if his older brother was actually attracted to Ren. He also wondered whether or not Beck would act upon his feelings if that were the case.

David removed his shoes and clothes and placed them on the porch. Caden admired his brother's raw power, as his huge muscles visibly worked in tandem while he strode out into the yard and knelt on the ground. While the others watched in the illumination cast by the porch light and the glow of the moon, his dark skin appeared to expand and contract for a few seconds. David's body became a blur. Moments later, a handsome dark German shepherd stood in his place. The canine glanced at Caden, dipped his muzzle, and then sniffed the air.

To Caden's dismay, David didn't take off running. They all headed for the barn. It was only once they'd arrived there that they realized they hadn't brought the key for the lock. Thorn teleported to the house then reappeared a few minutes later with Rory's keys. In a matter of seconds, the lock was off and the doors were parted. Ren found the switch that turned on the lights, and the barn was instantly illuminated.

"Looks like the inside of a barn to me," Sawyer muttered. "Riding mower, tools, generators, odds and ends...."

"David, sniff around here while I check out the loft," Caden directed. Once he'd confirmed that nothing unusual was in the upper area of the structure, he returned to ground level and asked the dog, "Well?"

David pawed at the dirt in the center of the barn. When Beck asked him if he smelled Elias or Rory on that spot, the German shepherd moved his head back and forth to indicate that he hadn't. However, he pawed at the spot again.

"It must *feel* different to him," Beck offered.

"The portal," Thorn added excitedly.

"Now we know where it is, but where are Rory and Astrid?" Caden asked. "Where are Elias and Dominic?"

David trotted out of the barn and began to explore the property. The others stayed close behind him, scanning their surroundings but seeing nothing out of place.

"Why didn't you bring any weapons with you?" Ren asked.

"I have a gun tucked at the small of my back in the waist of my pants," Beck told her. "If you recall, I also have the power of pyrokinesis, so I'm always packing heat."

Ren laughed, and Beck's lips twitched.

"Did you actually just crack a joke?" Sawyer asked. "We need to write this on the calendar." Shaking his head in amusement, he added, "I have a knife in a sheath on the side of one boot."

"And I have a gun strapped to my lower left leg," Caden told her.

"I didn't bring any," Thorn confided to Ren. "If I need anything, then I can teleport back to the house to get my weapons. As long as inanimate objects are in my pockets, strapped to me, or held in my hands, then I can teleport them wherever I need. As you know, up until yesterday I couldn't teleport living beings with me." Darting a glance at David, he said, "I wonder what would happen if I teleported you in your canine form. Would I become a German shepherd?"

Somehow, the dog managed to convey the dubiousness he must have been feeling. Thorn smiled and said, "It would be great if I could take on the talents of those I teleport and not only absorb their injuries."

"Maybe someday," Ren said encouragingly.

The six of them went from cottage to cottage and checked the outbuilding where Rory kept the gasoline locked up. There was still no sign of her, Astrid, Elias, or Dominic. They walked back to the main house, and David shifted into his human form and then dressed.

"That spot in the barn is definitely the portal," he said, as he buckled his belt. "It has the weirdest energy vibe I've ever felt. A human wouldn't be able to detect it, but I damn sure could."

"So, our mission is two-fold," Beck said. "First, locate Rory. Second, find, interrogate, if possible, and then kill Elias. That will ensure the safety of the gateway."

"I don't think just killing Elias is going to ensure anything," Caden said.

"What do you mean?"

"The portal needs protecting. One of us residing at each point to stake our claim, if you will."

"And what happens when we die someday?"

Caden forced a smile. He had to believe that Rory was still alive and that they all had a future together at Nostalgia Road. If he didn't hold onto that thought, then he was going to lose his mind and, therefore, be ineffectual in the fight against their adoptive father.

"Our kids will protect the points one day," he said. "We're going to live here, love here, and love life here."

"You now have the gift of prophecy?" Sawyer teased.

"Maybe I do," he answered thoughtfully. "Or maybe it's only that I want it so badly that it's the future I see for us. But I do see it, and I do think it can be our reality. The Brodys of Ireland settled in this location in order to safeguard this part of the world. They changed their name to Roosevelt in an attempt to protect themselves. When all this is done, Nostalgia Road will belong to the Brodys again."

"Some by birth and some not," Thorn offered. "We may not have Brody blood in our veins, but I think we've more than earned our place in the Brody line."

"But what'll we do here?" David asked. "This is a rural area."

"I'll have a bar to own and run," Sawyer proclaimed.

"I can work anywhere just as Rory does," Thorn added. "Hm. Maybe she and I could combine our computer talents to form a new company."

"I'm thinking about ranching," Caden confided. "I've always liked horses. That was one reason I chose to have my apartments in places like Texas, Wyoming, and Montana. It allowed me to ride or travel to ranches during any downtime I might have."

Beck shrugged and said, "I'll be damned if I know what I'd do out here, but I'll figure it out. So will you, David. We can always travel and come back, all of us."

"Not me," Caden said. "All I want is a normal life in a normal place."

"Says the killer with supernatural abilities," Ren smirked. "None of you is normal, and you may not like it in Sage. But I think all of this was meant to be. Let's find Rory so that at least she and Caden can get started on their happy future."

Caden didn't mention what he knew all of his brothers were thinking – that none of the Brody brothers would be satisfied until they knew the truth about their origins. That was a conversation best left for another time. If none of them survived, then it would all be a moot point.

"So, how do we find Rory?" David asked. "If I couldn't sniff her out, then could she be held in the same place where Caden was being held?"

"It's a definite possibility," Beck noted. "Thorn, can you teleport there and check?"

"If I knew where 'there' was, then I could. As it is, I have no idea." Eyeing Caden, he suggested, "Why don't we try the link in reverse? Rory linked with you but took me along. Maybe you can link with her and take me with you."

"I don't take on an astral form," Caden pointed out.

"I think it's worth a shot," David remarked. "Maybe your souls will link or something and guide you to her. Thorn can hold your hands like he held Rory's. If you make it, then you allow him to connect with her then break the link. Give it a shot."

Caden and Thorn went to the kitchen and sat facing one another. They clasped hands. Then, they closed their eyes and opened their minds.

25 Rory

"Well, well, well," said an unfamiliar male voice. "I'm glad you're finally awake. I thought perhaps my spell had worked a little too effectively. Actually, it was probably more effective on you than the others because we're related."

Rory opened her eyes and blinked rapidly in an effort to clear her vision. She felt chilled from the inside out. It was an odd sensation. She wondered if it was the result of being the target of a spell. Regardless, she didn't like the feeling.

The room was dark, but a muted circle of light was above her. A tall, fit, older man with gray hair, a gray moustache and short beard, and gray eyes stared down at her. He was wearing what looked to be expensive, dark blue slacks and a bright white dress shirt that had its top two buttons undone. His sleeves were rolled up a few times. Rory knew the man must be Elias Brody. When she realized she was lying on some sort of table or platform and couldn't move, panic seized her.

"What is this?" she asked hoarsely. "Where am I? Why can't I move my arms and legs?"

"You, my great-niece, are in part of an old bomb shelter built by the family of your one-time rapist, Dominic Ambrose. I made some modifications to their construction in order to suit my purposes. I've been waiting for this opportunity since I found out the truth regarding our family. I was seventeen, and I'm now seventy-one. I've had many years to make certain things align so that I get what I want." With a half-shrug, he added, "As for why you can't move, it's because I'm restraining you with my psychokinesis."

"What do you want?"

"Power, of course. I'll use you to open the portal and take control of all of the primal energy that surges forth."

Knowing that she wouldn't like the answer, Rory nonetheless asked, "How will you accomplish that?"

"I understand you want answers. First, we must be properly introduced." Brushing a lock of red hair away from her face, he said, "I'm your great-uncle. You may know of me as Charles and as

Elias. I'm certain you and my adopted sons have been working on piecing together the puzzle of our family's destiny."

"You said I'm your great-niece. So, you didn't get Ike's wife pregnant?" she asked hopefully. "We figured out that you came to her disguised as Ike's ghost after his murder."

Elias scowled and said, "It was my intention to impregnate her, but I found I was a fraction too late. If only I'd killed Ike a month earlier, then your grandmother would have conceived *my* child. Such is life. I made the most of my night with Ike's sweet young bride and gave her some of the best sex she'd ever had. I gained the satisfaction of knowing that I'd killed Ike and brought his woman more passion than she'd ever experienced with him even though they truly loved each other."

Rory heaved a mental sigh of relief. Her father had been Ike's son, not Charles's. He hadn't carried the seed of evil and passed it on to her and Nolan. She and Caden could still have babies someday, assuming they survived whatever Elias Brody had planned for them.

"What do you want to be called?" she asked. "Charles or Elias?"

"Charles died in infancy, didn't he?" the man asked sardonically. "The day my parents sent me away, I became Elias and have remained Elias. The only thing I changed after I murdered my adoptive parents once they told me the truth was to begin using our family's rightful surname of Brody."

"Please, let me up," Rory said, trying hard not to sound as helpless as she felt. "I'm stiff. I have no superpowers that could hurt you. At least let me stretch."

Elias considered her words for a few moments, and then her invisible restraints vanished. Rory sat up slowly, fighting conflicting urges to scramble away from the man, to hit at him, and to run in search of a way out of her confinement. Her pulse rate and breathing were becoming more rapid, and she couldn't seem to slow either.

I have to stay calm and keep him talking. I have to get him to explain as much as I can until Caden and the others rescue me.

"Nolan told Caden that Dominic is a ghost who's working with you."

"*For* me!" Elias corrected. "I knew he'd be a valuable asset to me from the first time I saw him. I promised him greatness someday

214

in exchange for his…assistance with my plans. Of course, he didn't realize he'd have to die first, but that's life." He smiled and said, "Ah, you got the joke. Dominic himself didn't when I initially told it to him."

"When did you first see Dominic?" Rory asked tightly.

"Hm. I believe he was fourteen. He was a smug punk even then."

"How could you have seen him when he was fourteen?"

"Because, my great-niece, I'd periodically drop by this rural area to check on your father after he was born. I continued to do so after you and Nolan came along. I knew one of you would hold the key to my success."

"When did you approach Dominic about helping you?"

"When the two of you were seventeen. I didn't tell him I was related to you, of course. I merely said that I was a very wealthy and powerful man who could help him attain greatness someday. Being narcissistic, he thought I was a talent scout for a professional football team. I promoted that misconception and told him I'd guide him toward the fulfillment of his destiny. And I did."

"How?" she asked, her voice barely a whisper.

"I met with him once a month. His parents were absorbed in their own lives and paid little attention to him. Dominic longed for a strong male role model, so I provided him with one. I gave him an allowance and offered him advice."

Rory felt her stomach drop. Somehow, she instantly knew that Elias had orchestrated her rape. What she didn't know was why he'd done it. She could think of no logical reason.

As if reading her thoughts, Elias continued, "I was the one who suggested Dominic take the prettiest bookworm in his school on a picnic lunch date. He'd been lusting after you for a long time, but he didn't want to sully his reputation as a jock and a stud by going to lunch with a girl who was beautiful but wasn't in his social circle. You were very innocent and chaste, not his usual type at all. I told him a picnic would give him privacy to get what he wanted without parading you around your small community. I intuited what he would do with you in a remote location whether you protested or not."

"You set up my rape," Rory said flatly. "Why?"

Elias smiled darkly and said, "To get your virgin blood, of course. I needed it in order to proceed."

"My virgin *blood*?!?" Rory cried. "We're not living in The Dark Ages!"

"Ah, but that's where our supernatural roots lie," Elias responded calmly. "Our family has always had the gift of supernatural powers. I've actually traced it back for centuries. The only difference between me and the rest of the family is that our bloodline was dedicated to doing only good. I was always dedicated to doing only what was for my own benefit."

"*Why* did you need my virgin blood?" Rory asked, as tears slid down her cheeks. "You told Dominic to…to bring you some back?" Repulsed, she cried, "That's unconscionable!"

Smiling, Elias said, "I never claimed to have a conscience. And, yes, I told Dominic to prove to me what an able student he was by bringing me back something with your blood on it. I'd expected the picnic blanket but got a pleasant surprise when he returned with not only that but also your pink cotton underwear. I gave him a car for his ingenuity."

"A car," Rory echoed in disbelief. "You engineered the rape of your great-niece who didn't want to have sex before marriage and then gave her rapist a *car* as a reward afterwards because he brought you her bloody panties?"

"Yes."

Attempting not to pass out or throw up, Rory asked, "What did you do with my blood?"

"Used it to cast a spell that confirmed you were the descendant who would allow me to open the portal."

"You're sick!" Rory hissed, wiping futilely at the tears on her cheeks. "You were probably the one who killed Dominic in the first place."

"Smart girl!" Elias said with a grin. "Yes, I needed him in his ghostly form, so I ended his life in that car accident."

Her head spinning, Rory asked, "Why kill my parents? Why leave Nolan alive until yesterday?"

"Once I knew that you were the lynchpin for my operation, I could have killed them all. However, that would have put you in a disadvantageous position. You hadn't even graduated from high school, yet. I waited until you got your bachelor's degree and started your business. Once I knew you could handle staying alone on the family property, I caused the plane crash and eliminated two loose ends in the process."

Rory rushed forward and hit at Elias's chest, as she yelled, "Loose ends? They were our parents! And Nolan was your nephew!"

Despite Elias's age, he was preternaturally strong and had no trouble fending off Rory's blows. He grabbed her by the shoulders and pushed her to the ground then stood, towering over her. She trembled with residual anger, revulsion, and grief.

"Your father had done his job by fathering you, the tool I need in order to get what I want."

"And Nolan?"

"Nolan was a wild card. I considered approaching him as I'd done with Dominic after he did nothing about your rape, but I wasn't quite sure how he'd react to me. He had been close to you and his parents, and I didn't want to make my presence known just then. So, I watched and waited. After I found out he'd threatened you and Caden with the gun, I knew I had to eliminate him. The fool might have inadvertently killed you in his blind rage, and then decades of plotting would have been for nothing."

"Where is Nolan now?"

"The police will be finding his body any minute, if they haven't already."

"And Dominic?"

"Dominic is taking care of some finishing touches for me. Soon, I'll be transporting you to the barn where the portal is. My sons and your half-Asian friend have already searched it and won't suspect I'd bring you there so soon."

"What is Dominic's reward? What could you possibly offer him that would make up for taking his life?"

"Immortality. He may be dead, but I'll have the ability to return his human form to him once I've opened the portal. He'll be my right-hand man. In exchange, he'll have wealth, power, women, and whatever else he wants."

Rory shuddered, asking, "What about your adopted sons? I don't understand. You took them in and trained them. If they survived, then you rewarded them by legally adopting each one.

Why get them to kill evil people in the name of good if you're really evil yourself?"

"Those who survived were loyal and talented. I trained them to kill evil people in order to help me eliminate my competition. I explained that they were doing that work in order to gain vengeance for the victims, and they were. However, my ulterior motive was to thin the herd, if you will. I know there are many more out there who are threats to me, but at least some of the worst offenders have been crossed off my list as well as more mundane murderers."

Rory shivered again and then reminded herself, *I need to stay focused, to keep my eyes on the prize.*

"Were the stories you told your sons about their real families true?" When he didn't answer, she demanded, "Tell me where they came from then. I know you plan to kill me, so what difference does it make if I know?"

"It would take way too much time," Elias told her. "However, I suppose I could give you a summary. Would that suffice?"

"Do I have a choice?" she asked, each word tinged with fury.

Ignoring her anger, Elias said, "The story I told Caden about his parents *was* true. They were honest people with little money who already had six children. The mother went to a *traiteur*, a faith healer, when she began to have problems early in her pregnancy. The *traiteur* did tell her that the baby was fundamentally flawed and might die before birth. She did say that if the boy lived, evil might claim him." With a malevolent gleam in his eyes, Elias said, "And evil did. The woman brought Caden to me shortly after he was born. I knew he would survive my training the moment I held him in my arms."

"Was Caden the name his birthparents gave him?"

"No. I named him Caden. In Welsh, it translates into 'spirit of battle,' and I knew he'd be an excellent fighter. And I was right."

And Spirit is the element he represents, Rory thought. *Coincidence? I doubt it.*

"Why a Welsh name?"

"Because his parents' last name was 'Welsh.' I thought I could honor them in that way since they did unwittingly give me a strong and brave son."

Shaking her head, Rory got unsteadily to her feet and asked, "What about Beck?"

"Ah, my Beck," he murmured. "His mother was a teenaged prostitute working the streets of Tokyo who didn't want to have an abortion, even though she probably had no idea which John had fathered her child. I convinced her pimp to let her continue with the pregnancy. She didn't know I was behind his decision. Actually, the girl didn't know I existed. She thought she would somehow manage to keep her child. However, her pimp took the mixed-raced baby from her as soon as he was delivered and brought him to me."

"You...you bastard!"

"Technically, no. I was born to parents who were legally married." When Rory glared at him, Elias sighed and then said, "I thought you had a good sense of humor." As she remained silent and furious, he said, "Never mind."

"How did you select the boys you wanted to train?"

"I *felt* my sons as they began to develop in utero and targeted them for removal and relocation to my home."

"David?" she asked in a shaky voice.

"His Mississippi mother had eight children by eight different men. Very stereotypical and sad circumstances. I stole David from his crib when he was only a few hours old."

"Sawyer?"

"His mother slept with every man she found appealing in her father's motorcycle club. She was also a junkie. The State of Texas was going to take the baby away anyway, so I simply took him off their caseload a little early."

"And Thorn?"

"Thorn. Hm. Thorn is different. All of my other surviving sons came from homes that were rife with poverty, illegal sex, or drugs and alcohol. Thorn's parents were both computer engineers who worked in Silicon Valley. I knew that obtaining him wouldn't be as easy as it had been with my other sons."

Fearing the answer, Rory asked, "So, how did you get him?"

Elias hesitated, and Rory's gut tightened in anticipation.

"I had no choice but to kidnap his mother just before her due date. I rendered her unconscious then took the baby."

"What do you mean by 'took the baby'?"

Looking calm but somber, Elias said, "You watch the news. You've seen stories about crazed women kidnapping pregnant women to take their babies. I'm sure when they found her body, the police assumed the person responsible was simply another case of a lunatic who'd lost a child or couldn't have one of her own."

Oh, my God. Oh, God. Please, get me out of here. Please, let Caden and the others kill this thing that calls himself a man as soon as possible. Please!

"I told Caden the closest version of the truth about how he came to live with me. The others all thought they were foundlings. They have no idea I targeted their mothers soon after they were conceived. I could always tell if I'd been right about their potential the first time I held them."

"But what about the boys who didn't survive? Why keep them if you knew they wouldn't make it?"

"I had to provide the ones who would with suitable training partners. None of my charges were to form friendships outside of the brotherhood they shared or to become emotionally involved with women. Their lives were to be dedicated to me and to their goal of killing murderers."

"So, you kept the boys you knew wouldn't make it then disposed of them when they'd outlived their usefulness?"

"Basically, yes. I never fostered hatred or cruelty toward those boys. No one except me knew who would survive and who wouldn't. My sons grieved when I killed any boy during training, but I explained that they had to learn to mourn quickly and then let the grief go in order to get their jobs done."

"They were children!"

"I was an *infant* when I was thrown out by my own family."

"Because you were evil."

"True," he replied as though he were passing the time of day with her.

"Did you do something with the boys' blood?" Rory blurted out.

It was a question she'd had on her mind ever since she and Ren had been told of the Brody boys' ritual of cutting themselves and mixing their blood whenever a new brother was adopted. The boys hadn't suspected that Elias had known of this practice, but Rory had. His recent mention of needing her virgin blood had heightened her concerns.

Elias narrowed his slate gray eyes and said, "Very perceptive. You are an extremely bright woman, but I hadn't expected you to make that connection."

"Tell me what you did with their blood," she demanded.

"I used my abilities and knowledge in order to heighten their strengths, which were already impressive. However, I had a feeling that this might also lead to other heightened abilities. I simply wasn't quite certain of what those were. So, I instructed all of my sons to use condoms when they had sex. Partly, I wanted to prevent them from contracting things like HIV or other STDs. Partly, I wanted to prevent them from getting women pregnant since that would definitely lead to emotional attachments. Mainly, I didn't want to chance having them connect with a woman by having unprotected sex, a union that might lead to a physical and psychic bond."

Like the one I now share with Caden.

Elias stepped forward, reaching to lift Rory's chin with his index finger, but she jerked her head to one side, denying him the opportunity. He studied her for a moment before saying, "I understand your hatred of me. I expect it. But I also don't care." When she turned her back to him, Elias said, "I'm going to leave for a while. When I return, we'll be off to the barn. I promise I won't make you suffer long, Rory. I admire your courage. For one so wholesome and innocent, you're quite versatile and resilient."

"You don't have to be hardened or evil to be versatile and resilient," she countered without moving.

"No, but it often helps."

Rory heard an odd swishing noise. When she turned, Elias was no longer in the dimly lit room.

Suddenly, she felt as if she were being literally pulled apart. Stifling a cry, Rory collapsed to the ground. When she looked up, Astrid was crouching beside her.

"Sorry about that," Astrid said with a grin. "I couldn't think of any other way to stay with you except to go *inside* you. I was hoping that devil wouldn't detect me, and he didn't appear to notice. What an evil sicko he is! I'm sure he was happy to kill me and Anderson so that we didn't mess up his big plans."

"Astrid?" Rory gasped. "No *wonder* I was so cold! I've had ghosts pass through me but never stay!"

"It was really weird, almost like playing hide-and-seek and hiding in a dark closet. Actually, it was kind of cool."

"Well, I'm glad you enjoyed the ride," Rory said dryly. She added with a smile, "Thank you. That was quick thinking. You heard everything while you were in there?"

"Yes. I'll go to Caden and tell him everything." The ghost paused, frowned, then said, "I don't know how to get from you to Caden."

"I'm thinking he's going to try to link to me as I did with him. Why don't you, um, go back inside me. When he links to me, then you…I don't know…jump to Caden?"

"I'll try it. I hope he does it soon," Astrid said with a worried look on her face. "I doubt if we have long before you-know-who comes back."

"I hope whatever Elias has planned can be stopped. I don't want to die, but I'd rather die than let Elias absorb all that power from the portal and be loose in the world."

Moments later, Rory shivered as Astrid returned to her hiding place inside Rory's body. Cold, frightened, and repulsed by what her great-uncle had told her, Rory sat on the table, hugging her knees to her chest. She prayed that Caden would act immediately. The longer he waited, the more she feared Elias Brody would soon be unstoppable.

26 Caden

Caden felt Rory but couldn't see her. He could tell that she was cold, and, for a moment, he feared that she was already dead. Then, before either he or Thorn could attempt any sort of deeper connection with her, *he* was unbearably cold. The frigid blast shocked him and broke the fragile link he'd established with the woman he loved.

"Caden!" Beck barked. "What the Hell is happening?"

He heard David ask, "Should we move him and Thorn from the kitchen floor to the living room?"

"No," Thorn groaned. "I'm okay, just slightly disoriented. I don't know what to think of *that* experience."

Caden shivered, and Astrid suddenly appeared in the room. He found that he was no longer freezing and pushed himself up, resting his back against one cabinet door as he got his bearings. He would try to stand in a minute.

"It worked!" Astrid crowed. "That was perfect!"

"What worked?" Caden asked, still not feeling quite right. "Where have you been? Do you know where Rory is?"

"We don't have much time, so let me fill you in," Astrid said in an authoritative tone of voice. "It's like this...."

For the following twenty minutes, they listened to Astrid's monologue. By the time she finished telling them what she'd done and what she'd overheard and discussed with Rory, all of the Brody brothers and Ren were horrified and enraged.

Caden looked worriedly at Thorn. It had been bad enough to hear the details regarding Elias's part in Rory's date rape, the murders of the Roosevelt family members, and his manipulation of his sons in regards to reaching his ultimate goal of gaining unlimited power. However, the tales of his adopted children's origins were all extremely disturbing, and what Elias had done to Thorn's mother had been the worst.

"You hanging in there, Thorn?" Caden asked quietly.

"Barely," his younger brother answered without lifting his eyes to look at anyone else in the room. "He killed my mother to get me, and the way he did it…"

"We're going to take him down tonight," David said, his words clipped. "We'll make him pay for killing his family members, lying to us, taking us from our rightful families, and murdering your mother."

"We'll *obliterate* him," Sawyer said with conviction.

"If we simply kill him, then we lose our best chance of getting into the folder regarding our true origins," Beck pointed out. "I want him to talk before he dies. I need to know my mother's name and any other information about my birth and kidnapping."

"I'm sure you all want to find your real families," Ren said. "But you may not have the time to get that information. It might come down to a choice between simply killing Elias Brody in order to stop him from murdering Rory and becoming all-powerful or finding out more of the truth about your parents."

"That isn't a choice," Thorn said. "I won't hesitate to kill him in order to stop him, even if it means I never know who my parents are."

"I think I speak for the rest of us when I say that we all feel the same," Caden said. "As much as we want to know all, stopping Elias is our top priority."

The others nodded their agreement. Caden pushed himself up off the floor and then extended a hand to Thorn, who accepted it and allowed his older brother to "help" him to his feet. Physically, Caden knew he was capable of standing on his own, but he figured Thorn might need the emotional boost of the contact. Sure enough, he offered Caden a grateful nod and a sad smile.

He's not going to be able to stop thinking about what Elias did to his mother, Caden thought. *It might cripple him during the fight. Conversely, it might make him more deadly. And what will happen to him afterward? He already had some issues with self-confidence. How will he deal with knowing his mother lost her life because Elias wanted to take him?*

Pushing his concerns about Thorn away, Caden declared, "We have to think about Rory and the portal now. Nothing else. It sounds like things are going to go down soon. How should we approach this?"

"We need to get a variety of weapons and plant them in various locations in the barn," Sawyer suggested. "We have no idea which ones we'll need or if we'll even need them."

"But if we plant the weapons, then Elias could use his psychokinesis to turn them against us," David pointed out.

"True, but I agree with Sawyer that we have to be prepared for anything," Beck said. "We should bring some weapons but know that Elias might try to turn the tables on us."

"What do I do?" Ren asked.

"Stay here," replied Beck. "You'd only be a liability in the barn, someone else we have to protect."

"Someone else who could be used as leverage against us," Thorn added. "He's right. You need to stay in the house."

"What if Elias or his flunky, Dominic, comes for me while I'm here alone and unprotected? He could kidnap me and use me as leverage against you that way, too."

Caden watched Beck give Ren an appraising look then an acknowledging nod. They all liked and respected Ren, but Caden continued to suspect that Beck felt something more for the woman. The question was: Would he allow himself to act upon the attraction he felt once the showdown with Elias was over?

"You might be sealing your death warrant by coming to the barn with us," Beck told Ren. "It's your choice."

"I understand the risks. I know it's dangerous, but I also know I might be able to help in some way. I'm not only worried about Rory and you guys. I'm worried about what Elias Brody might do if he succeeds. This town is my home. I want to make sure it stays safe." Offering a sardonic smile, she added, "Besides, if Elias wipes out Sage, then it would *really* hurt my business."

Beck chuffed out a laugh. Caden and the other brothers stared at him. As the eldest brother, Beck had always taken his responsibilities seriously. He knew that if he didn't, his brothers and innocents might be more likely to die. At some point in their young lives, Beck had slammed the door to that part of himself that could relax and enjoy life. Caden was relieved that Ren seemed to be able to reach that place within his brother and hoped that she was aware of how she affected the man. He vowed to talk with her as soon as things were settled in order to unobtrusively suggest that perhaps she and Beck get together.

Caden almost laughed out loud. He was now going to add "matchmaker" to his list of fraternal duties. He'd always been the one in the family to make certain all the brothers stayed emotionally connected to one another. He'd been the peacemaker and the planner of joint missions. Beck led by example, but it had always been Caden who'd made their unusual familial situation work. Caden supposed it was part of his personality and wasn't going to stop doing everything he could in order to ensure that the brothers remained close. The only difference was that they would now be able to live near one another again. They could live in a sort of family "compound" at Nostalgia Road.

A hell of a lot different than Elias's compound in New Orleans. No fighting and killing here, not after this is done.

"Caden, did you hear me?" Beck asked.

"No. Sorry. I was lost in thought."

"Well, get with the program. We need to work out a plan, set things in motion, and take care of Elias once and for all."

"I'm with you."

"We're all with you," David agreed. "Let's do this."

An idea struck Caden, and he said, "Ren, stay close to Beck. That way, he can direct you as to what you need to do and make sure you're safe. Astrid, you act as Ren's protection detail."

"With pleasure!" Astrid said with a grin.

Beck appeared momentarily confused by his younger brother's suggestion then gave a half-shrug and said, "If you think that's the best plan. I trust your judgment."

The next thirty minutes were filled with discussion, the finalization of what they hoped would provide them with a workable plan to stop Elias, and the consumption of many cups of coffee. Then, the brothers scattered to retrieve the weapons they'd agreed to bring to the barn. Soon, Caden, Beck, David, Sawyer, Thorn, Ren, and Astrid were in the old red structure, readying their trap.

"Take your positions," Beck directed. "Ren, *don't* move or make any noise unless you're told to or we're incapacitated and you have no other option."

The woman bristled at his brisk tone but then relaxed and said, "I understand."

They watched as Ren climbed up into the loft and tucked herself behind an old trunk that had been stored to one side. Astrid disappeared behind the trunk once Ren was out of sight.

The brothers exchanged knowing glances. Elias would sense both Ren and Astrid, just as he would sense his sons and know that they had weapons at the ready. Their only hope lay in finding a weakness that would enable them to overpower the man. He was way too strong and enigmatic for them to defeat without some sort of luck or Divine intervention. Caden didn't care where help came from, as long as it came.

"This has to work," David announced. Turning to Caden, he said, "You know Elias is probably going to hurt Rory, but keep your cool. We've got it covered, remember?"

Caden nodded, knowing that what David said was true but hating that he'd have to watch Rory suffer. He reminded himself that she was going to be all right. As long as their plan worked, she would be fine. He couldn't allow himself to consider what he would do if the plan failed.

The five brothers took turns giving each other brief but tight hugs. Then, they retreated to the parts of the barn that corresponded with their positions in relation to the pentacle described in the first diary they'd read. Settling in, they waited for Elias to appear. They didn't have long to wait.

There was a flash of light, and then Elias and Rory appeared on the exact spot David had indicated was the gateway for the portal. Elias's left arm was around Rory's waist, and he held a long piece of metal in his right hand. Without hesitating, he drove the point into the center of Rory's chest and then quickly ripped it free. Rory's eyes widened in shock, but she didn't have time to scream. As blood began to gush from the wound, she said softly, "Caden, I love you." Then, she slumped forward in Elias's arms. Her long, red curls veiled her face, as blood dripped onto the dirt.

Wanting to howl, Caden forced himself to remain calm, remembering to stick to the plan he and his brothers had developed. Rory had known he was there, even if she hadn't been able to see him. She was counting on him to help save her, and that was precisely what he intended to do. He refused to lose her.

"Now!" Beck shouted, and the five Brody brothers stepped out from their hiding places.

For a moment, Elias and Caden locked eyes. Elias looked surprised by his sons' coordinated appearance, which confirmed that the older man had no idea about Thorn's teleportation of Caden, Astrid's involvement, and their sneak attack. Their adoptive father might have sensed their presence, but he'd been unprepared for their knowledge of where he'd be or what his exact intentions were. Caden experienced a fleeting feeling of satisfaction that vanished as soon as he saw Rory's astral body begin to appear.

No, not her astral body, Caden realized with horror. *Her ghost.*

"Thorn!" he cried, but his younger brother was already on the move.

The youngest Brody teleported from where he stood to a spot right in front of Rory. Without pausing, he yanked her from Elias's hold and then teleported her out of the barn. Elias snarled with rage as he darted a glance at the ground. Everything had happened so quickly that only a small pool of Rory's blood had collected on the spot over the gateway.

Elias hastily knelt and traced his right pointer finger through the blood atop the clay dirt of the barn floor. Caden couldn't see what the man was creating with his crude and revolting version of finger painting, but a blinding red light began to stream up through cracks that suddenly appeared in the earth. Elias laughed and called out, "Dominic Ambrose, come to me!"

The ghost materialized beside him. Dominic had been blonde with brown eyes. Thanks to the car accident that had taken his life, his skull had been split open and his nose completely shattered. His mouth was a gaping maw filled with only a few teeth. The dead man's chest cavity was visible, and it was evident he'd broken both arms and legs in the crash. The terrible injuries didn't seem to bother Dominic. His horrific mouth twisted with what Caden supposed was meant to be a triumphant grin.

"Go down through the cracks!" Elias commanded. "After the portal has opened fully, you'll emerge immortal and as unmarred as you were before you died!" Once Dominic had done as he'd been told, Elias grinned malevolently before shouting, "Finally! After over seventy years, I'll have my revenge and gain my true inheritance!

"You'll have shit!" Sawyer cried. "Fuck you!"

The older man laughed and said, "Sticks and stones, Sawyer. Allow me to demonstrate."

The weapons the brothers had hidden were suddenly lifted and pointed at their owners. Caden looked down the barrel of his SIG Sauer, while the blade of Beck's sword was across its owner's throat. Sawyer had the tip of a Bowie knife pressed against his chest, and David blinked down at his Luger pistol, which was trained on his midsection. No one moved. No one spoke.

Thorn teleported back into his original position in the barn with Rory by his side. Caden literally growled, wondering why the man hadn't left her at the main house. As long as Rory was in the barn, she was the one whose life was at greatest risk. Then, he looked closely at his youngest surviving brother.

Thorn had obviously assumed Rory's chest wound when he'd transported her but didn't have time to lie still and heal. The brothers had agreed in advance that they'd all be needed in order to stop Elias. So, Thorn had teleported back despite his precarious physical state. Rory knelt by him, supporting him as best as she could while he tried to stay upright.

He couldn't have come back alone, Caden thought. *He and Rory probably both knew she'd have to return with him so that he could help us to end this. How is he even still conscious? Christ, he's losing so much blood from that chest wound!*

"Ah, Thorn," Elias said indulgently as if he were talking to a small child. "Trying to redeem yourself by sacrificing your life in an effort to stop me?"

"He has nothing to atone for!" Caden shouted. "You murdered his mother. It wasn't his fault you killed her to get him."

"No, it wasn't his fault. It was her fault for running from me."

Thorn's fury radiated from him as he managed to grind out, "What are you talking about?"

"I knew you'd be the one," Elias said. "Just as I knew that one of my brother's descendants would provide me with the perfect offering to open the gateway. The moment I saw your mother and her husband at a gallery opening, I knew she was going to bear the child who would one day give me the means to achieve my goal."

Using his psychokinesis, Elias yanked Thorn from Rory's side. The invisible force hauled the younger man in front of Elias, who still knelt on the ground. He wrapped an arm around Thorn's shoulder to support him – and to hold the man over the place where the red light streamed through the cracks.

"Rory's blood was the key that began to unlock the gateway," Elias said. "When you teleported her and took on her injuries, you gave me exactly what I needed. But I knew that you and your brothers would come, would try to stop me. And I must have *your* blood fall on this spot in order to complete the opening of the doorway to my destiny. After all, you carry my DNA."

"*You're* my real father?" Thorn croaked.

Elias smiled and said, "I pursued your mother after we first met, but she insisted she was passionately in love with her husband. I tried to persuade her to join me for a one-night stand, but she continued to refuse. So, I made her believe she was dreaming when I came to her while her husband was away on business. I had to leave right after our encounter because he came home early. I then contented myself with watching from afar, waiting as you developed. Finally, I snatched her, knocked her unconscious, and performed a crude C-section that delivered you safely into my arms. Your blood comingled with Rory's will fling open the doorway to the other side. It will make me unstoppable!"

"What was my mother's name?" Thorn asked, as tears of physical and emotional pain streamed down his cheeks.

"Moira," Elias said. "She was quite lovely and brilliant. I hated to have to kill her, but it was the only way I could ensure my possession of you. You are the linchpin that will make all my years of research and plotting worthwhile."

He slammed Thorn to the ground, causing the man to cry out as his chest hit the dirt. Caden had frantically been trying to think of a way to stop Elias without injuring Thorn further but hadn't had time to work out a feasible plan. He knew his other brothers had been thinking the same thing. And now it was too late.

Except, instead of having the portal open wide, Thorn's blood appeared to be sealing the cracks. Elias looked disbelievingly at the ground then shouted, "No! You *have* to be my son! You *can't* be Moira's husband's child! I can't be wrong! I'm *never* wrong!"

"Looks like you are this time," Thorn choked out. "Screw you, you fucking psychopath!"

"No! No! No!" Elias roared. "I *won't* let this happen!"

His focus, broken by his frustration and rage, caused the weapons Elias had aimed at his four sons to fall to the ground. Beck nodded to each of them. Caden grabbed his gun and fired two rounds into the older man's chest before Elias regained enough control to use his psychokinesis to stop more bullets from hitting their target. Sawyer rushed forward and pulled Thorn away from their adoptive father. David shifted into German shepherd form, lunged forward, and used his teeth to tear at the older man's throat. Beck called for him to retreat. Once David had bolted away, fireballs formed in the air in front of Beck's palms. He hurled them at Elias, who was bleeding from the bullet holes and a gaping neck wound.

Elias screamed and writhed on the ground, as the fireballs found their mark. Suddenly, there was a burst of flame so intense that embers flew everywhere. When the smoke cleared, Elias was a smoldering pile of charred clothing, skin, and bones. Caden heard Ren throwing up in the loft and couldn't blame her, but he couldn't tear his eyes away from the body of the man who'd been his father for so long.

"We have to finish this," Caden declared.

"H-how?" Rory stammered, as she struggled to her feet.

Caden hurried over, enveloping her in his arms. He kissed her deeply before saying, "We have to get the portal to swallow Elias down into it. It's the only way to permanently contain him."

"I don't want to get stabbed in the chest a second time," she protested. "Thorn's not recovered enough to teleport me and save me again right now. *He* still has to recover."

"We know now that Elias linked us when he cast those spells using our mixed blood when we were kids," Caden reminded everyone. "I think if we brothers cut ourselves, mix our blood with Rory's, and pour it onto the spot, it will open enough to accept his remains then close up."

"But how can you be sure?" Ren asked, as she climbed down the ladder.

"I can't. But I'm thinking about what Hugh Roosevelt wrote in his diary, that six Brodys would stop the ultimate evil. He wrote that some would be Brody by blood and some wouldn't."

"We have no choice but to try it," Beck said. "If it doesn't work, then we'll figure out what will."

Rory, Caden, Beck, David, and Sawyer held out their hands. Thorn, who still lay on the ground bleeding from the chest wound he'd absorbed from Rory, extended one palm out for them to cut. Caden picked up the piece of metal Elias had used to stab Rory and probably Nolan, while David lifted Thorn and carried him closer to where Elias's smoldering remains lay. Then, Caden made a long, quick cut on each of their palms. Rory gasped at the pain and automatically flinched, but none of the brothers made a sound or moved. Holding their hands palms down, the six of them let the droplets of blood fall onto the dead man and then onto some of the earth beside him. An odd buzzing sound filled the air.

"Everyone move away!" Beck ordered. "Get as far back as you can!"

Caden lifted Rory and carried her toward one wall, while Beck grabbed Ren and swept her away toward another. David scooped Thorn from the ground and ran for one of the empty corners, while Sawyer and Astrid darted for the other. As they watched, the dirt underneath Elias began to sink.

Like a sinkhole swallowing everything above and around it, Caden thought. *Let's hope it stops with his body and doesn't swallow the whole damn barn!*

As they stared, Elias's remains and the odd piece of metal he'd used in his efforts disappeared into the ground, which then filled in again as though the surface had never been disturbed.

"You okay, Little Brother?" David asked Thorn, as they all congregated around the spot where the portal lay.

"I'm kind of in agony," Thorn groaned from where he lay in his brother's arms. "But my chest should heal abnormally fast if I mend as I did when I absorbed Caden's injuries. That's probably the only reason why I'm still alive with this kind of wound."

"That's not what I meant."

"I'm damned thankful he's not my father, but…but he thought he was. How could he be wrong about that but know that Rory's grandmother was already pregnant when he slept with her?"

"Remember, Elias said he had to leave right after he'd had sex with your mom because your father came home early," Caden said. "Your mother must have waked from her 'dream' of having sex with Elias and then made love to your father. Your biological dad's sperm made it to an egg instead of Elias's. It was just by chance that you were the product of love between your parents and not of Elias's own version of rape."

"He killed my mom because he thought I was his son."

"Yes, but that was because you *did* develop with supernatural powers," Beck commented. "Your mother evidently had her own abilities. Otherwise, Elias wouldn't have fixated on her. Another coincidence? I don't think so. If you hadn't been taken by Elias, we'd all be dead now and a great evil would have been unleashed upon the world. Instead, you saved Rory – literally – by teleporting her out of here and taking on her chest wound. You then saved everyone else by contributing your blood to ensure Elias stays gone forever. You saved Caden earlier when you teleported him out of his prison cell and assumed his injuries. You and Rory were the keys to everything, and I don't think that's by chance. What's tragic is that your mother paid the ultimate price so that many other lives would be spared."

"I'm sorry about your mom," Sawyer offered. "But you were destined to be here, destined to be a Brody brother."

"When I find my mother's grave, I'm going to have fresh flowers kept on it all the time."

"We'll all contribute," Caden said. "We owe your mother so much."

"My birthfather will hate me when I locate him," Thorn speculated. "He'll blame me for her death."

"You don't know that," Rory said. "He may simply be thrilled to know that you're alive and are such a good, brilliant, courageous man."

He nodded but said nothing, and Caden wondered what was going on in Thorn's mind.

You can't do any more for him right now, he thought. *We'll clear out of the barn and go home.*

Home. Nostalgia Road was going to provide the men with a wonderful new beginning. Now, if they could only uncover the truths about their pasts.

Epilogue

"Rory!" Astrid said in a hushed whisper. "*Rory!*"

Rory snuggled closer to Caden and mumbled, "I told you not to spy on me or come into my bedroom without asking permission."

"I know, but I think this is *it*."

Opening her eyes, Rory echoed, "It?"

"I think I'm getting ready to cross over. I feel tingly."

Rory slowly sat up and looked at Astrid. Sure enough, she could see *through* the blonde woman in the red cocktail dress. Astrid was obviously about to leave their current plane of existence.

"But the police are still investigating your death. No official conclusion has been released. All they've stated is that you were pregnant, didn't have alcohol or drugs in your system, and were murdered. They don't have any leads. They don't know it was Elias."

"That doesn't matter," Astrid told her. "*We* reached an official conclusion. The man who staged the scene and killed me, my unborn baby, and Anderson is dead and can't ever hurt anyone else. I can go now. I want to be with Anderson and see Glen, my first husband, again."

Rory smiled but said, "I'm happy for you but…."

"But what?"

Sighing, Rory admitted, "I can't believe I'm about to say this."

"What?" Astrid asked, frowning.

"I'm going to miss you. You've become a good friend."

The ghost smiled and said, "I'll miss you, too. You've been a wonderful friend to me, even when I didn't deserve it. Thank you, Rory. At least I helped make things right between us and for you and the others before I crossed over."

"We wouldn't have been able to do it without you."

Astrid tossed her blonde hair, allowing a momentary glimpse of the bullet hole on the left side of her head, before saying, "Glad I could help. Will you tell everyone 'Thank you' and 'Goodbye' from me?"

"Sure. Have a nice eternity, Astrid."

"I plan to. Have a happy life, Rory."

"I plan to."

Grinning, Astrid said, "Until we meet again. I can't wait to hear about your beautiful life with Caden and all those babies you'll have together."

Rory's cheeks flamed, but she merely nodded. She planned to have a *lot* to tell her friend when she met up with her again – many, many years in the future.

Astrid faded from sight. Once she was gone, Caden muttered, "That was a nice farewell."

Rory ran her fingers along the lines of his dragon tattoo and asked, "Why didn't you let us know you were awake?"

"Because that exchange needed to be between the two of you. I heard it. I know how she felt, and she knew how I felt about her. She might have started out as bitchy and self-centered, but she had a good heart underneath. I'm glad she was able to realize that before she moved on."

Rory lowered her mouth to his back and began to trace the outline of the red dragon with her tongue.

Caden groaned and asked, "Just what do you think you're doing?"

"I'm trying to get you hard so that we can make love again."

When Caden turned to face her, Rory could tell that he was most definitely ready to make love again. She squealed with delight as he grabbed her and rolled her onto her back.

Knock! Knock! Knock!

"Go away!" Caden called out in a rough voice before easing himself inside Rory.

"It's important," Thorn said, his voice muffled by the door.

"Later!" Caden growled.

"But it's *really* important," Thorn persisted. "What are you doing that could possibly be more –"

"We're having sex!" Rory said loudly, her face burning with embarrassment. "Please, come back later."

Caden and Rory lay entwined for a long time afterward. Finally, they rose and went to shower. Rory was thankful that no one else was around to see them heading for the bathroom. It wasn't as though the brothers didn't know what they'd been doing, but she still felt embarrassed by having them present in the house when she and Caden made love, especially since she no longer attempted to stifle her screams as she climaxed.

Each brother will be settled into his own cottage next week, Rory reminded herself. *They'll have made the cottages fit their styles and personalities over these past two months. Once they're settled into their homes, Caden and I will be alone in the house and can do whatever we want, whenever we want, wherever we want. At least Beck, David, Sawyer, and Thorn will remain on the property with us.*

A lot had happened since the showdown with Elias. Nolan's body had been discovered, but his murder, of course, remained unsolved by the local police. Harvey had made a full recovery and was back at work. His "invisible" assailant had already become part of local Sage lore. Nostalgia Road was no longer a Bed & Breakfast, and Caden was working on plans to set up a horse farm on one area of the property. Sawyer, who had bought Nolan's Bar from Rory after she'd inherited it, was having the place renovated and would reopen it in the future under the name 'Spirits.' Beck and David had been busy tying up loose ends regarding all of the brothers' business affairs and Elias's estate, which had been considerable. Thorn had been working to crack the encryption on the electronic files regarding the men's origins. Rory and Caden had married on the lakeside dock next to the family home in a private ceremony attended only by the brothers, Ren, Astrid, and the judge who'd officiated. In other words, things had been unbelievably hectic.

When Caden and Rory went downstairs that morning, they found the other four brothers seated around the kitchen table. Rory tried to push aside her embarrassment regarding the sounds of sex they'd certainly heard and told them about Astrid's departure. They nodded somberly, no doubt thinking of their lost brother, Anderson.

"Now that we've discussed Astrid and you two are, uh, done, I want to tell all of you my important news," Thorn said. "I was able to get into Caden's file in the 'actual origins' folder that Elias had on his computer."

"What?!?" Caden practically shouted. "When?"

"Just before you two became…occupied."

"What about the rest of us?" David asked, but Thorn shook his head.

"Not yet. He has the folder subdivided with different security blocks on each file. I'll just have to keep working on the thing in pieces until I'm able to access it all."

"What did you find out about my family?" Caden asked.

"The story Elias told you was mostly true. The information verified what he shared with Rory after her kidnapping by him. Your last name was Welsh."

"Are you going to change it?" Sawyer asked.

"If he does, then I'll have to change my name again," Rory said with a smile.

"No. Your family name was Brody, then Roosevelt, and now it's rightfully back to being Brody," Caden insisted. "I want to find out more about my birth family, but I'm keeping the *good* name of Brody, not the one with *bad* connotations to Elias. This land was settled by the Brodys who protected the world from evil, and that's who we all are. That's the name I want our kids to have."

"Me, too," she agreed. "I'm glad you feel the same way I do."

"Where were my parents?" Caden asked. "What are their names? What about my brothers and sisters?"

"Once I got into your file, then I was able to do a lot of digging on the Internet. Your parents and siblings are all still alive, living in Lake Charles. I have their addresses for you."

"We can handle things here if you two want to make a trip to Louisiana," Beck suggested.

"Thanks. Rory, are you up for this?"

She kissed his jaw and then said, "Let's go pack a bag or two. Thorn, will you make our plane reservations?"

"Sure."

Caden rested a hand on Thorn's left shoulder and said, "Thank you, Brother."

Thorn smiled, but the smile didn't reach his eyes. Caden knew the man was dreading what he would eventually find in his own file. He would have to make the decision regarding whether or not to seek out his father. He prayed that Thorn would be welcomed with open arms. Actually, Caden prayed for that regarding each of them.

Rory and Caden drove to Orlando and caught their afternoon flight. When they arrived in New Orleans that evening, they rented a car and then drove to Lake Charles, which Caden informed her was a city where the economy was fueled by petrochemical and natural gas plants, casinos, retail outlets, and other industries. They ordered dinner from Room Service, watched a movie, and then made love before falling asleep.

The following morning when they stepped out of the hotel into the humid September Louisiana air, Caden hesitated, confiding, "I don't know what to do. A part of me says I should call and introduce myself first, but another part of me leans toward simply showing up."

"I think we should just go," she said seriously. "We can check out the house from the outside, then see if you feel like you want to approach your family now. I know it's Saturday, but they may not even be home this morning. Let's do a drive-by and see."

He nodded as he unlocked the rental car but still seemed unsure. Following the GPS on his phone, Caden drove to his parents' address. Rory placed a hand on Caden's upper right thigh and gave it a squeeze.

"Are you trying to distract me by making me hard?" he asked with a somewhat forced smile.

"I can do that anytime," she said, pulling her long, red hair over one shoulder and beginning to braid it. "I was attempting to be reassuring. Everything will be fine, no matter what happens."

"What if my parents curse me and call me names?"

"I doubt if they will, but, if they do, then I'll be with you to hold you tonight while you cry."

"The only times I've ever cried were when I lost brothers."

"If you're hurt by your family's reaction, then it'd be okay for you to cry tonight because you're sad. That would be normal."

Caden nodded, raked his fingers through his ginger-colored hair, and stared straight ahead. Wanting to distract him, Rory asked, "How do you think your brothers are adjusting to life in Sage?"

"None of them have really gone into town much, except for Sawyer. Beck and David have been coming and going all over the country in order to get our ducks in a row so that we can live comfortably and safely at Nostalgia Road. Thorn's been glued to his computer in an effort to get into our files and track down other ventures started by Elias so that David and Beck could shut them down. With the remodeling of the four cottages and the focus on working with an architect to draw up plans for the stables and the placement of fences for our horse farm, their contact with the Sage residents has been minimal. I think they'll adjust once things settle down."

"*I* hope Ren and Beck get together," Rory remarked. "He seems to be affected by her in a personal way, and they are both half-Japanese and are both adopted. That gives them a lot in common."

"What they don't have in common is personality types. Ren is friendly, while Beck is reserved."

"Because he had to be," Rory noted. "You said so yourself. Perhaps if he and Ren start a relationship, he'll relax a little. I get the impression there's so much more to him than he allows anyone else to see."

"You're right on target there." Smiling, he said, "Sawyer won't lack for female companionship although he's not looking for anything serious."

"Sometimes love finds people whether they want it or not. Look at us. Did you ever think before we met that you'd fall in love, get married, settle down, and plan to have a family with anyone?"

"Nope," Caden admitted, the corners of his green eyes crinkling as he smiled.

"Me neither. Look at us now. I love you more than anything, and we're building a new life together. We're also trying to *make* a new life together."

"I know, and I couldn't be happier." Turning onto the street where his parents lived, Caden exclaimed, "Damn! Look at all the cars. Must be a crawfish boil or something, and it looks like it's centered around the address Thorn gave me for my parents."

"Well, that could be a good thing. If people are milling about, then no one will be suspicious if we take a peek. This looks like a nice, middle-class neighborhood, but I did see a *Neighborhood Watch* sign when we turned in."

"I saw it, too." Caden flashed her a grin and said, "*I* may look like a badass, but you look like the beautiful, sweet woman you are. Did you wear that cute little yellow dress to make them think we're normal?"

"No. I wore it because I know how turned on you get when I dress the way I like. I love you for it, Caden."

"God, if I could be in you right now, I would."

"I don't think that would make a very good first impression on your parents."

He laughed and said, "Probably not."

They were soon walking hand-in-hand toward the front door of the house in question. The exterior of the red brick home was neatly kept. It appeared that the owners of the houses in this neighborhood took pride in their property. Rory prayed that the occupants of the house they were heading for would take pride in their long-lost son.

Caden knocked on the door. They could hear people laughing and chatting, and his fingers tightened around hers. She stood on tiptoe and gave him a quick kiss on the jaw. Then, the front door opened.

The tall, gray-haired, green-eyed, middle-aged man had been smiling when he'd pulled back the door, but his expression went from jovial to shock the moment he saw Caden. The bottle of beer he had in his hand began to shake slightly. Otherwise, he remained frozen in place. Finally, he asked someone nearby to hold his bottle. Then, he stepped forward, took Caden's face in his hands, and said roughly, "Oh, my baby."

Caden stiffened but didn't pull away, as the man's eyes filled with tears.

"PawPaw, are you all right?" a small girl asked from beside them.

"Go get your MawMaw now," he answered. "Tell her our baby's come home."

The child looked confused but ran quickly through the crowd calling, "MawMaw!"

"We thought we'd lost you forever," the man said hoarsely. "We should never have let you go."

"Chester, what on –"

The short, heavyset woman with graying ginger-colored hair stopped several feet away from the front door then cried, "Oh, sweet Jesus! Oh, thank you, Jesus! Oh, my baby!"

She hurried forward and threw her arms around Caden's waist before bursting into tears. Caden never let go of Rory's hand, as his biological parents embraced him and those gathered at the house surged toward them. They were ushered inside and asked to sit on the couch. Rory glanced around and estimated that there were over thirty people crowding the large living room, about half of them adults and half of them children.

"What's your name, Son?" Chester Welsh asked.

"Caden Brody. This is my wife, Rory."

"Caden Brody," his mother repeated. "What a nice name. How did you find us? We've been looking for you ever since we let the *traiteur* take you away, but we were never able to find you."

"You looked for me?" Caden asked.

"Of course," his father said. "We tried to find the *traiteur* who took you but never could. We were heartbroken."

Elias probably killed the woman the moment she gave him Caden, Rory thought. *Another victim of such an evil man.*

"I'm your daddy, Chester, and this is your mama, Erin."

The man proceeded to introduce Caden to his three brothers, three sisters, eight nephews, and nine nieces. The Welsh children seemed ecstatic to finally meet their baby brother, the one their parents had been searching for since they'd given him up at birth.

"Your mama and I married at sixteen and started having babies right away," his father said. "We were only in our mid-twenties when she got pregnant with you, our seventh. After what the *traiteur* said, we feared for you. But we knew in our hearts that we'd made a mistake once you were gone. We looked for you; we hired private investigators whenever we had any extra money; and we even appealed to the police. We always prayed we'd find you, but, after thirty years, we doubted it would ever happen."

"You can't imagine how grateful we are that you found us," his mother said. "Oh, my little boy! Where have you been? Were you treated well?"

"I can't explain – yet," Caden said, his voice thick with emotion. "I'm just so happy to know you all now. I want to know you better, be close, and stay close. Rory and I live in Florida, but it's not far away by plane."

"You could live in Antarctica, and we'd make it work!" Chester declared. "Now that you've come back to us, we can't lose you again. Plus, we want to get to know your beautiful wife."

Rory smiled and said, "Thank you. I can't wait to get to know all of you, too. My family is gone, and Caden and I are working on starting a family of our own. I'd love for our kids to have grandparents, aunts, uncles, and cousins they can grow up knowing. Well, our children will already have four uncles, but one can never have too many loving family members, right?"

When the Welshes looked confused, Caden said, "I have four adoptive brothers who are like my own flesh and blood. I'd love for you to meet them all someday."

"And we'd love to meet them, too," Erin told them. "Right now, we just want to *be* with you. We have the rest of our lives to get to know one another and to know them."

"Caden Brody," Chester said. "Our son. We're so glad you found your way home."

Looking to Rory, Caden said, "Yes, I found my way home."

Knowing he was talking about finding his way to her as much as he was talking about locating his birth family, Rory kissed Caden and said, "We've each found our way home."

"We've also found that balance your father mentioned when he came to me a few months ago," Caden observed.

"Balance is an essential element in every happy family," Rory said with a smile. "And ours is definitely going to be one, big, happy family."

Other Books in The Essential Elements Series

Scorched Creek
Spirits Corner
Memory Lane
Homeward Bound

ABOUT THE AUTHOR

Lauren Cutrera, who also writes under the name Barbara Cutrera, has published over 20 contemporary romance, romantic suspense, paranormal romance, mystery, and fiction novels. Diverse people and plots highlight her works, drawing readers into the characters' unique journeys as they navigate their way through their struggles and triumphs. Lauren and her husband, Budge, are the proud parents of a grown son. They live in southwest Florida and have a cute and naughty Yorkie, Hadrian, who sleeps next to Lauren as she writes each day.

Check out all things Lauren (and Barbara) at www.laurencutrera.com

And connect with her there or on

Facebook: https://www.facebook.com/profile.php?id=100063631654302

Instagram: https://www.instagram.com/laurencutrera/

Pinterest: https://www.pinterest.com/laurencutrera/_saved/

OTHER BOOKS BY THE AUTHOR:

The Real World Series

Over, Under, Across & Through
A Good Man's Life
Mercy
Unfinished Business (Final Chapter)

The Gift Series

The Healer's Gift
Jordan's Way
Bound by Grace
The Nameless

The Seneca & Michael Duet

A Lovely Dream
A Lovely Reality

The Limitless Series

Sight Unseen
Better Left Unsaid
Unheard Of
Under Her Skin
Brainstorm
Out On A Limb

Standalone Novels/Short Stories

In A Manner of Speaking
Prim & Proper
Lucky
Compromising Positions
True: 3 Short Stories